"I hate th...
There...
and I'm drea...

She had sat up, her shift hanging off one shoulder. Ian closed his eyes tightly and turned on his heel. "Go to sleep," he said gruffly.

"Will you leave when I'm asleep?"

"I will stay." He took a lunging step and dropped into the small rickety chair.

"Are you cold?"

Ian jumped, for Olivia stood beside him suddenly, holding her blanket out toward him. Truly she could have overpowered him easily in that moment. What on earth was happening to him?

"Take the blanket," she said. "I shall be warm enough." Olivia draped the blanket around his shoulders, but he dared not move. He did not trust himself, for in his mind's eye he could picture perfectly what his body longed to do.

"Oh my God," he muttered, dropping his head onto his hands. She must be a witch, and he was under her spell. He had never felt such a need for a woman in his life.

"Good night," she said finally and moved away. And still, Ian did not move or speak, for he knew that if he did, he would go to Olivia's cot and slide down next to her, and forget who they were and what their circumstances were . . .

MALIA MARTIN

Much Ado About Love

AVON BOOKS
An Imprint of HarperCollinsPublishers

This is a work of fiction. Names, characters, places, and incidents are products of the author's imagination or are used fictitiously and are not to be construed as real. Any resemblance to actual events, locales, organizations, or persons, living or dead, is entirely coincidental.

AVON BOOKS
An Imprint of HarperCollins*Publishers*
10 East 53rd Street
New York, New York 10022-5299

Copyright © 2000 by Malia B. Nahas
ISBN: 0-380-81517-6
www.avonromance.com

First Avon Books paperback printing: September 2000

Avon Trademark Reg. U.S. Pat. Off. and in Other Countries, Marca Registrada, Hecho en U.S.A.
HarperCollins® is a trademark of HarperCollins Publishers Inc.

Printed in the U.S.A.

WCD 10 9 8 7 6 5 4 3 2 1

This one is for grandpa.

*I sure hope there are John Deere caps,
cowboy boots and little girls' bikes
that need fixing in heaven.*

... *no sooner met but they looked; no sooner looked but they loved; no sooner loved but they sighed; no sooner sighed but they asked one another the reason; no sooner knew the reason but they sought the remedy* ...

—AS YOU LIKE IT, V, II, 31

Prologue

Rutland Castle
Cornwall, 1580

> . . . be not afraid of greatness. Some are born great, some achieve greatness, and some have greatness thrust upon 'em.
> —TWELFTH NIGHT, II, v, 143

"**P**oppet, how will I ever keep up with you?"

Olivia giggled as Anne Ford read over her Latin translation. She pulled her legs up and crossed them beneath herself on the bench so she could sit higher. "May I read now, Annie?"

Anne laughed. "Of course, dearest child." She stared at Olivia for a moment, and a sad look suddenly pulled at the corners of her mouth.

" 'Tis sure who your mother is, child. Such a brain as yours could be sired by no less."

Olivia pulled a large, leather-bound volume toward her, keeping her eyes on the pages as she opened the tome. She did not like to speak of her mother. A woman she had never seen, never heard from. In her small ten-year-old heart, she wished Annie to be her mother. And so she closed her mind to anything that disturbed such a fantasy.

Annie, her beautiful Annie, stood and straightened her skirts. "I shall make us our noon meal, then, Poppet." Her Annie must be in a thoughtful mood, for she mentioned Olivia's mother again. "Your mother would laugh if she could see me now: nursemaid, cook, and all-around drudge. Of course, she knows well enough that I do this, for she asked me to."

Olivia shut her eyes tight and sent a small prayer heavenward that Annie would quit speaking of the terrible woman called her mother.

With a small wistful sigh, Annie moved off, and Olivia relaxed her thin little arms, her long fingers unclenching and showing the half-moons her fingernails had dug into her palms.

Olivia pushed herself from the bench and hefted the big book from the table so that she could read in the soft chair. Even as she lugged her heavy burden, Olivia walked as Annie had taught her, head high, shoulders back: like the ladies at court.

She had just gotten situated when Annie rushed back in, her long skirts kicking up a bit of dust. Olivia chewed on her lip, hoping that Annie did not notice the dust. Sweeping was Olivia's duty, and she had neglected the chore terribly.

"I knew it would happen someday. God in heaven, I knew this day would come."

Olivia quickly looked from the floor to her Annie's face when she caught the distraught tone of her guardian's voice.

Annie stopped in the middle of the room, a small piece of paper in her hands as she closed her eyes and leaned her head back on her neck.

Olivia sat staring at her quietly. There was something very, very wrong. And Olivia feared that she knew what it was.

"If only there was some other way!" Annie whirled around, her face distorted with emotion, and Olivia sank against the back of her chair.

Annie looked at her then, and blinked. "Oh, Livie," she said softly, and then smiled largely. "I should not scare you so, child, for all is well."

Olivia said nothing. She was smart. She knew full well that something was wrong.

"We have treasure to take with us," Annie

3

said, going to a chest set beneath one of the tall windows that looked out onto the seas below their lonely cliff. The woman pulled a large, heavy-looking bundle from the chest. She turned to Olivia and winked. "Our allowance is at an end, but I have saved a bit. And, it is well that my father was a rich man. Now hurry, child, for we are warned that his message precedes the evil which comes by only the miracle of a swift horse."

Someone banged loudly on the front door, jolting Olivia as Annie clutched her bag more tightly to her stomach. "Come quickly!"

Olivia jumped from her seat and curled her fingers around her guardian's. They scurried across the vast room to the large painting of Annie's great-grandfather. With a quick glance around, Annie yanked on the wall sconce, and one side of the portrait sprang from the wall.

Olivia knew of the hiding place. She knew of all the hiding places in the large castle. There were also tunnels that ran down through the cliff so that one could get to the rocky beach below without leaving cover. Her guardian's father had not been a rich man through legal means.

Annie hustled Olivia into the small room behind the wall and pulled the portrait so that it clicked against its latch once more.

"Now we must be still as mice, dear heart. I

4

do not want to risk opening the door to the stairs until this terrible man is gone."

Olivia did not have to ask who the terrible man was. She knew whom Annie had railed against. She knew what was happening now. She had only needed a moment to sort it out in her mind. Olivia crouched on the floor so that she could see through the peepholes. They were cut into the eyes of the little dog, which had been painted sitting at Annie's great-grandfather's feet. Breathing as softly as she could, Olivia peered through the dark cloth at the room they had just vacated.

"Be still, dearest." Annie squeezed her shoulder.

She heard the thump of boots in the hall, a strange sound, as a man had never trod the halls since Olivia had lived in the castle. And she had lived there for as long as she could remember.

And then a shadow fell across the doorway. The man strode through, his large frame making the room seem rather smaller than it ever had been before. He wore a long cloak and no hat, and he was alone.

Funny, that. Olivia had always pictured this moment with soldiers breaking down the doors, and hordes of terrible people violating her life, burning her books, taking her away to a horrible end: For she had definitely pictured this moment.

And Olivia had thought that, perhaps, *She* would be at the front of the throngs of invaders: tall, proud, and beautiful, as Annie had always described Her. Her red hair a brighter shade than Olivia's own, but her hands exactly the same shape, with long fingers and thin wrists.

Olivia stared down at her hand for a moment, her knuckles white, fingers clenched in a fist as she waited without breathing.

She heard movement and slid her gaze back to the peepholes. The man had picked up her Latin translation. Olivia could only stare as the weak light streaming in through the large windows glanced off the white parchment in the man's hands, illuminating his face in an unearthly way.

He was young. He was beautiful. It hurt her, actually, that he was so beautiful. Her throat burned with tears at the sickness of it. That evil should come clothed as an angel.

The man set the translation down slowly, reverently it seemed. Then with the tips of his fingers he caressed the top of one of her books that sat on the table.

Olivia furrowed her brow as she watched. Perhaps he had not come to hurt her? He did not seem like the villain she had conjured in her mind. He was not dark and ugly, with clawed hands that would snatch a young girl from her bedchamber and do unspeakable harm to her.

The man turned slowly and went to where Olivia had left the leather-bound tome she had been reading before Annie had interrupted her. He sat, picked up the book and opened it.

Olivia took a smooth, quiet breath. She could feel Annie beside her shaking. Her guardian, of course, could not see what was happening. As quietly as she could, Olivia glanced back at Annie and smiled reassurance. Annie just closed her eyes, raising a finger to her lips.

When Olivia turned back to the scene through the peepholes, the man was sliding a paper from the pages of the book. Olivia stiffened. It was a sonnet she had written, a silly scribbling, really. But the awful thing was that she had signed her name . . . her entire name. Annie had warned her about ever even speaking her name out loud. Her guardian would probably expire on the spot if she knew Olivia had written it down.

The man sat very still for a few moments before folding the paper and depositing it under his cloak. He stood quickly then, the book slipping from his lap and landing with a loud clap on the floor. Annie jumped as the sound reverberated in the high-ceilinged room.

Olivia did not move as she watched the dust

disturbed by the book billow along the stone floor. She felt her nose itch and quickly pinched her nostrils together with her fingers.

The man turned, striding purposefully toward the door, and Olivia relaxed her hunched shoulders in relief. And then she sneezed. Two short, high squeaks and then one long, nose-clearing blow, just like she always did.

Annie's hand tightened on her shoulder like a claw, and Olivia could do nothing but squeeze her eyes shut. Her mind was frozen with terror, and she could think of nothing at all to do but wait for the evil angel to crash through the wall and take her away.

"I am going to set the house afire," she heard a strong male voice say. "Seek safety."

Olivia opened her eyes in surprise, staring out through the peepholes. The man was looking directly at their hiding place. Gooseflesh rose along her arms, and her throat went so dry she despaired of ever swallowing again.

"Leave England," he said. "Do not come back, and I will let you live."

Annie's hand was clamped so tightly on Olivia's shoulder, she could no longer feel her arm. But Olivia still did not move as she watched the man turn quickly, his dark cloak sweeping out behind him like wings, and quit the room.

She blinked once, wondering if she dreamt,

then stood and looked up at Annie. Her guardian had tears streaming down her cheeks, and she grabbed Olivia in a tight embrace. "Oh, Livie," she whispered. She said nothing more, but held Olivia against her skirts.

They heard the bang of the large front door, and Annie released her quickly. "Come," she said, turning about in the cramped space and pulling a small wooden door open. It creaked loudly, and more dust swirled up from the floor. Olivia sneezed again, completely aware that hers was a funny way of doing a normal function. The two first sneezes, high-pitched and feminine and the last one a loud, long *whoosh* that cleared her head with its gusto. Annie usually laughed whenever it happened. Always waiting through the entire sneeze to give her blessing. Today neither of them laughed.

Annie shooed her through the opening, and Olivia grabbed the railing bolted to the wall and started down the steep stairs before her. The only sound as they went was the tapping of their hard leather slippers against the wooden stairs. They twisted their way downward carefully in the dark as the air became more dank and humid, and the banister became slick with moss.

As they got near the bottom, light began seeping through the blackness that surrounded them. Olivia hurried her steps since she could see better, her feet finally sinking into soft sand when she reached the cave that cut into the cliff under Rutland Castle. It was a shallow cave, with just enough room for a small dinghy tied to a metal divot set in the rock wall. The opening to the sea was small and low.

" 'Tis a good thing it is low tide, or we'd be sitting on these steps all night waiting to get out," Annie said.

Olivia just nodded. And then she began to shake.

"Ah, now, child." Annie knelt down in the wet sand beside her and wrapped her in a warm embrace. " 'Twill be all right, my dearest. I am going to take care of you like I always have."

"My books," Olivia said through chattering teeth.

"We shall get new ones!" Annie patted her back.

Olivia reached up to touch the ring that hung on a chain about her neck. As it always did, the small circlet of gold gave her strength.

"And we shall get you a tutor! We will live a better life, sweetling, for we will not have to hide any longer. We shall go to Italy. We will go as mother and daughter, and we shall live in grand style, with servants and tutors and anything else your precious heart desires. I am going to take care of you forever, dearest, by my will I am!"

Olivia giggled.

Annie grasped her shoulders and held her away. "And what is it you find so funny in this situation?"

"You have a William?"

Annie frowned.

"You said, 'by my will-I-am.' By my William! You have a William, Annie?" Olivia laughed again. "I never knew you had a suitor."

Annie just rolled her eyes. "You and your word games, Livie. I do swear. You are more trouble than I can shake a spear at."

"William Shake-spear, you say?" Olivia laughed merrily. "Ah, he sounds like a strong, warrior of a man."

"Oh you!" Annie stood and smoothed her hand over Olivia's crown. "Come on, now, we must get this boat free and out in the water."

Olivia, feeling much better after a good laugh, scampered over to untie the boat. " 'Tis a good name, though, Annie! Should we be the Shake-speare family? Ohhhh," she sighed gustily, "poor dear papa. He was such a strong man, large and lovely he was, William Shakespeare, before he tripped on the stair, broke his nose, and died of infection."

"Why did he not just trip on the stair and break his neck?" Annie asked, pushing at the dinghy so that it slid toward the cave's opening.

"Because, for one to break his nose and die of the infection sounds much more unbelievable."

Annie stopped for a moment and stared at her.

Olivia giggled. "In subterfuge, Annie, the unbelievable is much more believable."

Annie laughed shortly before leaning down and pushing at the boat once more. "You and that imagination, Livie Shakespeare. You're just like your father. If a man could spin a tale, 'twas that William Shakespeare."

Chapter 1

Windsor Castle
April 1597

> All the world's a stage. And all the men and women merely players; They have their exits and their entrances; And one man in his time plays many parts . . .
>
> —AS YOU LIKE IT, II, VII, 139

The glittering crowd roared with laughter, Queen Elizabeth's bellow louder than them all. Sir Ian Terrance crossed his arms over his chest and leaned against the stone wall beside him, his gaze scanning the people watching the play. He hated these things: too damn many people.

He scrutinized the periphery, his mind quickly

analyzing what his eyes saw. The archway leading to the outer hall, Whiting standing to the
right. Ian acknowledged his man with a nod and
kept going. A group of women next caught his
eye. He stopped for a moment and watched
them: Nothing suspicious there. Ian continued
his visual tour, a man stood just off the group of
chatting women. Ian was about to move on before he realized there was something odd about
the man.

Ian shifted a bit, glancing to where the man
seemed to be staring. The hairs rose on the back
of Ian's neck, and he looked quickly back at the
slight figure in the back of the room. He was
thin, tall, dressed as a gentleman—a shabby one,
but a gentleman all the same. And instead of
watching the play as everyone else in the room,
he stared rather obsessively at the Queen.

Slowly, Ian pushed away from his place
against the wall and began skirting the room toward the man. As he came near his quarry, a
slim white hand snagged Ian's arm.

"Ian!" the mouth that belonged to the hand
whispered.

"Andromeda." Ian shook his sister off of him.
"I am busy."

"But, Ian, have you seen Sir Richard?" His sister clamped her rather strong hand around his
arm once more. "He promised to sit with me,

and I obtained special permission from the Queen." Her shoulders slouched forward and her brown eyes dulled. "And now he is not here."

Ian groaned. "Andy, really, I do not have the time . . ."

"Find him for me, Ian, please."

"Zounds, Andy. 'Tis the man's night to revel. He has shown his bravery in battle and is now initiated into the Order of the Garter. Let him be."

"You are being more than mean, Ian. You are being terrible."

"I have the right as your brother to be terrible to you. Anyway, the way you have your talons in the man already, he has precious few nights of being a bachelor left. I am not about to go running out, drag him in here, and begrudge him his fun, Andy." Ian carefully extracted his sister's hand from his arm. "Now sit down and enjoy the play before the Queen realizes that you do not attend her."

"Fine. But if you chance to see Sir Richard, please . . ."

"I shall warn him that you stalk him, yes."

Andy stamped her foot and said as loudly as she dared, "Upon my life, Ian, you can be the worst toad."

15

"I know, I know. Now sit." He waved her away.

"You do not approve your sister's choice in a match?"

Ian jumped as he was watching to make sure Andy found her seat, and had not realized that the young man whom he had been going after had come to him.

He had a long, thin face, pale with a handful of freckles sprinkled across his nose and a dark auburn beard. And he sported a pair of sky-blue eyes that probably made the women weep at his feet.

"Pardon my large ears, sir, but I could not help overhearing."

Ian shrugged. "Sir Richard Avery is a fine enough man. It just pains me to see another male fall into a woman's marriage trap."

"And yet, this woman is your sister."

"And thus I know that whoever marries the girl will rue the day."

"And you, sir, I would guess that you have yet to be trapped?"

"I plan never to suffer such a fate." The people around them laughed loudly, and Ian glanced toward the stage. "Are you enjoying the play, sir?" he said, remembering his first intention of finding out the man's identity.

The man blinked owlishly, and then a smile

crept across his full mouth, and he laughed aloud.

Ian frowned. The man had a very soft laugh, and rather full, pouty lips. Perhaps he had been mistaken. It seemed that the man probably used his large blue eyes to catch himself those of the male persuasion. Ian nearly groaned out loud. Wonderful, the man probably thought Ian was trying to engage him in conversation and a little something else afterward.

But he must determine the man's interest in the Queen.

"Actually, I find it hard to stomach the characters," the man said.

"Really?"

"Yes, they were much more full-bodied in *Henry IV*. It seems a shame, really, that we must see them again so watered down." The man shrugged. "But I hear 'twas what the Queen wanted: a return of Oldcastle, that is to say, Falstaff, and Mistress Quickly. She ordered it, so 'tis done."

Ian's ears pricked up at the slight sound of bitterness to the man's words. "What is your name?"

Just then thunderous applause broke out around them. "William," the man said over the din. "If you'll excuse me. I must be going." He hurried off, walking the perimeter of the room toward the stage.

Ian followed behind, his instincts at full alert, but William disappeared behind the curtain at the side of the stage.

"Ian!"

Ian glanced over his shoulder when he heard his sister's voice. He scowled, held up his hand, and mouthed "one moment," before continuing after his quarry. But when he got to the curtain and peeked behind it all he could see were actors rushing about half-dressed. William, it seemed, had vanished.

"Damn."

"What is it, Ian?"

"Nothing, 'tis nothing. What do you want of me now, Andy?"

"You mustn't tell Sir Richard that I am anxious for him. Please, promise that you will not."

Ian wanted to strangle her. "If you don't wish the man to believe that you salivate over his very footsteps, then cease so doing, dear sister."

"Ian!"

"I have the remedy to our situation!" He placed his hands upon Andy's shoulders. "If I happen upon the poor plagued Richard, I shall say absolutely nothing at all."

"That shall be the day." Andy rolled her eyes.

"Touché, little sister. It warms my heart when you speak back to me so."

Andy whacked him on the shoulder. "You are the most terrible tease, Ian. But, truly, say nothing to Sir Richard. I had permission to sit with him during this play only, and I really should not be seen with him now that it is over." She glanced behind her to where the Queen sat surrounded by her courtiers.

Ian huffed a disgusted laugh. "If it upsets her, I would like nothing more than to arrange a secret rendezvous for the two of you."

His sister turned a worried gaze upon him. "Do not do anything stupid, Ian. It bodes ill that the Queen is constantly angry with you. Do not put her in a temper this eve."

Ian laughed without a trace of humor. "Don't worry your pretty head, Andy. The Queen adores being in a temper with me. It is why she keeps me around, I'm sure."

"You know that's not true, Ian. You are indispensable to her!"

"More pity to me."

Andy's soft brown eyes rounded in horror. "You should not say such things," she hissed under her breath.

Ian shook his head wearily. "Dearest Andy, have you not learned yet that I can say anything I damned well please? She will never let me go, ever. Believe me, I have done my worst, and she still has her claws in me like tenterhooks."

Andy swallowed audibly and looked around them quickly.

"But, alas, I'll not frighten you with my ill-placed words any longer. I go anon to find the identity of a certain young William." He said this last more to himself than to his sister, but she stayed him with a hand on his arm.

"William? Do you mean the man you were following to the stage?"

Ian stopped. "Yes," he said in surprise. "Do you know him?"

"Of course! He is Shakespeare. The one who has written such entertaining plays of late. The Queen is quite impressed with the man, though she is very upset he has run off without meeting her. Even ordered the play acted out this night . . ." She tapped her finger against her chin. *"The Merry Wives of Windsor*, I think he has called it."

"Shakespeare?" Ian could only stare at the now deserted stage. *"That* was Shakespeare?"

"Find out everything you can of this Shakespeare fellow, Sir Ian."

Ian jerked at the sound of the man's name. When one began hearing too much about an obscure person it was never coincidence. He had learned that well enough in the last seventeen years.

"Shakespeare, Your Majesty?"

"Yes, the writer of the plays." The Queen walked regally about the perimeter of the room, her blue eyes sharp, as she obviously made sure there was no one hiding behind the curtains. " 'Tis a matter of great discretion, Terrance. That is why I am asking you."

Ian truly wanted to groan aloud. He stared at the ceiling for a moment. *Thank you for the integrity you ingrained within me, Father, it has ruined my life.*

"Terrance!"

With an audible sigh Ian looked again at his ruler. She glared at him, but he did not tremble like everyone else. The worst she could do was cut his damned head off, and at this point Hell seemed a sight better than earth.

Then an image of his sister materialized in his mind's eye, and Ian gritted his teeth. Ending his life was truly the least this woman could do to him. He bowed his head before her angry stare.

The Queen breathed heavily through her nose. "You tax my patience, Terrance."

" 'Tis my calling, obviously." The words were out before he could stop them.

"Your *calling*," she said, her voice trembling

with rage, "is to protect me, do as I ask, and bow to me as your liege!"

Without lifting his head, Ian answered, "And I do all three, Your Majesty." He did not flirt or flatter, though, and that was what she craved. But he was not about to flirt with a sixty-four-year old woman. He did not flirt with any woman for that matter. Nor did he flatter. He had no use for women who required anything more than a good night of sweaty sex and a six-pence for their trouble.

Feeling that he had given the Queen enough of his demure act, Ian straightened. "What is it you want me to find out about Shakespeare?" he asked.

Elizabeth stared at him icily for a moment, then turned with a swish of her skirts and went to her chair. She sat, drumming her beringed fingers on the gilded arm.

"Find out who he is, where he is from," she finally said. "I want to know everything about his background." She looked at him, then her gaze slid away.

Ian blinked. He had seen something in her eyes that he had never seen before. Fear. And something else. Confusion, doubt, perhaps? No, that would make Elizabeth human. He must have been mistaken.

"Could you tell me what I am looking for?"

he asked. "It would make it a bit easier."

The Queen looked at him again, her gaze un-wavering and steely. "Just listen for anything suspicious. You will know it if you hear it."

Ian nodded, thinking of the way Shakespeare had stared at the Queen the night before. "Yes, Your Majesty."

She waved her hand, dismissing him. He bowed low, then turned and left through the privy chamber. Along with the usual cortege of courtiers, there were some ladies-in-waiting mill-ing about, though his sister was nowhere to be seen. Ian grimaced and hurried through. But just as he reached the door, he felt a large hand clap over his shoulder.

"Terrance."

Ian turned. "Crandle."

"How is she today?" the tall man whispered, pulling at his dark beard.

"Very much the same as always, actually, my lord." Ian moved as if to leave, but the Earl of Crandle did not let go of his shoulder, so he waited.

"She seemed agitated this morning."

Ian forced himself to hold back a long, both-ered sigh. These men of the Queen made him want to run screaming from humanity. Their lives revolved around the ruler's moods and whims. Pathetic creatures, all of them. Especially

Crandle of late, since the Queen had decided he was in disfavor. Usually the earl was her very most favorite only following Essex. After all, the man had been a young crony of Dudley's. And everyone knew that Dudley held a special place in the Queen's affections. There had once even been rumors that they would marry.

"Well," the earl urged anxiously, "has she told you what has perturbed her? Did she give you some sort of . . ." here the man waved his fingers in the air. "Some sort of, um, job which would tell us why she is upset?"

Ian frowned. "You wish to know what the Queen wanted of me?"

"Yes, yes, that would help to gauge her feelings most admirably."

Perhaps he had been an agent of the Queen for too many years. He was beginning to see plots in everyone's eyes. He squinted suspiciously at Crandle. "You know full well that I cannot tell you anything."

"Crandle, Terrance, what is it that you two are whispering about?"

Ian's scowl deepened at the sound of Essex's voice. If there was anyone more pathetic than Crandle, it was Essex.

"I'm just trying to ascertain what has the Queen in a pique," Crandle answered.

24

"And?" Essex turned his pretty face toward Ian.

"And I have informed the earl that I cannot divulge my conversation with Her Majesty." He glared at Essex. "As you well know." Essex had queried him for information on more than one occasion. "Now, I'm terribly busy." He nodded at the two gentlemen and strode off without waiting for their reply.

"Bunch of preening peacocks," he grumbled under his breath as he finally gained the fresh air outside. The sun shone brightly, and flowers were blooming in their beds. But Ian only pulled his hat lower on his head and put his hand to the hilt of his sword as he left the confines of Windsor Castle to make the journey to London.

In order to investigate this Shakespeare person, Ian would have to enter the world of actors, theaters, and writers. The thought made him clench the fingers of his free hand. Writers, poets: He had thought to be one once. Long ago in those naive dream-filled days before he left his father's farm in Derbyshire and ventured into the dark, stinking alleys of London.

Ian shook his head hard. "Don't think of it!" he said aloud. A woman in front of him gave him a wide berth, obviously scared that he was some sort of madman. He chuckled a bit, for he cared not what others thought of him. In truth, he had not cared about himself in a long, long time.

"Something happens to which we should be privy," Crandle whispered to his friend.

Essex waved the thought away. "Be patient, Crandle, you shall be in the Queen's good graces anon. She will not stay angry with you forever."

"It is not only that, Essex. There is something more. The Queen is preoccupied with something that distresses her."

"You see more than what is there."

"No, good man, I see through what is there."

Essex shook his head. "I know not of what you speak."

"I have told you, Essex, the Queen is not happy with you either. Though you were her favorite, you have fallen from that stature."

Essex frowned. "You speak nonsense."

"I do not, and well you know." Crandle looked slyly about as if to make sure that no one overheard their conversation. "Did she not let you wallow in your depression last winter? You ran off in a pique to your country house, and the Queen cared not at all."

"She cared."

"She cared not! And you, the earl of Essex, are her peer, 'tis sure. You have royal blood as well as she. And pure yours is, not tainted by bastardy."

Essex grabbed Crandle's arm and pulled him toward a wall. "Speak thusly and you shall hang!"

"I speak only truth."

Essex frowned.

"You deserve more for your troubles than such as she gives, Essex."

"And you should be careful of your words, Crandle."

"Then keep your ears to doors, Essex. Let us find out what upsets our Queen. For if it is something that mayhap could be used to further your own self, you should take note upon it."

"I need not further my own self. The Queen looks favorably upon me. 'Tis you she is angered with." Essex seemed to need reassurance, though, for he bit his lip for a moment, and then asked, "Do you not think so?"

"We should watch and listen, Essex, 'tis all I will say."

Chapter 2

False face must hide what the false heart doth know.

—MACBETH, I, VII, 81

S he heard the knock at her door and started, sending a smattering of ink across the page. "Faith!" Olivia blotted the page as she stood. Another knock sounded, harder this time. "I'm coming!" She marched to the door and opened it a crack.

The heavy portal swooshed inward, sending her sprawling on her backside.

"Sorry!" Ben Jonson said breathlessly as he shoved the door shut and bolted it.

"Are you in trouble again, Ben?"

"Yes." He peeked out her small window and then pulled down the darkening drapes.

28

Olivia sighed and scrambled up, rubbing her bottom. "Whatever have you done now?"

Ben shrugged, turning away from the covered window. "Just a little bit of a brawl. But it seemed I picked some gentleman to knock in the eye, and he was shouting the constable down on me."

"And I assume you'll be wanting to stay here for a few days?" She rolled her eyes and went to clean her quill. "I shall get nothing done with you here, Ben."

"Just a few days to let this little problem die down." Ben went to Olivia's small cupboard and pulled out a loaf of bread.

"You could always go stay with your wife," she said loftily, turning away from him.

"Do not start with that, Liv. She stifles me, and you have no way of knowing how that feels. Anyway, you have earned a few days of rest from what I hear. The special showing at Windsor was a smashing success, was it not?"

Olivia snorted. "Oh yes," she said sarcastically. "Bringing Falstaff back and marrying him off was such a lovely idea."

"Liv, you have an unhealthy way of criticizing our monarch." He made a slashing motion with his finger against his neck.

She frowned at him as he bit into the loaf and dropped down onto her small cot. "Do not call me Liv. You shall forget yourself one of these days and do so in public. Then where will I be?"

"Sorry, Will," Ben said around a gob of yeasty bread. He nodded toward the parchment littering her small, rickety desk. "What are you working on?"

Olivia shrugged as she pivoted on her stool and concentrated on shaving her quill. "I am trying to finish the second part of *Henry IV*." She sighed as she put away her writing paraphernalia. "My heart just isn't in it, though. I started writing this even before I wrote part one, and I am itching to start something new."

"Yes, I know what you mean. Though I have come to the end fewer times than you, it can get frustrating." He dropped back and kicked his boots onto the cot. "And now you are telling me that it does not go away, even with practice?" He groaned.

"Get your muddy shoes off my bed, you ingrate."

Ben pushed around so that his legs hung over the side, but did not sit up. He took another bite of bread, chewing and humming at the same time.

Olivia rolled her eyes. Men. They were disgusting, truly. It sometimes made her ill to try to impersonate the crackbrained fools.

"Some fellow has been asking questions about you, Li . . . Will."

Olivia stiffened, her heart pounding rapidly in her chest. She tried to keep her voice calm. "Really? Who is he? What does he want?"

Ben scratched himself and tore off another hunk of bread with his teeth. "Some agent of the Queen, actually." He grunted as he came up on his elbows. "Maybe you're finally going to get your due for all those little cracks about our fair Lizzie."

"Fair Lizzie?" Olivia snorted. Just the thought of the Queen made her stomach clench, so she shook her head as if to dislodge the woman's presence from her mind. "What was he asking about me?"

"Oh, wanted to know where you came from. Who your family was." Ben shrugged and dropped back onto the cot. "No one could give him any answers, of course." He let a beat of silence go by, then said, "And neither could I."

It was a bit of a sore subject that Olivia would not tell Ben any more of her background than that she had lived on the Continent for more than half her life. He had probed, but she had kept her mouth tightly sealed. It was hard to break a habit, especially when that habit was a way of keeping her head attached to her neck.

She turned away from Ben so that he would

not see the terror that must surely be evident in her eyes. An agent of the Queen asking questions of her background? Lord above she had been too bold in putting Annie in *The Merry Wives of Windsor*. She had used the name Anne for one character and Ford for another. She had not been so bold as to use both names for the same character, but still it had obviously sparked the Queen's suspicion. Of course, she had also used a few of Annie's traits in the character of Anne Page. She had probably just done something rather stupid.

She had probably just hastened her own death.

"Who is he, this man who is so interested in me?"

"That large nodcock, Sir Ian Terrance."

"Sir Ian Terrance? I don't think I would know him on sight."

"The one that walks around behind the Queen like the frigging angel of death. Always wears black, never in fashion."

Olivia nodded. "Ah, yes, I spoke to him, actually, at Windsor last eve. I have heard he is one of the Queen's top men."

"Aye, that he is. It's funny, too, for I hear he is brash with his tongue and often offends Her Majesty. But he has been made a knight, been given two estates, and his sister is now a lady-in-waiting. And he began as nothing more than a farmer's son."

"He must have proved his worth in some other way than twittering about the Queen with a mouthful of foolish flattery."

Olivia heard rustling as Ben sat up. She turned, and the serious look in her friend's eye made her even more nervous. "He's a bad one, Will. There is no telling the men he has killed. I nearly pissed my pants when I heard him asking questions about you. What if they suspect you're a woman?"

Olivia laughed, the sound full of much more bravado than she felt. That was the least of her problems.

"I mean, I saw through your costume. And, although I've made some brilliant additions to your mannerisms and disguise, I don't think it would stand up to anything like an . . ." Ben coughed. "Interrogation by Sir Terrance."

"Not to worry, Ben." Olivia stood and strode to the changing screen at the corner of the cramped room. "I shall ask a few questions of my own, find out exactly what they want from me. Perhaps I offended Her Majesty somehow in *Merry Wives*."

She slipped behind the screen and took off her shirt. Then she untied the cloth that bound her small breasts, letting out a deep breath as it came undone.

"Can't say as I can think of a single thing that might offend in that light comedy of yours, Will. Although, I must say you are amazing. Finishing it in such a short time, and doing such a fine job, too."

"I am none too thrilled, personally," she said as she pulled her flannel night rail over her head. "I plan to rewrite the thing before selling it to a troupe."

"Ah, and now I will have to plunge to my death over a cliff. 'Twas a wonderful piece of work, and you hate it. What must you think of my dreary attempts at greatness?"

Olivia came out from behind the screen, fluffing out her short-cropped auburn hair. "Ben, you have talent and you know it. With practice you shall be great. With practice I hope to reach that pinnacle as well."

Ben stood, his eyes taking in her appearance like a hungry man looking at a plump chicken. She knew that he cared for her in a way that she did not feel for him. Only three years younger than she, he still seemed like such a child. And, truly, she would never know the love of a man.

Olivia pulled a heavy blanket from the chest against the wall and threw it at her dear friend. "You get the floor, Ben."

"Yes, of course." He blinked and looked away from her quickly, then huffed and puffed as he laid the blanket on the floor and yanked off his boots.

Olivia walked about her small room snuffing the candles, then with a bone-deep sigh settled on her cot. She closed her eyes and quietly sent a prayer toward heaven asking God to please take extra special care of Annie. When she finished, she had to bite her lip to keep from crying. With this new little twist in her life, she wished more than anything that Annie were still around at least to share her secret.

It had been seven years, though, since Annie died. Seven years since Olivia had come back to England with no money and only a dream to write plays for the theaters. Seven years since she had taken on the persona of her fictitious father, William Shakespeare.

"Liv?"

"Yes?"

"You've already achieved greatness. In my eyes, at least."

Olivia smiled and reached her hand down in the darkness to curl her fingers around Ben's. "Thank you, Ben. I could never do it without you."

Ben slowly brought her fingers to his lips. "Glad I could be of help."

*   *   *

He could definitely use some help. Unfortunately, Elizabeth had been quite stringent when she refused to allow him to recruit that help. Ian sagged against the dirty brick wall of the Rose Theater and watched a group of ragged urchins playing some sort of game in the street. For a moment in the Rose, Ian had thought that he had struck a gold mine of information.

"Oh, yeah." Some young boy dressed as a woman player had nodded. " 'Tis Shagspeare you be askin' about?"

Ian had nodded tentatively, unsure because of the lad's mispronunciation of the name.

"From Stratford, 'e is." The boy had shrugged and wiped his runny nose on the velvet sleeve of his dress. " 'as a wife and kids, 'e does." The boy had frowned. "Bit o' a tight fist with the money."

That had got the boy a cuff on the ear from another of the actors. "Plays ere ofen enuf. Think 'es tryin' to build 'is own theater 'cross the river," the other actor had said.

But when they had gotten down to descriptions, Ian had realized they were speaking of two different people. He closed his eyes for a moment and kneaded the back of his neck with his fingers. It was too bad, really, for it had been the first actual breakthrough in finding out who the hell this Shakespeare fellow was.

"I hear you have been asking questions about me."

Ian opened his eyes quickly and looked into the bright blue eyes of the one and only William Shakespeare. He nodded slowly. The bloke was tall, for Ian was very used to towering over others, but Shakespeare reached at least to Ian's nose. Ian recognized the man immediately: the blue eyes, aquiline features, and dusting of fragile-looking freckles over his nose were memorable to say the least.

"What do you want to know?" Shakespeare crossed his arms over his thin chest and leaned his weight on one hip. His gaze skipped down the front of Ian, then back up. "We were never properly introduced."

Ian could see no reason for keeping his identity a secret. His clandestine activities had been over for some time, as everyone knew exactly who he was. Except for, it seemed, this young chap before him.

He stuck out his hand. "Terrance, Ian Terrance."

"Ah, yes." Shakespeare grasped his hand for a brief second. "Sir Ian Terrance. Sorry to have run out on you so quickly that night at Windsor," he said without an ounce of sincerity.

" 'Twas nothing."

"But it was, obviously, for you have scoured

the city asking questions of everyone I have ever worked for," the man said with a lift of his dark eyebrows. "You must have left something unsaid to . . . search for me so diligently."

Ian was very used to interrogating and intimidating, and it had been a very long time since someone, especially a someone so much smaller than he, had tried to turn the tables on him. It left him strangely amused, though, rather than angry.

"I admire your work, Mr. Shakespeare."

That finally stopped the man. He pinched his mouth together for a moment, and then smiled dashingly. "I am glad, Sir Terrance. My life's work is to please."

"In truth, Mr. Shakespeare, I sense brilliance in your work." He bowed slightly to the shorter man. "Genius, even."

"I am flattered."

"Would you like to take a drink with me?" Ian asked, gesturing to a pub across the road.

Shakespeare looked at the small, dark alehouse, then back at Ian without answering for a long tense moment. William Shakespeare had not been fooled by his honeyed words; the man knew that Ian wanted more than just to speak with someone he admired. The writer of plays tilted his pointy little chin covered with a sparse, dark red beard, "I should enjoy a drink, sir. I find myself terribly parched."

"After you then, my man."

Shakespeare nodded tersely, his summer blue eyes hard on Ian before he turned quickly on his heel.

"Ho there!" came a strangled yell from the street. Ian blinked as William stepped directly in front of a large cart pulled by four pounding steeds.

Ian's mind processed the driver's scared bellows and fruitless tugs at the horses' braces as his body went into immediate action. He launched himself at the man in the street, grabbing and yanking him back against the theater as the neighing horses thundered by within inches of them both.

"Faith, man, you should watch where you step!" Ian yelled as he gasped for breath. He had William plastered against the wall of the theater, his large body covering the slighter one of his quarry.

Ian could feel the man's chest shuddering beneath his own, and he took a hurried step backward.

William placed his long thin fingers against his temple, and said nothing, his whole frame trembling. They stood silently for a while, neither moving while they both caught their breaths, then William's hands slid down the sides of his face and he blinked at Ian.

"Thank you," he said.

Ian frowned, staring at the man. And then his mouth quirked, and he arched his eyebrows. "You are welcome. But before we go anywhere you ought to know that you seem to have lost your beard."

William's eyes widened in horror, and he slapped his hands to his chin, finding his beard literally hanging from a thread. He turned quickly away, his hands working furiously against his face. He coughed a few times, cleared his throat, and mumbled something unintelligible. Finally, he turned back to face Ian.

The beard had been reclaimed. Unfortunately, it was a bit crooked.

"Very embarrassing," William said, his voice a noticeable octave lower than before. "I burned my beard on a candle last week and have been wearing a replacement until the real one grows back."

"I must say, that *is* embarrassing." Ian peered at the beard in question. "Quite remarkable, though, how you managed to singe off your beard and not mar your face in the least."

"Remarkable, indeed. Incredibly so."

"Well, I guess we should make sure you have no other injuries after such a close call." Ian smiled. "I mean the close call with the cart, of course. Not the candle." He took a step back and ran his gaze up and down William's form. The man immediately crossed his arms high over his chest.

Odd, that.

"I'm fine, sir, I thank you for your concern." He stopped, brow furrowed as he gulped down an audible swallow. With the new tilt of his beard, Ian noticed the smooth line of William's throat. "I must pass on the offer of a drink, though. I think I shall return home, actually, as I'm a bit . . . um, shaken."

"You must let me accompany you, Master Shakespeare. I fear in your perturbed state you may straightway throw yourself in front of another cart."

"No, really, I shall be fine."

"No, really, I insist!" Ian gestured that Shakespeare should precede him. With obvious reluctance, the man turned down the street.

"Shakespeare is quite a unique name, sir," Ian said as he fell into step beside the young man.

"Yes," was all William had to say.

"Although there is a man, an actor I'm led to believe, who has a strikingly similar name. Shagspeare, the men at the theater called him. His first name is William, as well."

"Yes, we were often confused when I first came to London."

"And when was that, young William?"

"I am not young, sir. In three years I shall be thirty."

"Really!" Ian cast a sideways glance at the smooth-looking cheeks above his companion's crooked beard. "You seem much younger."

William cleared his throat again, and then made a great play of winking at a bawdy woman across the street.

"But, then, your plays are very well done. They seem to come from the mind of someone even more mature than you."

"Thank you," William said, hurrying his pace. "Perhaps, though, I seem young to you only because you are so old?"

Ian stopped in his tracks as William continued on down the street. When the man did not stop, Ian rushed to catch up with him. "I am not old," he said rather indignantly.

"How old are you?" Shakespeare asked.

"Six-and-thirty."

"That is old."

Ian frowned. "It is not that old."

Shakespeare shrugged as they jogged around a corner. " 'Tis younger than the Queen, I shall grant you that."

Ian was not sure he wanted people seeing him

as, "younger than the Queen." He pushed aside his pique though, to get on with his investigation.

"From where do you hail, old William?" Ian asked.

William stopped at the edge of the street, looking both ways carefully this time, before he started across. They reached the other side, and began hurrying along before the man finally answered, "Cornwall, actually, a very small town in Cornwall."

"Really?" Ian said casually as his heart seemed to stop for a moment, and then beat wildly. The very name, Cornwall, always caused such a reaction.

Even after all these years, Ian remembered standing in a sunlit room on a cliff in Cornwall, readying himself to kill for the first time in his young life.

He remembered the sonnet, a good piece, really, written in a childish hand. A name that caused his blood to run cold. The high, feminine sneeze of a terrified child that had pierced his soul with its innocence, and caused him to disobey an order.

It had been the first time and the last, but he hated to think of it now, for it reminded him of his own loss of innocence.

It reminded him of who he had been.

Ian shook his head and took a deep breath, trying to calm his racing heart. "Your speech does not hold a Cornish accent, I must say."

They were now practically running through the maze of streets. "I've spent much time on the Continent," Shakespeare panted. "When I was young my family sent me to live with a guardian in Italy. We traveled extensively—Switzerland, France."

"And you returned just lately?"

William sliced a glance at him, then shook his head sharply. "No, actually, I have been here nearly seven years. England is truly the only place a person can earn his way writing plays."

"And what happened to your guardian? To travel you must have had money." Ian tripped on an upraised cobblestone, but caught himself. "Why did you suddenly find the need to earn your way?"

William stopped. "My guardian, a woman, died. Her money had been spent on my upbringing, and my family is gone, sir." The man folded his arms across his chest. "I found the need to support myself because I am a man of pride and, I do hope, talent. Queen Elizabeth's England beckoned me."

Ian stiffened. The writer of plays had put a strange inflection upon his last sentence, which caused a shiver to race down Ian's spine. "Really?"

They stared at each other in silence for a moment, and then William turned on his heel and started quickly down the street once more.

Ian had to jog to catch up with the man. "I have visited France," he said conversationally. "I enjoyed the women there."

Shakespeare slowed his pace and shot him an amused-looking glance. "Truly, Terrance? I had the feeling you did not enjoy women at all."

Ian arched his brows at his companion. "Quiet, obliging women who know exactly how to pleasure a man, I enjoy very much. Although, I must ask, of course, that you tell no one that I ever said such a thing. I am known to be a tyrant to the female sex, and I should not like them ever to believe I said anything so positive about them."

Young Will came to a halt in front of a glovemaker's shop. "Your secret resides safely with me, sir," he said between breaths. "I must thank you for your escort, Sir Ian." William pointed to the rooms above the shop. "I am home, be it ever so humble. We shall have that drink someday when I am feeling better up to the task."

"Task? Interesting choice of words, Shakespeare."

"They are my job, Sir Ian." He smiled, or tried

to, at least, and turned down the alley beside the glovemaker's shop.

He most definitely could not be a woman. For a brief moment, Ian had thought that perhaps . . . The man did have a complexion that reminded one of milk. And he had actually blushed a few times, and not in a way that any self-respecting man might blush, but with a light wash of rose-tinted color that bloomed prettily . . . Ian stopped abruptly in the street and shook his head, hard.

What in the devil's name was he thinking?

Shakespeare was no woman. A woman could not devise such intricate plays, could she? It was that slim white throat that had put the strange thought in his head.

Boys had slim white throats and smooth cheeks. Perhaps Shakespeare was just a boy, younger than most thought. Or maybe he hid behind his disguise for another reason. Did he put himself out as the writer of the plays while another actually wrote them? How did this all involve the Queen? For it most certainly seemed that it did.

Ian wracked his brains as he made his way to the Queen's private chamber, intent on getting the monarch to divulge something of why she was suspicious of the man called Shakespeare. The whole thing was getting more mysterious by the moment, and though he enjoyed puzzles, mysteries surrounding the Queen made him distinctly nervous.

Passing through the presence chamber on his way to the Queen's private chamber, Ian spotted Sir Richard. He hunched his shoulders and hurried his steps, trying to blend in with the tapestries, but it did not work.

"Terrance! A word, if you have the time?"

"No, actually, I am quite hurried at the moment."

" 'Tis important, man." The soldier cupped Ian's elbow in his hand and steered him farther away from the people milling about the room. "Of a delicate nature, what I must say to you."

Ian sighed.

"Your sister, Andromeda, how goes her heart? Do you know?"

"Toward jewels and gowns and not much else, really."

"No, Sir Ian, I speak of . . ." The man cleared his throat and looked about him. "I wish to know if your sister finds favor of any young men at court?"

"It does not matter much, actually, because she has little to put herself forth with."

Avery frowned. "You will provide a dowry, will you not?"

"What I can. It will not be of great consequence. And you know, of course, that her father was a farmer, a tenant at that."

"I have name and fortune, Sir Ian. 'Tis not what I must have in a wife."

"Then why have one at all?"

Sir Richard ignored that statement. "And your sister, if you will allow me to say, is quite lovely. Her manners are fair, and her voice is like a song from heaven."

"Do not take to writing sonnets, Avery, 'tis only I you speak to, not Andromeda."

"Will she accept my suit, then?"

"If you wish to give it, I am sure it will not be turned away." He shook his head. "Why you would want to shackle yourself is beyond my comprehension, though."

Avery slapped him on the back. "Oh, you, Terrance. Walking about here in your dark clothes and cynical tongue. Why do you eschew the joys of court? The Queen favors you, sir. You could have any woman at your feet."

"So that I may trip and fall? Thank you, no, Sir Richard. Now, I must be off to conference with that great woman who shows me so much favor."

"She has been in bad temper of late, Terrance. Watch your step."

"I know what to do with Her Majesty. It is you we must worry about since you throw yourself

into the jaws of Hell better known as matri-
mony."

Avery laughed. "You slay me, Terrance."

"Better a fellow soldier than a weak woman,
Avery." Ian walked away as Avery laughed
louder, for he saw others coming toward them,
obviously ready to share the joke.

And then he saw Andromeda coming for him
and he hurried his pace, slipping into the hallway that connected the presence chamber to the
privy chamber before his sister could corner him.
That he would rather speak to the Queen than
his sister was a testament to how much he enjoyed being used as cupid.

"You have found nothing?" The Queen raged
as she paced her private chamber. "Nothing at
all?"

"Nothing of much consequence," Ian answered. He took a sip of wine, savoring the taste
before he continued. "I know that the man is a
score and seven, he is from a small town in Cornwall, and he lived on the Continent for a time."

The Queen halted mid-stride. "Cornwall, you
say?"

Without making eye contact, Ian stared down
at a book that lay upon a small side table. "Yes,
Your Majesty." He, of course, knew the signifi-
cance of Cornwall for the Queen.

His breathing slowed suddenly, and he blinked. Could this young Shakespeare have something to do with . . . ? Holy Mother of God.

"Well that *could* explain it," the Queen whispered. "Of course, he would be rather young to have known Anne, but he could have known *of* her . . . put her name in a play, because as a child he found her lovely to look at?" She pressed two fingers against the bridge of her nose for a moment.

"Still, it plagues me! Does he know something?" This last, the Queen said in a fierce whisper, jangling Ian's nerves.

"It might help me, Your Majesty, if you could tell me what it is I am looking for," he interrupted her musings, his voice harsh to his own ears.

She twirled on her heel, her heavy skirts fanning around her as she shook her head vehemently. "You are looking for anything that should be made known to us!"

"Isn't that everything, Your Majesty?"

She stopped, her entire body still and her blue eyes leveled on him. "Do you speak lightly to us, Sir Terrance?"

"Never." He put his goblet down carefully and strode forward. "It would help me, though, if I knew what you found worrisome about this Shakespeare person."

With a shake of her head, the Queen resumed her pacing, halting suddenly before the book Ian had looked at before.

She took it up and held it out to him. "Read the foreword, Terrance. Do We have ought to worry about here? What think you?" Her voice had lost a small bit of its imperial tone.

Ian took the book from her, gliding his fingers across the embossed title: *A History of Henry IV*, penned by a man named Hayward. Ian opened it slowly and read the Latin dedication on the first page. It was to the earl of Essex, and it was obvious the author adored the man.

"The book concerns Richard II's deposition. A subject I find highly deplorable," the Queen stated.

"Yes, but it *is* history, Your Majesty. What has upset you so about the dedication?"

"Just look, Terrance!" She said, pointing a thin white finger at the book as if it were some sort of vermin. "Read the sentence that begins 'Most illustrious Earl.' "

Ian glanced back down at the page and began reading. "Most illustrious Earl, with your name adorning the front of our Henry, he may go forth to the public happier and safer."

" 'Tis treason!" The Queen raged, her entire frame shaking. "He says that if Henry IV had possessed the name and titles of Essex, his right to the throne would have been stronger." She dropped her voice to a whisper. "He implies that Essex *does* have a right to the throne. Treason, I say!"

Ian closed the book slowly and thought through his words carefully. Something was causing the Queen upset. She would have never read such implications into the dedication otherwise. "Hayward is probably referring to his work, the book, I mean, when he says that he has put Essex's name to the front of it."

The Queen just shook her head and turned away from him. "The rack. I shall put this Hayward person to the rack!"

"Your Majesty, there would have to be a trial first. And I really don't think . . ."

She sliced her hand through the air, and Ian stopped speaking. Elizabeth moved away from him, staring out her window for a long moment. "Fine then, I shall just throw him into the Tower."

Ian blinked down at the book of history in his hands. "I am sure Hayward meant nothing by his words. And you know that Essex would never think to usurp you . . ."

"He knows things," she cut him off ominously.

There was something more happening here than just an ill-written dedication, Ian thought, placing Hayward's book upon a side table.

"Find Hayward." The Queen did not turn around, but she held her skirts so tightly that her knuckles showed white. "Now. Take him to the Tower." She paused. "And Shakespeare. I want them both in the Tower."

"Your Majesty, I . . ."

Elizabeth waved a regal hand in the air, cutting him off. "Begone," she said without turning around.

Ian stared at the back of her head for a long moment, then left, as Her Majesty had demanded.

Chapter 3

Asses are made to bear, and so are you.
—THE TAMING OF THE SHREW, II, i, 198

"**A** comedy, I think." Olivia sat with her feet upon her writing table and her eyes closed. "A good one this time. I am in the mood for some merriment. And it shall be set in Italy. For I do miss the warmth of the Italian sun." She smiled as memories flitted through her mind.

"And what of the second part of *Henry IV*?" Ben asked from his languid position on her cot.

"Oh, 'tis finished already. I was just revising," she said offhandedly, dropping her feet to the floor and edging her chair forward. "I have had inspiration for my hero, he shall be quite the devil." She giggled as she took up her quill and dipped it into the inkpot.

"Inspiration you say?"

"He shall be a confirmed bachelor, and despair as his friends find mates." Olivia brandished her quill. "But 'tis because of insecurities he hides well within his heart that he feels thus."

"Hmmm."

"Oh, and my heroine." Olivia scratched a name down upon the parchment. "Beatrice. Yes, Beatrice, she is also very sure that she will never marry." She continued writing, becoming so entranced by her characters that she completely forgot that Ben was in the room until he began to snore quite loudly.

Olivia looked up quickly from her work. Ben lay on his back, sprawled across *her* bed, and, of course, he still wore his wretchedly muddy boots. She sighed, dropped her quill, and snuffed out the candles at her desk.

Stretching her arms above her head, Olivia went to stand over her friend. She bent and shoved against his shoulder with her hand. "Ben?" She hit him harder when he did not even make a sound. "Ben!"

The man drew a long, drawn-out breath, turned over, and snuggled deeper against her pillow.

The rat. She would have to take the floor this night. With a disgusted click of her tongue, Olivia went to change her clothes. She put on her nightgown, as she refused to wear men's clothes to bed, and then went to tug Ben's boots from his feet.

A rancid smell emanated from her friend's hose, and Olivia squeezed her eyes shut as she backed out her door, determined to leave the smelly shoes on the small landing.

But when a well-muscled arm clamped around her waist, and a hand snaked around to hold her mouth shut, the mud-encrusted boots flew through the air. Olivia blinked, hearing only the soft thud as Ben's boots hit the dirt beneath her second-story landing.

"Damn!" a male voice hissed in her ear. She felt herself twirled around and shoved up against the wall, the hand at her mouth staying fast. "I am looking for Shakespeare, not some lightskir . . ."

She stared into Sir Ian's eyes, and, with a full moon pouring down upon them, he stared right back.

"What the bloody hell?" he sputtered, pulling his hand away from her mouth as if she had burnt him and staggering backward against the rickety railing.

"You ought to be careful," she said. "That railing won't hold your weight.

Terrance straightened. "You're wearing a woman's night rail, for the love of God! What are you, some kind of . . ." and then he stopped and stared down at his arm. His eyes hopping back up to rake her body. "Bloody hell," he whispered.

Before Olivia knew what he was about, Sir Ian reached out and cupped her breast in his large hand.

She gasped at his touch, her breath sticking harshly in her throat, her hand going instinctively to cover his.

"You're a woman," he said, his tone like that of a child in wonder.

For some odd reason Sir Ian's quiet words made Olivia wish to cry. Without moving, she closed her eyes and felt, suddenly, exquisitely feminine. Her breast seemed to swell, her nipple tighten as she stood in the darkness with this man's hand hard against her.

"I'm a woman," she said, opening her eyes. Reality in the form of Sir Ian's rounded, shocked eyes made Olivia's grip tighten around his hand. She tried to push him away. "You have found proof, now unhand me."

Olivia backed away, but Ian just followed her.

He shoved up against her, pinning her against the unforgiving wall, his hand still cupped against the soft plumpness of her breast.

Olivia felt a moment of panic as she held tightly to Sir Ian's wrists, trying desperately to wrench his hands from her body. She tilted her head back to stare into his eyes. They were dark above hers. In the light, she knew, they were as green as jade, but now they seemed made of onyx.

"You are a woman," he said through his teeth, the boyish tone gone completely. His breath held a light scent of mint that washed over her face pleasantly. Strange, that she should think of that.

Strange that she should find something pleasant as her life started to rush by in her mind.

She would never get to finish that last play. And *The Merry Wives of Windsor* would forever be regarded as a sorry piece of rubbish. She ought to have revised that first, before starting on her new piece.

There would be no more writing. There would be no more life. The Queen had found her.

Her thoughts focused suddenly on the man's body pressed against hers when he trailed his hand down from her breast to her waist, then her hip. There would be no man, no love . . . no children. But, of course, she had accepted that many years before.

"You cannot be!" her captor said harshly.

And then it hit her. This man of the Queen's was quite surprised she was a woman. He did not know who she was.

His hand rested once more against her breast.

Olivia curled her shoulders forward and clenched her fingers around Sir Ian's wrists.

"You are! But the plays . . . your writing it is . . ."

"Good?" she asked.

He scowled. "Someone else writes them, yes?" he said harshly.

Idiot man. Olivia narrowed her eyes, took a deep breath, and brought her knee up as hard as she could. Finally he set her free as he collapsed, staggering backward awkwardly.

"No, sir. I have written the lot." He was leaning against the railing again, gasping for breath. The wood creaked beneath his weight. "Except that hideous poem *Venus and Adonis*. I do not write poetry. But I let whoever used my name know of my discontent when I wrote *The Rape of Lucrece*." She laughed, disgusted, and shook her head. "To use my name in wooing that young nodcock Southampton. How vile, truly." She stopped for a moment and watched as Sir Ian hobbled toward the stairs.

"*Your* name, madam?" Ian gasped, still bent over and clutching his manhood. "In truth, 'tis your quick knee that bears your true name!"

Olivia laughed. "Preferest thou the knee of my false name to the sharp spear of my true name?"

"By my troth, neither, woman."

She chuckled again, flirting with the thought

59

of escape as the Queen's agent sat with a grunt on the top step and put his head between his knees. Obviously Sir Ian would not give chase. She felt her lips curl into a grin. Oh, and men thought themselves so superior. One small kick, and they were like babes.

"Sweet Lucifer!" Sir Ian hissed, as he sat up straighter. Well, it seemed he was breathing once more. She had probably just missed her only chance at escape.

But she did not wish escape. Truly, Olivia had hoped for this end when she had stepped aboard the ship bound for England. She knew that someday she would be sentenced to death ... again. But this time, she was going to see her mother's face before it happened.

Olivia sat next to the great Sir Terrance. He flinched.

"You took liberties which I did not give you permission to take," she said, pressing her hand to her chest.

He glanced at her sharply, his gaze going immediately to her breast. Olivia felt her face heat. "Believe me, I shall not touch you so again."

Olivia folded her arms in front of her. "Good."

He turned away, and Olivia studied Sir Ian in profile. Even struggling to come back from a major blow to his manliness, he was a powerful figure, this Sir Ian Terrance. Of course, she had noticed before, but now she would always remember the feel of his large, strong hands cupping her breast whenever she saw him.

Although, that might not be very often now that she would probably hang at the end of the rope before the next day shone bright.

"You could be hanged for impersonating a man," he said roughly. "If it is as you say, and you wrote those plays . . ."

"I have said that I did." Olivia laughed softly. "Why do you not believe me?"

He stood without any outward sign of discomfort. "You are a woman," he said with continued disbelief.

Olivia leaned her elbows on the step behind her and squinted up at the man who would probably kill her. "How cogent of you, Sir Ian, to have noticed," she said sardonically.

His lids dropped, shielding his eyes, and his mouth pressed closed, his mien changing before her eyes. "Whom do you cover for?" he asked, the incredulous man suddenly becoming the Queen's agent from the menace in his tone to the feral look in his eye.

Olivia shuddered, in that second knowing very surely that her life would never again be the same. If she were allowed a life at all, that is.

"You did not write those plays. You couldn't have. Who did, madam? And why do you go

61

about in his place? You, a woman? And what has this to do with the Queen?"

She said nothing.

"Whatever the answers, you have humiliated the Queen. She will not be happy."

Since the man did not seem to realize that it went much beyond that, Olivia held her tongue. Surely, he would take her before the Queen. Obviously that woman wondered about Shakespeare, but had taken none into her confidence.

Sir Ian swooped down and hooked his fingers about her upper arm. "I can get these answers from you easily enough." He lowered his face close to hers. "I have made strong men weep. You would be child's play."

"You have a rather small opinion of women, do you not, Sir Ian?" Olivia blinked slowly, putting all of her effort into making her gaze hard. "I have seen twenty-seven years and have yet to weep."

"You have yet to experience my . . . questioning."

"I have experienced worse, sir, believe me."

Sir Ian stared steadily at her, his eyes those of a different person now that the game had turned deadly.

"Who are you?"

"I am a writer of plays."

He narrowed his eyes and drew her slowly to

her feet. His grip on her arm hurt, but not unbearably.

"What is your name?"

Olivia took a deep breath, let it out, and then said, "Beatrice." She looked at his mouth for a moment, so close to her face. It was a mouth that could have been beautiful—the mouth, the face, really, of an angel, had Sir Ian not the cynical twist to his lips, the hardness in his eyes, the darkness in his being of one of the devil's own.

Evil cloaked in beauty.

The thought provoked a searing memory of the man sent to take her life so many years before. But he had been truly beautiful. He had been her salvation.

This man would be her downfall.

Olivia moved closer to him, her brow quirking up as she asked, "Who are *you*, Sir Ian Terrance?"

He stopped breathing. She could tell, for she no longer heard the faint rasp of air leaving his nose, no longer felt the soft slide of his breath against her cheek. She saw something in his eyes, though. And knew that she had hit a chord.

His lips thinned as he dragged in a harsh breath. "If I took you to the Queen now, she would probably have you killed."

"Probably," Olivia said without feeling.

"For whom do you cover?" He squeezed her

arm so that the pain was much more fierce.

Olivia had lived with death too often to fear it now. "I cover for myself, Sir Ian." She cocked her head to the side and smiled. "Because your brain is the size of a gnat's, you will probably never believe me, but I, a woman, write plays. I use the name of a man because the world seems of the same small mind as you, and would not allow such a thing."

His brows came together, and his gaze hardened even more. "Enlighten my small mind then, Miss Beatrice. What has this to do with the Queen?"

Sir Ian's grasp on her arm had loosened, and Olivia crossed her arms before her. She tapped a finger against her sleeve and curled her lips in a bit of a smile. "Why don't you ask the Queen?"

Sir Ian's gaze went to her hand. She glanced down, studying the ink stains on her fingers and in the corners of her nails. When she looked back up, Sir Ian was staring at her. He had noticed the ink stains as well. She arched her brow.

They stood silently contemplating each other for another moment, and then Sir Ian pulled her forward harshly. "Come with me," he growled, and started down the stairs.

Olivia stumbled, and then fell against him, but he grabbed her.

"I . . . will you not let me . . ." She was going

to ask that he let her dress or put on a coat . . . shoes, something, but then, and for the first time since Sir Ian had grabbed her, she remembered Ben. Dearest Ben asleep on her cot. She would not have him brought into this mess.

At the bottom of the stairs, her captor stopped and took off his dark cape. He swirled it about her, and she caught the subtle smell of this man who had become her enemy. It was a good smell, unlike that of most of the men she knew. It was clean, with a touch of musky soap and leather. And then he picked her up, tucking her against his wide chest. Olivia made a small sound of protest, but he curled his arm about her and pressed his hand against her mouth.

"Keep your silence!" he ground out between his teeth.

She thought of biting him, but realized with a sinking sense of destiny that this man would give her no more reprieves. Her only hope was to wait. She would have to put her faith in the hands of her mother now. The woman who had sent someone to kill her when she was all of ten years old.

What was he going to do? Ian marched through the darkened streets of London with his ominously still burden. He *should* take her straight to the Queen. He should dump her bottom in a cell in the Tower.

But what if . . . Ian did not even want to think it, but the facts were sitting heavily in his arms. Shakespeare, the person Queen Elizabeth seemed more fearful of than any person yet alive, was a woman. A twenty-seven-year-old woman.

Ian shifted her weight in his arms. A damn heavy woman.

Did the Queen toy with his mind? Did she know her daughter still lived? Was she just waiting for Ian to figure it out before she laughingly cut off his head?

But no. He knew her better than that after all these years. Elizabeth was not sure, but she was suspicious. Just as he was. For in truth, he was not sure. And how in the hell would he find out. He could not just come out and ask Miss Beatrice if she was in any way related to the Queen.

It was a coil, indeed.

The part of Ian that had been the Queen's agent for eighteen years wanted to turn his steps toward the Tower. If this woman in his arms was who he now suspected, then a hangman's noose would await him. And he would step up to the rope with the same determination with which he had done all of his duties.

But the part of him that was brother and son, trembled at the prospect of death and humiliation. His sister would be shunned, his mother would be destitute . . . again.

Ian realized that he needed to know more before he could figure out what to do. And he must find out the truth before the Queen.

He would have to disobey a command. It was only the second time in his life that he would do such a thing.

This was turning into a real-life nightmare.

He could only thank all the gods that by some miracle, *Beatrice* had decided to keep quiet so Ian did not have to figure out a way to carry her and shut her up at the same time. Still, she kept her arms folded across her chest instead of putting them about his neck to relieve some of the weight from his arms.

He scowled down at her. He could swear she was concentrating all her effort on being as heavy as possible. She caught his gaze upon her, narrowed her eyes, and looked away.

Damn petulant woman.

Ian cut across the street, down an alley, and up the stoop of the back door to his house. "You must weigh twelve stone, at least!" he said with disgust as he dropped her to her feet. Keeping his hand around her arm, he fitted his iron key into the lock and jiggled it open.

"I'm tall," she said between her teeth.

Ian pushed open the door and glanced at her. Well she certainly was not fat. There were no womanly curves or soft fleshy areas to Beatrice.

Ian snorted and shoved her inside ahead of him.

His housekeeper, Gretchen, would be asleep, fortunately. His only other help for his small town house was Mary, and she would be there in just a few more hours. Ian sighed heavily. He would have to take Miss Beatrice the pretend playwright up to his own room and hide her away until he figured out exactly who she was.

And he was tired, dammit. He wanted to sleep.

"Come." He pulled her along through the small kitchen to the hall and then up the front stairs.

"Your manners are atrocious," Beatrice grumbled as they went.

"As atrocious as yours are deceitful." They reached the first floor, and Ian headed toward his chambers at the end of the hall.

"Where are you taking me?" Her voice held the first trace of fear, and Ian had to laugh.

"Don't worry your pointy little chin. I would not ride your bony body if you were the last woman on earth."

"Your charm slays me."

He stalked into his room, dragging her behind him, and made sure that he bolted the door. "Since I possess nothing even close to charm, you must be easily taken in by those who try for the talent." He bared his teeth at her, let her go, and surveyed the room for a blessed moment of silence. Gretchen had left a lamp burning, and a fire banked in the grate for his arrival. The room was not fancy, though, and did not have much more furniture than a bed and a chair. "Now what do I do with you?" he murmured.

She chuckled, and he cut a quick glance at the girl. She had her hands planted on her hips, her hair stood out on her head like straw, and huge, white feet stuck out from under the hem of her gown.

"You don't know what to do with me, sir?" She laughed again. "Truly, you must not come to this conclusion often." She gave him a self-satisfied smirk. "I mean, a woman half-naked in your room, of course."

He arched his brows. "Quite courageous of you, Bea, since you have no idea how I might react if provoked."

She rolled her eyes and plunked her skinny bottom upon his favorite leather chair. Crossing one long leg over the other, she propped her elbow on her knee and leaned her chin on her palm. "Oh, I am sure I know how you react. That great cynical tongue lashes out and whips at those in the sorry state of being near you." She pursed her lips and lifted one fine brow. "Well, lash away, dear sir. If there is one thing I can deal with nicely, 'tis words."

"Oh, yes, that's right," he said with derision as he strode toward a chest at the end of his bed and pulled out a few of his garters. He turned on her, advancing slowly. "You are a great one with words. A genius even. Weaving your wit and intelligence into the words of such as Henry IV and Falstaff." He laughed as he came to stand above her. "Amazing, truly," he gushed.

And then he bent quickly, placing his hands upon the chair arms and pressing Beatrice against its back. "Forgive me if I do not believe you in the least," he said in a low voice.

She stared back at him, all humor washed away, but nothing close to fear lurked in her eyes. "You're forgiven," she said without taking her gaze from him.

"Really?" And then he kissed her. He was not sure why, perhaps to remind her of his dominance, because she did not seem to be scared. And dominance definitely gave him an edge when his prisoners were afraid of him. Whatever the reason, his composure vanished when his lips met hers.

They were soft. Much softer than he would ever have thought, since she looked to be all sharp angles and hard planes. And she tasted rather nicely of something sweet. A fruit, perhaps, an apple.

He kissed her hard, feeling himself stir, and

70

then released her mouth without ever touching her body. He opened his eyes and realized that she had probably not closed hers at all, for she stared at him in shock. Her blue eyes dark and wide. Her mouth opened slightly, glistening with the wetness of his own lips.

Had he been trying to prove his dominance? Ian had a profound moment of uncertainty as he blinked and then straightened, slowly. It had been a very long time since the touch of a woman's mouth had made his knees weak. Ian searched the shadowed face of the woman before him for a long, silent moment. And then he shook off the feeling, curling his fingers around the garters in his hand. It must be the seriousness of the situation, for the woman did not appeal to him at all.

Of course she did not.

He enjoyed curves and softness and mouths that only opened to ask him what he wished.

This tall, thin woman with the biting tongue did not appeal to him in the least. But her thickly lashed, large eyes were rather lovely, and so Ian looked away, his gaze snaring on her glistening mouth. He swallowed, his mind instantly remembering her soft lips against his own.

Frowning, Ian squinted past his captive at a spot on the wall. He pulled a garter through his fingers, snapped it taut, then wrapped it around her arm and the chair.

She did not move. Nor did she speak. A wonder, that. Ian quietly tied her other arm, and then her legs, securing them tightly to the chair.

He stepped back when he was finished. "Will you keep your mouth quiet this night, or shall I gag you as well?"

She said nothing, so he just nodded. "Fine." He moved away, snuffed out the lamp, and sat on the edge of his bed to remove his boots. He stayed still for a moment, though, trying to reclaim his sanity. He should not have kissed her.

"Could I have a blanket?" she asked in the dark.

His conscience stirred, and it angered him mightily. He had not heard from that part of his being in a rather long while, and he liked it that way. He grabbed the heavy blanket from atop his feather mattress and took it over to her. He spread it over her body, then stumbled back to his bed, banging his shin upon the side so hard he knew there would be a bruise. " 'Sblood," he hissed.

"That will probably leave a mark," his prisoner said from her place off to the side. Amusement wreathed her words, and Ian scowled.

"Not as permanent as the mark about your neck when you swing, Miss Bea."

That brought a lovely sound of silence from his chamber partner. Unfortunately, his newly lively conscience decided to talk to him through most of the rest of the hours until morning finally came.

He had just gotten to sleep when a scrabbling at his door had him sitting upright in bed, his hand reaching for the dagger beneath his pillow.

"Sir Ian?" a small voice called through the door.

Ian shut his eyes for a moment trying to remember where he was, what day it was, what year it was? Why was he so damned tired? Why the hell did his groin ache?

"Sir Ian is rather detained at the moment," a feminine voice piped up from beside his bed. Ian's eyes snapped open, and he stared at the woman still bound to his chair.

"Oh, goodness. I shall return later with your morning coffee, Sir Ian." He heard Mary's light footsteps retreating down the hall. Ian scowled at his houseguest.

"I need that coffee now, by my troth."

"By all means, call her back." Beatrice shrugged, her smile the perfect picture of innocence. "I am sure your servants have found worse in your room than a poor gel tied to your chair."

Rather than get into a verbal joust with Beatrice, Ian closed his eyes and rubbed his hands roughly against his face. The tiny bit of sleep he had managed to get had done nothing to help him solve the small problem he found himself facing.

He opened his eyes. Namely, Beatrice.

Ian threw back the thin coverlet he had used the night before and pushed himself to the floor.

"My, my, aren't you a manly one?"

Ian frowned, looked over at the termagant, and then followed her gaze to his fully engorged manhood, straining against the hose he had forgotten to take off the night before.

Ian yanked at his shirt, but it did not hide anything, then he scowled at Beatrice. She lifted her brows. "Do not tell me that I have inspired such lofty signs of affection from you, dear sir."

Ian grunted and turned away from her, deciding to walk over the bed rather than go around the piece of furniture and get within spitting distance of his fair chamber partner. "Do not flatter yourself," he said as he crawled across the rumpled linens. "I would find myself in such a state should a squealing pig sit where you do."

"A pig?" Beatrice asked. "I did not think you would have high standards, Terrance. But, a pig?"

Ian rolled his eyes and went to unbolt his door. He stopped, though, his hand on the lock. He

74

could not order Mary back in the room. He did not want it widely known that he kept a woman tied to his chair in his bedchamber. And his servants, though more discreet than most, could still spin a tale with the best of them.

"Confused, Sir Ian?" Beatrice asked. "That, dear sir, is a door. You open it. You go outside. You could try to run through it, but I would advise against it."

"Keep your inconsequential thoughts to yourself!" Ian opened the door. "Don't move," he commanded Beatrice.

She looked at him as if he were daft. "I hadn't planned on it."

Ian made a sound halfway between a growl and a sigh. He had not had enough sleep to deal with the likes of Beatrice. Throwing her a look of disgust, he marched through the doorway and slammed the portal shut behind him.

And from behind the door he heard two small, high, feminine sneezes, then one long, gut-wrenching one. Ian stopped, his feet rooted to the floor. He remembered that sneeze for it had been a sound which had changed his life forever.

And in that moment, Ian knew exactly who Shakespeare was. He was not a man, and he was not Beatrice. Shakespeare was the Queen's bastard daughter, Olivia Tudor.

Chapter 4

Misery acquaints a man with strange bedfellows.
—The Tempest, II, ii, 40

She would kill him. As soon as her hands were free she would wrap them around that thick neck of his and squeeze. They would have to pry her bloodless fingers from his dead body. Olivia shifted as much as her bonds would allow, realizing that along with her hands and her feet, her bottom was now numb.

Olivia closed her eyes and tried desperately to think of anything other than her need to use the chamber pot she had seen poking out from underneath Sir Dense Head's bed.

And then with a bang she heard a door close somewhere beneath her. Olivia opened her eyes, staring hard at the floor as if she might be able to see through the thick wooden boards. She heard footsteps below, most definitely in the house. Something heavy banged against a wall, making the floor beneath her feet shudder.

Olivia frowned. With the way things had been going for her, it was probably too much to ask that the heavy-sounding person belowstairs turn out to be some small, fragile housemaid who would willingly let her loose of her bonds so that she might delightfully relieve herself—oh, and that part of Olivia's short daydream was what she wanted most at this moment—and take off at a stiff run, putting this awful chair and the horrible Sir Ian behind her forever.

The thud of footsteps on the stair made Olivia straighten as best she could. The foul curses that vibrated up the stairwell and through the bedroom door made her cringe. No biddable maid would know the words Olivia was hearing, much less use them. She sighed and waited for the arrival of the great lout she knew to be her captor.

The latch on the door lifted and Sir Ian barged into the room, his face dark with stubble, his eyes bloodshot, and his breath so thick with the smell of ale, Olivia pursed her mouth and wished beyond reason she could pinch her nose closed against the stench.

"You disgusting pig," she said instead.

Sir Ian blinked his rheumy-looking eyes as if to bring her into focus. "You're still here," he said, slurring the words together.

The rage that boiled through Olivia's veins in that moment was beyond any she had ever felt. "You are drunk!" She banged her feet against the ground as best she could, trying to vent in any way possible. "You filthy bastard, you . . . you . . ."

Sir Ian placed a hand over his eyes as he slammed the door and toppled toward his bed. "Shut up."

"Shut up?" Olivia squirmed, the heavy chair only creaking slightly at her movement. "Shut up, you say? I am going to kill you! How dare you leave me here, *alone*, all day while you imbibe like the sniveling rat that you are!"

Sir Ian plopped onto his bed facefirst and did not move. "Rats imbibe?" he asked, his words muffled by the bed linens.

Olivia was about to scream something, anything, at the back of his big ugly head, but she stopped as she took a breath. If she screamed, she very well might lose control of her bladder. And so she huffed a disgusted breath and clenched her fingers around the leather arms of Sir Drunkard's chair.

His rather nice chair. Olivia smiled suddenly. "Since you sent your maids off this morning and left me alone, Sir Ian, I have spent the day saving up some rather pungent waste that would most likely ruin your obviously expensive chair."

The man did not even move.

"Sir Pig's Breath? Did you hear me?" Olivia asked sweetly. "I am about to relieve myself upon your chair."

Still he did not move.

Olivia took another deep breath and screamed with all her might. "I am going to piss all over your stinking chair, you lowly, mud-eating pig!"

Olivia blinked. She had screamed so loud, black spots danced before her eyes, and she realized that she was very hungry on top of the immediate need to urinate.

"For a supposed writer of plays, your vocabulary is quite limited."

Olivia narrowed her eyes upon the man who lay on the bed. He had lifted his head and turned it toward her. She scowled. Even piss-eyed drunk, Sir Ian Terrance was a beautiful man. A light brown curl slipped over his forehead and dangled in front of one thickly lashed eye.

"You have used the word *pig* in almost every sentence uttered since I entered the room."

Olivia tapped a finger against the arm of her prison. "I am much better with words when given a moment to search my mind for the perfect one. As I have been generously given an entire day to search my mind for the perfect word for you, I have done so, you swine."

He grunted, very much like a pig, actually, and dropped his head back onto his bed.

"God's teeth!" Olivia muttered, then started to take in another breath for another scream.

"Don't!" Sir Terrance held up his hand, palm facing her. "I'll help you, just give me a blasted moment, you termagant."

"A moment? 'Tis a moment you want?" Olivia stamped her foot again. "I've given you an entire day, you . . ."

"Pig, yes, I've heard." The man moaned and groaned as he rolled over and sat up, bracing his hands upon his knees.

"Have you been at the back of an alehouse all day, man?" Olivia asked, as Sir Ian finally straightened into a standing position. He wavered a bit, then made his way slowly toward her.

"Aye," was his short answer.

"And what about me? You left me with no one to take care of my needs? I would rather be in the bloody Tower!"

"Wouldn't we all?" He stopped a couple feet from her chair and took a few deep breaths.

"At least in the Tower I would have food and be able to relieve myself!"

"So you would like to believe." Sir Ian closed

his eyes, almost toppled to the ground, and opened them quickly.

"I *insist* that you take me to the Tower!" That had been her whole reason behind letting the man take her so easily the night before. Olivia had always known that she lived on borrowed time, and with the Queen's agent finding out that Shakespeare was a woman, that time had been yanked completely away from her. Destiny had obviously decided that it was time for her to meet her mother.

But now she had spent an entire day tied to a chair, with no Tower or Queen in sight. "Why have you not taken me to the . . ."

"Give your lungs a break, woman," he interrupted her.

"I could easily give my muscles a break, you lazy lackwit, and piss all over your chair."

"Yes." Sir Ian rubbed at his temples. "You've announced that intention already."

Olivia clicked her tongue against the top of her mouth, ready to launch into a verbal battle with the man, but stopped suddenly, as a coherent thought pierced through her anger.

The man was drunk.

She was sober.

He was about to untie her.

If he was not willing to take her to the Queen, she could very well get to the woman herself.

And Sir Ian Terrance had just made that easier, being the drunken lout that he was.

Olivia closed her eyes for a moment to thank God for Queen's agents who enjoyed spending the day at the pub. A puff of putrid breath had her opening her eyes again. Sir Ian was bent over her, eyeing the knots about her wrists.

"Hold your stinking breath when you lean close," Olivia muttered.

He squinted up at her, rolled his eyes, then returned his regard to her hands. With a low growl, he set about trying to untie her.

Olivia pushed herself as far back in her chair as possible, but even then, the man's hair grazed her chin a few times. And, unfortunately, his hair did not smell like his breath. It was soft, actually, and smelled of spice. For some unfathomable reason the feel of his hair against her chin made her heart flutter in her chest.

She made a disgusted sound in the back of her throat. She must be delirious.

With earnest determination, Olivia stared at Sir Ian's head and tried to plan her escape. She could not just take off running, for she truly needed to use the chamber pot, and she would definitely have to let the blood flow into her extremities for a few moments before she was able to go anywhere.

Sir Ian grunted again, and yanked on the garters that held her to the chair. The callused edge of his finger brushed the tender skin just below her palm, and a strange ripple of awareness feathered along Olivia's arm. Her breath caught, and her body shuddered.

Sir Ian lifted his face, putting their mouths scant inches apart. With a hard swallow, Olivia suddenly remembered the night before. The kiss.

It had been her first kiss from a man, and it had been from an enemy, but it had still rendered her unusually mute. Now, even with only the memory, Olivia's skin bristled, and her breathing went shallow.

Sir Ian stared at her for a long moment, and then his gaze drifted down to her lips. Would he kiss her again? Of course she did not wish him to. She could not want such a thing. Olivia wet her bottom lip nervously.

There was something in Sir Ian's eyes as he looked at her mouth. A man had never looked at her like that before in her life: as if he saw more than just a woman or a skinny girl. As if he saw something he wanted.

And then he let out a huff of breath, the alcohol content of which verily set her eyes to watering, and Olivia reeled back with the reality of her situation. "Dear God in heaven," she said, "go chew some mint before I pass out."

He just glared at her and went back to the task

of undoing the knots that held her bound. With another grunt, he finally loosened the ties.

Olivia groaned with pure ecstasy as she rotated her hands, then clenched her fists and relaxed them. Heaven . . . for a moment.

And then Hell.

Needles poked at her nerve endings, and Olivia held her hands away from her body as if she would like to give them to someone.

And then Sir Sweet Mouth thrust the chamber pot into her arms. "Well, get it done with then."

The chamber pot clattered to the wooden floor, and Olivia let out a small gasp of pain.

Sir Ian squeezed his eyes shut at the noise, pressing his fingertips to his temples. "Why did you do that?" he grumbled.

Olivia glared at her tormentor. "It *hurt*, you overbearing oaf!" She inched forward in the chair, using her elbows as leverage. The minute she went to stand, though, she felt herself crumple.

With every working muscle in her body, Olivia made sure she fell back into the chair rather than at Sir Thick Brain's feet. And then a very unladylike curse crossed her lips.

"Here." Sir Ian thrust out a large hand so that it nearly touched her nose. "I'll help you."

She had never heard a more grudging offer of help in her life. Olivia managed to raise her arm and bat the man's proffered hand away. "I'd rather sour myself."

"Not on my favorite chair, you won't," he ground out as he wrapped his fingers around her upper arms.

"Don't you dare!" Olivia squealed just as he heaved upward. "Oh!" Her feet pounded as the blood rushed back into them, the needles in her hands nothing compared to the spears in her feet. Blackness obliterated her vision, and Olivia cried out again.

And then, for the first time in her entire life, she fainted. Or she must have, anyway, because the next thing she was aware of was a hard, strong body plastered against every square inch of her own.

Olivia blinked, or, at least, she tried to. All she could see was darkness. And then her entire body began shaking: her arms swaying, her hands bouncing off another being, her feet smacking against something hard.

"Wake up, dammit!"

Olivia shook her head, and realized that her face was smashed against Sir Drunkard's tunic. She let her head fall back on her neck and looked up at the unshaven, bleary-eyed face of her nemesis.

"Wake up!" He gave her another good shake,

her feet whacking against his shins so hard he grimaced.

Served him right, the mannerless lout.

"I am awake!" she finally cried. "I'm awake, I'm awake . . . I live!"

At least he stopped the shaking. And then he gently placed her feet against the ground.

"Ohhhh," she groaned, and he immediately lifted her again.

And they stood there, silent, his arms wrapped tightly around her, her body hanging like a rag doll's. And she could not do a thing about it.

With that knowledge, Olivia let her forehead drop against Sir Ian's chest and relaxed against his body.

It was a good thing he was strong. She could feel the muscles of his arms around her torso. She could even feel the tightened muscles of his stomach against her own belly. Oh, yes, Sir Ian was definitely strong.

And aroused!

Olivia pushed her head back, and stared, shocked, into her abductor's eyes.

"I'm not a damned priest!" he snarled at her.

She felt her lips curl. "But I am not a squealing pig."

"So you say."

Olivia narrowed her eyes, very ready for another battle.

"I'm tired," he cut her off before she even formed the words. "My head aches, and I am in a foul mood, miss whatever your name is. Shall we take care of your immediate problem?"

"I told you my name. 'Tis Beatrice."

"Indeed." He trudged over to a screen in the corner, pushing the chamber pot along with his foot.

As they went, Olivia flexed her fingers and toes and knew that she would at least be able to relieve herself in privacy. She hoped.

With a grunt, Sir Ian shoved the chamber pot behind the screen. "Can you stand now, do you think?" he asked.

Olivia just nodded, and he put her down slowly. She rocked like a mast in the breeze for a moment, but Sir Ian kept a hand firmly about one of her arms.

"I think I am all right now," she said finally.

"Fine." He let go, and she felt bereft, alone and not at all strong.

What an awful feeling.

Olivia glanced up at her captor for a moment. She had actually enjoyed the feel of him close to her. How very strange, for she certainly did not enjoy *him*.

"Why are you looking at me like that?" he growled.

As if any person on the face of the earth could enjoy Sir Growly Bear's demeanor.

"I was waiting for you to turn back into an inconsiderate swine." She smiled. "And you have."

"Always willing to accommodate my guests." He smirked at her and turned on his heel. "If you need assistance, just open that shrewish mouth of yours and give a yell."

Olivia rolled her eyes and shuffled behind the screen. And then she stood there waiting to hear the door of the bedroom close behind her sweet-mannered new friend.

And she waited. "Aren't you going to leave?"

"I don't become stupid when I drink, Miss Bea."

Olivia felt her anger flare. She placed her fists against her hips. "You do not expect me to relieve myself with you only inches away, surely!"

"I *expect* you not to forget that *you*, my Lady Tongue, are a PRISONER in my home!" The sentence was said in a sickeningly sweet voice until he hit the word prisoner, which was yelled so loud Olivia swore dust fell from cracks in the wall.

"Well don't go getting yourself in a huff about it, Sir Lord-of-the-Manor."

Something crashed against a wall, and Olivia flinched. She must say she enjoyed speaking her mind, but she knew when to stop. She might not be exactly prudent, but she most definitely was not stupid.

Olivia situated the chamber pot, pulled up her nightgown, and went about her business. She winced at the sound that seemed to resonate in the room as her waste splashed against the empty pot. And she knew that when she finally rounded the corner of the screen her cheeks were a flaming red.

But then she saw her captor passed out cold on his bed, and all thoughts of embarrassment fled.

"Sir Ian?" Olivia called out softly. The man did not stir at all. Olivia backed toward the door, skirting the bed widely. A board squeaked beneath her feet when she reached the portal, and she stopped short, forcing all her muscles to freeze.

But still Sir Ian did not move. In fact, he snored. Not loudly, but Olivia could detect in the quiet the definite sound of air moving in and out of Sir Slug's nose.

Olivia reached behind her and grasped the door latch in a tight, slightly shaky fist as she sent a small prayer of thanks heavenward. And then she tried to move the latch.

Nothing happened.

Olivia frowned and put a bit more strength

into getting the door open. Still, it would not budge. She whipped around, shaking the latch, but it was not going to move. Olivia sighed. It was locked.

She turned back around, thinking that she could perhaps jump out the window, but she came face-to-face with Sir Ian's chin.

Damn.

"Looking for this?" he asked, dangling a large iron key before her nose.

Olivia went to grab it, but Sir Ian closed it within his fist and chuckled. "Don't think so, Miss Bea." And he dropped the key down the front of his hose.

Olivia could see the bulge of the thing she wanted most in the world snuggled right next to another bulge which she wanted nothing to do with. She snapped her chin back up and narrowed her eyes upon her captor. "You are a . . ."

"Pig. Really, if you are going to keep pretending to be a playwright, the least you could do is also pretend to have a larger vocabulary."

"I do not need to . . ." She stopped abruptly when Sir Ian placed a finger against her lips.

"I am a tired and out-of-sorts pig at the moment, Miss Bea. And I wish not to hear another word from your shrew's mouth for tonight, at least. You may practice your vocabulary on me in the morning, I promise."

Before she could even think of what he had said to her, the man bent and picked her up. Startled, she grabbed at his tunic, obviously catching chest hair in her fists as well, for Sir Bully grunted in pain and dropped her onto his bed.

She bounced once, then settled onto the divinely soft feather tick. And then he was beside her, locking her into a vise of strong arms and legs as he lay down on the bed.

Olivia blinked, shocked at their intimate position. She had never been so close to another human being in her entire life. Every inch of her back was touching some part of the man. One of his long, hard legs was hooked over both of hers, bracing them against his other shin. Her bottom was snug against his loins, and he had both arms around her shoulders.

She squirmed, but could not move.

"Stay put. I need to sleep."

Olivia could only stare at the opposite wall. How dare he! "You cannot do this! I . . . I . . ."

"You what? You have a reputation to protect?" He chuckled, and Olivia felt the rumble of it against her back. "Be quiet and sleep."

Olivia stayed silent for a moment, more out of shock than any need to obey the overbearing man at her back. Within seconds he was snoring softly once more.

Olivia listened to the sound of his breathing

for what seemed hours, letting the man fall into a deep sleep.

When she figured he must be dead to the world, Olivia waited even longer.

"Sir Ian?" she finally asked.

He did not reply, and Olivia began to roll slowly out of her captor's grasp. But the man just clamped down harder.

She squirmed.

"Let me sleep, woman."

"Of course I shall let you sleep, Sir Tyrant," Olivia said softly. "And then I shall slit your throat and be done with you."

Again, the man laughed. "You have me shaking in my boots."

Olivia pursed her lips together and said nothing. Again she waited for the man to sleep, only this time she was going to make sure he was deep in slumber before she tried anything.

She moved a bit, settling herself more comfortably in Sir Ian's arms, noting that he must have the most wonderful feather bed in all Christendom. His snoring began again. Not an awful, thunderous sound like Ben's snoring. No, Sir Ian's snore was more a soft sough of sound, soothing really. Especially combined with the feel of his chest rising and falling against her back.

Olivia relaxed a bit more. If he felt her relax,

perhaps he would go into a deeper slumber, right? She let her head drop to the side, and Sir Ian moved a bit so that he pillowed her cheek on his shoulder.

This must be what a caterpillar felt like as it wove a cocoon about itself, Olivia thought, as her eyelids began to droop and become almost unbearably heavy. Her stomach grumbled in the silence, reminding her that she hungered. But she had been hungry before.

And that slight discomfort was not enough to keep her awake, for soon her lids dropped for the last time, and Olivia settled more heavily against her captor. She slept.

She slept the most contented sleep of her life, actually. Which seemed very strange to her when she awoke still surrounded by Sir Ian's embrace. It had been the first night in her entire life she had slept with the sure knowledge that nothing would be able to hurt her in her vulnerable state.

Very strange indeed.

Chapter 5

The state of man, like to a little kingdom, suffers
then the nature of an insurrection.

—Julius Caesar, II, i, 67

The woman in his arms was no soft, snuggly
creature, that was for sure. Her body was
not one that would turn his head had he ever
seen her trot down the street dressed as a woman
ought to be dressed.

Personally, he had no use whatsoever for
women, other than the obvious. And that deed
was done better with a lot of cushioning—something that this tall, gangly thing within his embrace lacked altogether.

The fact that his body did not seem to understand that he was not at all attracted to the fishwife who called herself Beatrice was beyond his comprehension. That his hand tracked a course along her side, stopping for a moment at the indentation of her waist, his fingers splaying over her hipbone, then continuing up to cup the small curve of her breast was something that Ian could not fathom in the least.

She did have a nice mouth, her lips pouty. He had thought them rather feminine on the face of a man, and now that they adorned the face of a woman, he found them nearly irresistible. Of course he must resist, but in this silent, unhurried moment with his hand upon Olivia Tudor's warm body, Ian had to admit that he wished he didn't.

"What is it you think you are doing?"

If nothing else, at least she could not speak when he covered her mouth with his.

Ignoring the woman's question, Ian gave into a small temptation and palmed her breast. It was small, but rounded and wonderfully warm. Through her light gown, he felt Olivia's nipple pucker against his fingers. His own body stirred, and he had to slow his breathing before he could speak. "Checking to see if you are awake," he said.

"Oh!" She batted at his hand and rolled away from him. And he let her.

She scrambled off his high bed easily. A feat not many of the few women he had brought here had been able to do, short as they were. But the tall, proud Olivia Tudor slapped her feet to the ground and straightened, her fists curling as she planted them at her waist.

Her hair swirled about her head, a short tangled mess of rust-colored locks, and her night rail's ties lay loose and hanging down her front so that the neck of the garment gaped open. All in all she should not have appealed to him in the least. But in the last couple of days, it seemed, nothing was happening as it should.

He found himself wishing he could pull her back into his bed, comb her hair with his fingers, and take the garment from her tall body. The small taste he had gotten of her lips made him want more, and the slight touch of her body had made him curious to see her. She would have small, high breasts, legs long enough to wrap around him easily, and a slender waist he could surely encircle with two hands.

And she was the Queen's bastard daughter, his prisoner, and most probably the woman who would be his downfall.

He must keep that at the front of his thoughts and not allow any more flights of sexual fantasy.

"You will not use me like some alehouse whore, you ingrate." She pointed at him. "I demand that you take me to the Tower this instant.

I demand that you release me into the Queen's custody!"

Ian propped himself up on his elbow. "You are quite a demanding bedfellow."

She shook her head, disgust showing in her eyes. "I am sore amazed you could ever be such an esteemed agent of the Queen as your reputation belies. For truly, you are a lazy, loathsome, and despicable man. You have caught me, Sir Ian. I, Shakespeare, am a woman. The Queen would laud your work. But you lock me in your room and go out drinking." She tsked, folding her arms in front of her body. "You are disgraceful."

"And you, Madam Shakespeare, are quite in a hurry to get your head lopped off."

She glared at him. "Rather that than spend another minute in your company."

Ian watched her for a moment. She had to know that the Queen would kill her. And yet she showed not one ounce of fear. She was a pain in the arse, but he did have to admire her courage.

That, of course, did not help his predicament in the least. He shared none of Olivia's desire to march into the lion's lair with a mutton joint tied to his neck. He'd prefer to take a weapon with him if possible.

Ian sat up slowly, his head pounding and his stomach growling. It surely had been a stupid idea to while away a precious day at the back of a pub, but he had gone into the dark, cool place to think, and ended up drowning his problems as he had not done in many years. It had felt damn good yesterday afternoon.

This morning he faced the prospect of an angry Queen . . . he glanced over at the scowling Olivia . . . as well as that Queen's fishwife of a daughter. All with an ache in his head that would have brought a smaller man low, he was sure. Of course, if the Queen played games with him, the ache in his head might be gone sooner than expected. At that very moment there could be soldiers marching to his door—a chopping block their final destination.

Groaning with each step, Ian left his irate captive glaring at him and went behind the screen to empty his bladder. He had told Gretchen to go visit her daughter for a few days, and had given Mary a few days off as well, so there was no fresh, warm water in the bowl on the stand by the window. Olivia Tudor had definitely upended his comfortable life.

For that, Ian gave her a dark glance as he stomped past her. She stood with her back to the window, her eyes a wide, innocent blue. She had obviously been checking escape routes as he made water. Good. At least she wasn't curled up on his bed whimpering. He was not sure he could keep being the tyrant she accused him of being if she went all whiny on him. God knew his sister had figured that out early enough.

He splashed some cold water on his face. "You'll kill yourself jumping from there. The ground is far away, and stone as well."

She squinted her eyes and curled her lip. "What's the difference between dying out there or dying in here?"

He chuckled and went to don a fresh tunic. "It would actually be very helpful to me if you'd jump out that window, but seeing as how it's locked, and I'm willing to feed you this morning, you may want to leave that for later." He extracted the key to his door from his hose. "Would you like to break your fast?"

She stared at him for a long moment, her brow furrowed in obvious puzzlement, her wonderful bottom lip held at the mercy of her teeth. She ran her fingers restlessly through her hair, causing the auburn locks to curl in all directions.

He had always preferred women with long hair, but Ian found himself, once more, enjoying the way Olivia's hair tossed about her head, and he felt the distinct need to explore the hollow of her throat at the base of her slender neck.

Ian looked away quickly. He should not have gotten drunk. It had to be the fact that his mind was still bleary with drink which made him now

MALIA MARTIN

have to turn his body so Olivia would not see his arousal.

She brushed by him and started down the stairs, and Ian took a deep breath. He must keep his mind focused, or there were many things that could go wrong. She stumbled a bit, and Ian reached out to steady her. Her arm beneath his fingers shook. He had not fed her since he had abducted her. A stab of guilt pierced his conscience.

He tightened his grip on her arm and hauled her up so that she did not fall headfirst down the stairs. "Got some rashers on my way home last night," he mumbled, pushing his guilt aside and wondering why the hell his conscience had suddenly set up residence and intended to stay.

"Amazing. Dead drunk, and yet you still remember food. Men are quite incredible creatures."

Ian just grunted, very grateful that Olivia's small moment of vulnerability was over. Her harsh tongue he could take. Anything else made him nervous.

He sat Olivia at the table and dumped a loaf of crusty bread in front of her. Keeping one eye on his captive and another on the sharp knife in his hand, Ian carved off a hunk of cold meat. As he watched her eat, he contemplated his situation.

He had the Queen's supposedly dead bastard daughter sequestered in his home without his Monarch's knowledge.

Did the Queen know that Shakespeare was her daughter? Why had she sent *him* to find Shakespeare? And how many people would attend his beheading?

In truth, Ian could hardly believe the situation in which he found himself mired. Once upon a time he had been a boy living only by the strains of his heart, but he now prided himself on his levelheaded analysis.

"What thoughts bring such a fierce look upon your face, Sir Ian?"

Ian took a bite of meat before slowly focusing on Olivia. He chewed, noticing how the sunlight from the high windows deepened the rich color of her hair. He had never seen the Queen's true hair, for she kept her head shaved and wore wigs. He wondered if her hair color could possibly be as beautiful as her daughter's.

Their eyes were of like nature, though Olivia's were larger and her lashes thicker.

The daughter's lips were surely a gift from Lucifer himself.

"You planning a murder, perhaps?" she asked with a quirk of her much contemplated lips. "Or surely something just as dire with such concentration upon your brow."

Ian didn't answer, as Olivia shrugged her slender shoulder and popped a piece of bread into her mouth.

He wanted to make love to her. It was as simple as that, and as complicated. Ian frowned. Why on earth would his body choose to ache for a skinny lass with a shrewish mouth?

A shrewish, beautiful mouth.

"But, of course, murder would not be dire to you, now would it, Sir Ian?" she said, her tongue darting out and licking up a stray crumb from her upper lip. " 'Tis but business as usual, right?"

"Right," he said, not truly listening to her. Her gown gaped open at the front, and he couldn't help but watch and wait. What might he see if she but leaned a little more forward?

"Whyever did you become an agent of the Queen, Sir Ian?"

Ian heard the question, just barely, and slid his gaze back up the woman's throat, over her full mouth and to her summer blue eyes. "Money," he said simply.

She blinked, the answer obviously a surprise to her. "Really?"

He smiled. "I was young, a student on scholarship. My father a farmer. He died, and I was supposed to go home and support my mother and sister." Ian shrugged. "The Queen likes impoverished students. They are smart and in need."

Olivia leaned forward, and Ian let his gaze once more travel below her neck. "What did you study?"

"Poetry."

Silence greeted his answer, and in the sudden quiet Ian realized what he had been saying, and thinking. He pushed away from the counter and turned from the witch who sat at his table. She had lulled him into saying things that did not matter and had not been spoken of in years.

"Why are you not married?" she asked.

Ian scowled. What did the girl want of him? "I am married," he said shortly. "To my work. One who does what I do should not bring another into it."

"Not the sentiments of a poet."

With a harsh huff of breath, Ian shook his head. "I am no poet." He busied himself wrapping the meat.

"Could I have some water?"

"Of course." He probably had a pitcher of goat's milk that was still good stored down in the priest's room. Gretchen kept food that might go bad down there since it stayed so cool. But Ian did not dare leave Olivia that long. He poured her a large cup of water and handed it over to her.

Their fingers brushed, and she shuddered again as she had when he untied her the night before. Ian pulled his hand back. They both felt it, the attraction. What an unneeded twist to a convoluted plot.

And then he thought of the goat's milk in the priest's room and snapped his fingers.

Olivia jumped as Ian went over to throw back a corner of the rug that lay beneath the kitchen table. He rolled it back until it caught on the table's legs, then bent and yanked at the brass ring embedded in the floor.

It moved easily, for Gretchen used the door often, showing a dark hole in the floor. Ian glanced up at Olivia. "Are you done, then?"

She shifted, her eyes on the dark hole in the floor as she nodded warily. "What is that?"

"The tenants before me liked to entertain the clergy."

"Ah . . ." Olivia nodded. "Catholic sympathizers. What a boon to you, Sir Ian. Such a lovely home you received since they were found out."

Ian frowned at her. "I *bought* this house, Miss Bea. I did not find the priest's room until after I moved in."

"And did you tell your lovely Queen of your findings? Did you tell her of the Catholic sympathizers who lived here before you?"

Ian stared levelly at the woman before him for

a moment. "No, I did not." He raised one brow as he awaited a reply, but she said nothing. "Come," he said, finally, holding out his hand.

She shook her head vehemently. "I am not going down in that hole."

"Would you rather sit all day tied to a chair?"

"I am not staying all day in a hole."

"You are going in the hole."

"No, I am not!" Olivia's eyes rounded, and the look she cast him was frightening, truly. If he had been anyone else, he might have been scared.

But Ian just gave a little laugh. "Yes, you are," he said as he rounded the table and reached for the termagant.

Ian limped into the Queen's guardroom. If he wanted to stay a whole and sane man, he had to rid himself of Olivia, and very soon.

At the moment she was safely locked away in the priest's room with a chamber pot, enough food to last her a week, candles to last through the year, and some parchment and quills. She had asked for the last bit, and he had given them to her because his conscience had demanded he do it. His conscience was becoming a damned nuisance.

"Ian!"

'Twas another damned nuisance that came

hurtling toward him, her large eyes distressed as she grabbed his arm.

"I am busy, Andy. I will speak to you later."

"No, Ian, the Queen is terribly angered with you!" His sister tugged at his arm, pulling him back the way he had just come.

"The Queen is always angry with me."

"Oh, Ian, this time she is truly angry. You cannot go in there now."

"If she is angry, 'tis best not to keep her waiting, Andy, you know that."

"You did not come to her at all yesterday, Ian." His sister managed to yank him into a deserted room. "You missed her masquerade! She is beside herself."

Ian closed his eyes for a moment and dug his fingers through his hair. "The masquerade," he muttered.

"Yes, the masquerade! Ian, the tantrum was something I wish never to witness again. How *could* you have forgotten?"

"Do not even ask." Ian opened his eyes and sighed. "Thank you for warning me." He started toward the door, but Andy held him back.

"You cannot just walk in there, Ian. You must find something . . . a present . . . a letter. I have it!" She brightened and clapped her hands. "You shall write her one of your sonnets."

"Sh!" Holding his finger to his lips, Ian

glanced around quickly, but, of course, they were alone. "Really, Andy, I should never have told you about that."

"Indeed, if you hadn't told me, who would sell them for you?"

"Anyway, I shan't be writing sonnets to the Queen." He shuddered in distaste. " 'Tis bad enough trying to write odes to that young devil, Southhampton, for Lady Eloise."

"Still, they were lovely."

Ian could only stare at his sister. "You read them? I told you to give them to the lady without reading them, Andy."

"Marry, how could I refrain from reading them, Ian? Your talent is extraordinary, truly. I really do not see why you hide it so."

"I have not the time for this argument. I do it to pad *your* dowry, sister. I do *not* want to be known as the writer of sonnets, and that is all I will say on the subject."

"Fine, but you still have the problem of the Queen's distress. You will have to grovel, brother dear."

Ian made a sound of disgust. "I am not going to grovel. And I will not buy her a present. Do not worry about me, Andy, I can take care of myself well enough."

"Obviously, you cannot!" She shoved him in-effectually. "You missed the Queen's masquerade, and you came prancing in here without even remembering!"

"I most definitely did not prance."

"Ian! Be serious! This situation is dire."

Ian frowned at his sister's tone. Her last few words had risen to a high pitch that, if he was not mistaken, was usually the predecessor of a good cry. Oh, for the love of all things holy. Ian rubbed his temples. "Calm yourself, Andy."

"Do not tell me to be calm!" Andy twirled about, her skirts swishing. "Don't you dare tell me to be calm, Ian. You have no idea what I endured last night."

Ian rolled his eyes. "Come, Andy, you had all the hardships associated with going to a party."

"In faith, you *would* make light of it, Ian." Andy paced the room, her slippers slapping against the marble floor. "Because of you, the Queen threw a terrible fit. It was awful, truly awful. And, of course, she aimed her anger at me since I'm your closest kin. And then . . . Oh, and then!" Andy cried the last word as if in torment and bowed her head into her hands, her shoulders shaking.

Ian could just stare. If women were permitted, his sister really ought to try the stage. "And then what?" he asked, truly intrigued.

"Oh, Ian . . ." Andy's voice trailed off pathetically as she dropped with a poof of silken skirts onto a spindly-looking chair. "Sir Richard was there."

Ian sighed silently, and then dragged another chair close to his sister. "So these hysterics are about Sir Richard?"

Andy glared at him indignantly. "I am not in hysterics!"

Ian sat and placated his sister, "Andy, you are in hysterics. But I am listening to them. Even with the Queen in the other room waiting to throw me in the clink, I am sitting here listening to you. So tell me what happened."

"He was there, Ian, and, of course, I knew he was there. By my troth, I did not know what he would be wearing." She sniffled. "And then there was this lion. And he was tall and broad-shouldered. I could see blond hair. I swear I saw a wisp of blond hair."

Ian nodded although he really was not following his sister's line of thought.

"But it was not him, Ian. The lion, I mean. It was not Sir Richard. And I ended up in the lion's arms, I do not know how. I truly thought him to be Sir Richard, which would, of course, not mean that I should throw myself into his arms. But, I did, and it wasn't! It wasn't Sir Richard! It is all a jumble in my mind now. But everyone saw, because . . ." Here his sister held her hand to her

109

forehead and paused a moment. "Heaven help me, Ian, the Queen came upon us."

"You and Richard?"

Andy blinked at him, then glared. "Are you not listening at all, Ian?"

"I'm listening, I'm listening."

" 'Twas I and the lion she came upon. And, oh, what a terrible scene." Andy lowered her voice to a whisper. "She yelled at me in front of the entire assembly, because she was already in a temper over your disappearance." Here Andy shoved a finger against Ian's chest harshly. "She sent me away, and Sir Richard has not spoken to me since. I'm overwrought, Ian. I think Sir Richard must believe, like everyone else, that my intentions lie toward the lion."

Ian nodded again, only this time he thought that perhaps he had figured out a bit of what his sister was ranting about. "And who, exactly, was the lion?"

"The earl of Crandle."

Ian grimaced.

"Exactly! I am doomed." She sat up quickly and grabbed his hands. "Unless you intercede, Ian, which, of course, you must do since you are the reason everything went wrong in the first place."

Ian tried to pull his hands from his sister's grasp, but she tightened her fingers around his.

"Certainly I do not have the power to be the sole reason for everything to go wrong, dearest sister."

She narrowed her gaze. "You know you do, Ian." Obviously she then decided to take another, softer approach, for her eyes rounded and she smiled. "Ian, dear . . ."

"No."

Andy pouted. "You do not even know what I am going to ask."

Ian pulled his hands from his sister's grasp and stood. "I know exactly what you are going to ask. I want nothing to do with your love affair, Andy. I have enough trouble at the moment. Can it not be sufficient that I soothe the feathers of a ruffled hen?"

"Just speak with Sir Richard for me, Ian, please."

"No." He turned and started for the door.

"Please, Ian?" his sister asked as she followed him through the door and back toward the Queen's presence chamber.

"Why don't you go tell the man yourself, Andy?"

"You know I could not possibly do such a gauche thing, Ian. You must help me."

Ian turned to face his sister again. "Really, Andy—"

"There he is!" She cut him off with a hiss.

"Who?" Ian asked and glanced around. "The lion or Richard?"

Andy glared at him. "Go talk to him, Ian, please."

With a heavy sigh, Ian nodded. "Fine, I shall speak to him. But, really, I must conference with the Queen first, Andy. Hard as it might be to believe, I have another life apart from yours which needs a bit of straightening out as well."

"Just do not put her in a temper, Ian. She has been in a foul mood ever since the Garter ceremony, and it is fraying my nerves."

"And we would not want your nerves frayed." Ian smiled, and his sister scowled, but before she could berate him, he turned and left, striding purposefully toward the entrance to the Queen's presence chamber.

Obviously, though, he did not stride quite purposefully enough, for Sir Richard intercepted him.

"Sir Ian, a word, if you would?"

"I . . ." Ian's mind flashed back to his sister's impassioned plea. "Yes, Sir Richard?"

"I spoke with you a few days ago, Sir Ian, about your sister?"

Ian placed both his hands on Richard's shoulders, stopping the man mid-sentence. "Listen, man, I have no patience for all of this drama. Lord Crandle is of the same height and breadth

112

as you, as well as sharing your same color hair. Add to all that the fact that he wore the costume of a lion, and Andromeda could not tell that he was not you. Hence, she ended up in the arms of Crandle."

Ian shook Richard lightly, as if to make the man see sense. "She thought it was you last night, man. She loves you. Go to her now, for the love of God, and set things straight, or I will go stark raving mad." Ian shoved the man lightly in the direction of Andy, then took off once more on his own mission.

Chapter 6

They say, the best men are molded out of faults;
and, for the most, become much more the better
for being a little bad.

—MEASURE FOR MEASURE, V, I, 442

There were times when Ian truly believed
the Queen to have some kind of unearthly
powers. There was a crowd of people this day in
her presence chamber, and she stood with her
back to him. And yet the moment he entered, she
said, "You did not come to Our masquerade,
Terrance."

The room became deafeningly quiet, and then
everyone was gone, and he was alone with
Queen Elizabeth. How nice it would be to clear
a room so easily.

"No, Your Majesty. I was about your business."

"Your business is to make Us happy, Sir Ian. We are most happy when Our men come to Our parties."

He bowed, though, truly, he wanted to dispute the fact that he was one of her men. "I must beg you to forgive me, Your Majesty."

"Yes, you must beg."

He kept his head bowed, but said no more.

"Come, Terrance, we shall continue our conference in my private chamber." She swirled about and walked out into the hall, which was lined by guards.

Ian kept his eyes forward as he followed the Queen, his head up and his walk purposeful. Most of the people at court feared him, and it was important for him to keep that perception alive. Even when in the Queen's disfavor, he made sure that he did not act like the other simpering fools the Queen called men.

It had made it much easier for him to do his job, the fact that most people looked upon him as a man who gave no mercy to his enemies.

He followed the Queen through her privy chamber, where Lord Essex sat in conference with one of his many cronies. They halted as the Queen passed them, but Essex had eyes only for Ian.

Ian nodded at the man as they passed, and Essex acknowledged the salute.

And then came the tall doors of the Queen's private chamber. The Queen dismissed her chamber ladies with a wave of her hand, and went straight to her favorite chair, which sat upon a dais.

Ian waited while she arranged her skirts, and then she said, "We noticed that you brought Hayward to the Tower, but Shakespeare is not there."

Ian took a moment to answer. "After bringing Hayward in, I went to Shakespeare's apartments. The writer of plays, it seems, has disappeared," he said finally.

"Really?"

His left hand started to shake, and Ian fisted his fingers. Fear had never been a part of his conferences with the Queen. This was a new experience for him. And he knew well enough that it was fear making his legs seem weak as he watched the Queen stand up and stroll about her chamber.

"Have you questioned Hayward?" Ian asked, deciding that, for the moment, he did not wish to speak or think of Shakespeare.

"Yes." The Queen stopped to stare out one of the windows.

Ian waited for a moment.

"We have let him go," she said finally, without moving.

"I am happy that you found no grounds to believe he, or anyone else, plots against you, Your Majesty."

"Yes." She caressed the windowsill, running one hand up the casement, then stopping. One, long thin finger tapped, a sapphire ring glinting as the Queen's long nail *clink, clink, clinked* against the polished wood.

Ian did not move. She loved to make people squirm, and he knew that he could not. She must not think anything was wrong.

And it was pretty much all wrong at the moment.

"Where has this Shakespeare person disappeared to, and why would the man wish to leave at all, Terrance?"

"I am making inquiries into both of those questions myself, Your Majesty." He answered quickly this time, intent on seeming normal.

He hated lying. He hated it. He could remember his father just looking at him when he had lied as a child. There had never been harsh words or whippings as his friends had received. No, with John Terrance it had just been that look of complete disappointment. And then the words would just tumble out of Ian's mouth as he confessed and promised never to lie again.

Clink, clink, clink. "Do you think that the answers to your inquiries will in any way pertain to Us?"

"Do *you* think they might?" he asked.

She turned and glared at him. "Do not be impertinent, Terrance. When We ask you a question, We expect an answer, *not* another question."

The interview was going as many before them had, which was quite calming, actually. He was not placating or flattering, and the Queen was getting angrier and angrier.

Still, there was a feeling of anxiety about the woman that Ian had not experienced before. "I am sorry." He bowed his head. "I do not know the answer to your question, but I shall, of course, continue my inquiries and report as soon as I know anything."

She turned away again. "Do that, Sir Ian." Ian glanced up at her straight back from under his lashes.

"I am going to search the man's rooms this afternoon," he said.

The Queen took in a sharp breath, but said nothing.

"I shall take some men with me . . ." He, of course, would do no such thing, but he was interested in the Queen's reaction to the possibility.

"You shall go alone," she said quickly. "Bring

everything you find directly to me. Show it to no one else." She seemed to be physically shaking, her fingers fisted in the material of her gown. "I'll expect you back before I break my fast."

Ian turned to leave, but stopped when he felt a light weight on his arm. He glanced down at the sapphire ring and blinked. Truly, he could not remember a time in all of his years as a Queen's agent when she had touched him.

When he finally looked into her blue gaze, her hand had returned to intertwine with her other and rest lightly upon her skirts. "Be discreet, Sir Ian. And, please, do not leave me wondering for longer than a day again."

Ian only nodded, unable to say anything. Please? And she had referred to herself as *me* rather than the customary royal *We* or *Us*. She stood before him now suddenly very human and vulnerable, and it scared him as nothing else had before. He left as quickly as he could, stopping on the other side of the door to catch his breath.

Ian plunged his fingers through his hair and noticed that there were several people staring at him. He straightened quickly and strode through the room, keeping his gaze hooded and his expression hard. A woman near the door skittered away from him as if he might step on her, silly widget: but good. Now was not the time to lose his reputation as the dour and dark Sir Ian, a man who smiled rarely and gave clemency never.

"She had a man put in the Tower yesternight!" Crandle whispered to his friend over dinner.

Essex took a bite of roasted duck and chewed for a moment. "She has many people thrown in the Tower."

"Yes," Crandle looked around them, and then slid closer. "But this man did nothing but pen a tribute . . ." he hesitated for just the right amount of time to procure Essex's complete attention. "To you."

"Who is this man?" Essex asked with interest.

Crandle only shrugged. "He is no one, really, a writer of histories. Hayward, I think his name is."

"Ah, yes, I gave him money to write some rubbish he thought essential to life." Essex accentuated his boredom at the subject with a wave of his spoon.

"Well, it seems, that he implied in his foreword that you have a right to the throne."

"But, of course, I do!" Essex sniffed with disgust.

"Yes, you do. But it angers the Queen, obviously."

Essex took another bite of his dinner, chewing thoughtfully.

"And, of course, the intrigue continues between the Queen and Sir Ian."

Essex quit his chewing and narrowed his eyes upon his friend. "I saw Sir Ian today. He conferenced privately with the Queen for only a few minutes, but the Queen stayed sequestered for the rest of the day." He lowered his voice even further. "Has your man found anything out about Sir Ian's hostage?"

"He sits his post, still, and shall move when the timing is right."

"Good." Essex tapped a finger against the table. "I know many of the Queen's secrets Crandle."

"These are good things to know, Essex."

"She treats me badly of late."

"And she no better than the bastard daughter of an adulterer."

" 'Tis true these things you speak, Crandle."

Crandle sighed and shook his head. "I think often of how much I miss a man's guiding hand at the helm of good England. And you, Lord Essex, would have been one of the men chosen, were it not for Henry's upstart daughter."

"You are right, of course."

"And she does treat us like small dogs, to be led about by our noses, does she not?" Crandle clicked his tongue against the roof of his mouth

121

in disgust. "She has belittled our entire sex, I say."

"Your thoughts are mine exactly."

"She laughs at us, I think," Crandle said.

"Ah, but will she laugh last? I think not," Essex returned darkly.

She heard his footsteps above her and quickly blew out the candles. He tromped about the hall for a moment, then entered the kitchen.

Olivia held her breath.

Light pierced the darkness, a sharp blade of whiteness against the wood floor. Olivia waited, making sure she stayed in the shadows.

"Miss Bea? Where are you, woman?"

He was not drunk this night. Too bad; that might have helped her. A black boot stepped into her vision. She crouched, waiting for her moment to jump.

His other boot hit the stair. "Beatrice Shrew? Are you sleeping, or just lying in wait to kill me. Death by quill, it shall be quite painful, I'm sure."

All of a sudden, the man was a talker. Olivia scowled. *Just come down the stairs, you big oaf.*

He started down the stairs, and Olivia smiled. His boot came down square in the middle of the chamber pot waiting on the third step down. Perfect.

"What the . . ."

Olivia did not wait as the chamber pot slid on the butter with which she had coated the steps, but jumped from her hiding place and whizzed up the stairs as quickly as she could.

She passed the tumbling form of her captor, her heart beating at least twice its usual tempo and put on some speed as she realized that she was going to succeed.

Just as her head popped through the floor of the kitchen, she felt something snag her ankle. She saw table legs and the rolled-up rug, and then blackness again as she fell, her belly and breasts hitting the stairway and knocking the breath from her lungs.

"Tell me the damned thing was empty. Give me that, at least."

Olivia blinked and looked up at the gaping hole of freedom above her. Then she gulped in air and tried to breathe. She could feel Sir Ian's fingers like a steel trap around her ankle.

"You are starting to cause me great pain, Miss Bea."

Olivia sighed and leaned her forehead against a stone step. "I shall be candid with you, Sir Ian . . ."

"Oh, please, hold nothing back."

"I am rather alarmed that you have imprisoned me in your home, sir."

"You would rather I throw you in the Tower, perhaps?"

"I wonder why you have not."

"A question I must ask myself as well now as I sit here wondering if I shall ever walk again."

Olivia only sighed. "If your bones are as hard as your head, sir, you shall be fine, I am sure."

Ian tugged on her foot. "Are you going to answer my original question, or leave me wondering what vile stuff I now sit in?"

Olivia had to laugh. "You are covered in butter, dear man, nothing more vile than sour milk, I promise you."

" 'Tis vile enough." He yanked again on her foot, and she slid down a step. "And I can tell you now who will be cleaning it up."

Olivia scowled and pushed up on her knees. Ian's hand tightened around her ankle as his other hand grabbed her thigh. She slapped at him, but he only pulled her down toward him.

"Let go of me!"

"Right, and then you shall kick me in the head and make your escape."

"Well, I shall kick you, yes." Olivia chuckled as she said, "but 'tis not your head I shall aim for."

His hand tightened around her leg and then pulled her quickly toward him. In the space of a moment, Olivia was plastered to her captor's

124

body, his arms anchoring her to him, his legs locked around her own.

The laugh that had begun now clogged her throat as she stared through the dim light into Sir Ian's eyes.

"No more kicking, Miss Bea. Or I shall forget my gentlemanly ways."

"Ah, you are a gentleman, then? I had wondered."

"Hmmm." The sound that came from Ian's throat was more of a rumble, and she felt the vibration of it against her own chest. It made her realize completely their rather intimate embrace.

She squirmed. "I shall not kick, Sir Ian," she said breathlessly. Her head knocked against his chin. She glanced up at him once more and suddenly Ian's face was very close to her own. "I promise I shall not," she said with all the sincerity she could muster.

But he was not looking at her, at least not into her eyes. Instead his dark gaze was heavy upon her mouth. And, virgin though she was, Olivia was not stupid.

She swallowed hard. No man had ever looked at her thus, and she had to admit that it did rather take her breath away. Especially when the look was issued from the hard-planed, strong-jawed face of Sir Ian Terrance.

She remembered, suddenly, the quick, hard

kiss he had pressed to her mouth two nights before. It had been her first kiss, and truly, very
much too short. She really ought to know more
about such things, being a writer.

And so she closed the few small inches that
separated her mouth from Ian's and kissed him.
His lips were very soft, fitting perfectly, it
seemed to Olivia, against her own. His scent of
musk and mint permeated her very being, and
she moaned softly, settling her body more fully
against his.

It all felt so wonderful, his mouth, his strong
arms about her, his body beneath her. She was
beginning to understand lust and need in a way
she had never fathomed. It was as if her body
would quit functioning if Ian took his lips from
her. And then he opened them, his tongue coming out to invade her mouth, and her heart dou-
bled its rhythm.

Ian's arms tightened about her body, his hands
in her hair, and then on her back, her waist. She
could feel his desire hard against her stomach,
and reveled in the power it made her feel. With
a sultry groan, Olivia curled her hands in the
fabric of Ian's tunic and moved against his hardness. He made a low growling sound, then broke
their kiss.

With a small sigh, Olivia let her forehead drop
to Ian's chest. It heaved with the force of his

breathing. "You have been chewing mint," she said softly.

"I seem to remember you berating me last night for the smell of my breath." He moved slightly so she rested more intimately against his stiff groin. "I am quite accommodating, when I try."

"Hmmm." Olivia circled her arms around Ian's neck and waited in silence as her pulse finally slowed to a more normal rate. She wished more than anything to continue their kiss, but it would be folly, surely. "This is all very strange, is it not?"

"Quite." Ian moved his own arms down and cupped her backside with a large hand. "I do not usually find skinny creatures such as yourself appealing."

His words touched a sore spot of her vanity she had not known existed. She wanted him to think her beautiful, seductive, irresistible. "And I do not find overbearing oafs appealing, as a rule," she said, hiding her hurt behind words.

"So we do not find each other appealing then."

"Not at all."

They stayed silent for a long moment.

"As a matter of fact, dear Miss Bea, I find you a royal pain in the arse."

"Royal?"

"Royal."

Olivia tapped her teeth together. Did he know then? Did he know who she was? Was that the reason for her imprisonment in this man's home?

That, of course, would never do. If she were going to die, she would not do so without seeing her mother, at least.

"Do you plan, then, on taking me to the Tower?" she asked hopefully.

"You obviously have heard things about the Tower that are completely untrue," he answered. "You seem to think it is in some way better lodging than my own terribly hospitable, if I do say so myself, home. I must disabuse you of this notion, Miss Bea. The Tower is awfully drafty. And there are implements of torture which the guards actually enjoy using on the inhabitants."

Olivia twirled a lock of Sir Ian's hair about her finger, noting the lovely softness of his honey-brown curls. How strange to find things about this awful man that she actually enjoyed: the feel of his hair against her fingers, his lips against hers, and the very new feeling of safety when he held her in his strong arms.

And, of course, this last part must mean she had gone completely mad. This man had ruined what had been a rather nice life. In fact, he would most probably kill her sometime in the near future.

The ironies of life were truly beyond her ken.

"You have never kissed a man before, have you?" She heard her captor's question through the haze of her own musings and stiffened with a touch of indignation.

"Of course I have!"

"No, you haven't." Sir Ian pushed himself up, still keeping her within his embrace. "You say that you write plays, plays which I have seen portrayed on the stage. These plays depict love, betrayal, murder, jealousy. And yet, you are an untried girl." He set her down on the cot that lined the far wall. "It is hard for me to believe that you are who you say." He straightened to his full height, planting his fists against his hips.

So much for feeling safe, or feeling anything other than disgust for Sir Ian. "Tsk!" Olivia pulled the blanket from its folded position at the end of the bed and threw it over herself as she flopped over to face the wall.

"I am *not* an untried girl!" She kicked the wall, just for emphasis, and bruised her toe. "Go away," she said, feeling like a child again and hating Ian for initiating her regression.

It seemed that every intelligent thought or action fled when this man was within ten feet of her. It was tragic, really.

"I read the beginning of the new play, *Beatrice*. I found it on the desk in your apartments."

Olivia blinked at the wall, wishing with all her

heart that she was a huge, strong man and could take down Sir Ian with one blow. O, that she were a man.

"I hate for people to read my work before it is done," she told him sulkily.

"Your work?" Sir Ian had moved away from her. She heard him doing something near the stairs. "Again, I am skeptical. Who lives with you in your apartments? Who writes those plays?"

He gave a little grunt, and Olivia peeked at the man over her shoulder. He was cleaning the mess of butter off the stairs. Ha! Let him clean. Next time it would not be so benign as butter on his damn stairs.

Olivia huffed a disgusted sound and turned back to stare at the wall. "I'll tell the Queen anything she wants to know. *You* will get nothing from me." She pulled her blanket up to her chin. "Including kisses, you ingrate."

"I can barely stand the disappointment."

"Oh, shut up and leave. I wish to sleep, Sir Cynic."

"As you wish, Lady Virgin."

"Oh!" She thrashed herself up, throwing her blanket aside when it tangled about her feet, but only saw the bottom of Sir Ian's boots as he reached the trapdoor.

"Pig," she said again, just as he dropped the door and secured the latch.

She really did need to think of better names for the man, but he made her mind feel like mush. Olivia flopped back on her small cot and squirmed around trying to get comfortable. She was going to miss Sir Ian's lovely bed, that was for sure.

She had snuffed the candles before trying to make her escape, and now her small tomb beneath the kitchen was dark as pitch. She would never be able to find the candles again either, so she was stuck until her gallant captor decided to make another appearance.

Olivia pulled the blanket up around her once more. She was glad now that she had taken her ring to the jeweler when she heard that Sir Ian asked questions about her; otherwise, he would have probably found it when he searched her room above the glovemaker's shop.

Still, he had read her work. She shuddered. And the odious man did not even believe it was hers. She kicked the wall again, softer this time, just to vent, and then closed her eyes.

She hated such thick darkness. She missed having a window, something, that would let in air and a bit of moonlight. This priest's room was a tomb, truly it was.

And then something began scratching. Olivia's

eyes snapped open, and she lay rigidly on her cot. It was a rat, of course it must be. And it was probably huge: bigger than huge. The thing was probably the size of a dog. Holy Mother of God, she could not sleep down here in this tomb with a rat bigger than a small horse.

"Ian!" Her scream reverberated in the small room, and whatever had been making the scratching noises stopped. That didn't mean it was gone, though. In fact, it now knew exactly where she was. Olivia stood up straight on her cot, bracing herself against the wall. The thing was obviously sneaking up on her, its huge fangs dripping saliva as it thought of the juicy meat covering her bones.

"Ian! Ian! Ian! Ian!" She screamed so loud her ears hurt.

She heard pounding, and then blessed light poured through the opening in the ceiling. "What the bloody hell is going on?"

"I refuse to sleep down here!" she cried defiantly.

"What?"

"There are rats down here, large ones that want to eat me. I will not sleep down here."

"Yes, you will."

"No, I will not!" Olivia could see Ian outlined against the light above, and he dug his fingers through his hair in obvious frustration.

"I must get some sleep," he said finally. "Now lie down and close your eyes. Rats are much more afraid of you than you are of them." And he dropped the door.

"Ian! Don't leave me down here! You can't do this to me!"

The door opened again. "Quit your screaming, woman!"

"Then don't leave me down here with these beasts!"

Ian sighed heavily. "Do you have the stairs coated with butter again?"

Olivia blinked. In her terror she had forgotten to even try for escape. It would have been a good idea, actually. "No," she said, disgusted with herself.

Grumbling, Ian backed down the stairs, testing each step with a tentative toe before putting his full weight down. When he got to the bottom, he came over and stood staring at her for a moment.

"You cannot be afraid of the dark."

"Of course, I am not!" She folded her arms across her chest. "I'm afraid of rats."

She thought he rolled his eyes, though she could not see in the dim light, but she definitely heard the little disgusted huff of breath. "Lie down. You're going to break the cot standing on it like that."

She frowned at him. "I do not appreciate your

mean insinuations that I am overly large."

"You are a bloody Amazon, now lie down."

"I am tall."

"You're tall, and you have feet bigger than mine." He grabbed her and flipped her onto her back. "Now lie down, dammit."

Olivia lay for a moment stunned.

"Here." Ian draped the blanket over her. "Now go to sleep."

Before she could protest, he plunked down next to her cot, leaning his head against the side, his legs stretched out before him.

Olivia blinked in disbelief. She rolled to her side, facing the back of Ian's head. "Do you think my feet are ugly, then?" she asked.

Ian snorted and rubbed his forehead with the palm of his hand, but he said nothing.

Olivia sighed and turned onto her back to stare at the ceiling. Her captor had left the trapdoor open, so a bit of light filtered into the small room. It felt very good to have light, and even better to have someone near who was not of the rodent variety. Well, not truly a rodent.

They sat in silence for what seemed a long time. "I've always wanted to be beautiful," Olivia found herself saying. "It seems from the time I can remember I've been tall and awkward." She stopped speaking, but Ian said nothing. "I must say I do have very lovely hair." She felt the soft,

134

short spikes of hair on her head. "I wish you could have seen it long. Before I had to dress as a cabin boy in order to get to London, my hair reached all the way to my bottom."

Olivia sighed. She was rambling, and she did not know why in the world it suddenly mattered so much that Sir Ian knew that at one time she had had lovely hair.

"Where were you that you had to take a ship to London?" Ian asked.

"Everywhere."

Silence took over their small space for a while then.

"Your hair is a pretty color," Ian finally said.

Olivia turned toward Ian, wondering if she was hearing things. Perhaps the rat had decided to start speaking? It certainly was not Sir Ian Terrance saying something nice to her, was it?

"And your feet are not ugly."

Well, perhaps the world would end this very night. Sir Ian Terrance had actually complimented her. She thought he had, at least.

Again, silence took over their conversation. Olivia sighed heavily, her eyes becoming heavy.

"I think my sister has found a suitor," Sir Ian said softly, almost to himself.

"Sir Richard? From the Garter ceremony?" Olivia asked quietly.

"Yes." Ian dropped his head back so that his

hair lay against her cheek. Olivia reached up and ran her fingers through his silky locks.

" 'Tis a funny story, actually."

"I love stories," Olivia said.

"Well, it all begins with a lion and a fair maiden . . ."

She was most definitely a witch, Ian thought as he told her the story of his sister. The soft touch of her fingers in his hair had shocked him completely. He could remember his mother running her fingers through his hair when he was small. She would sit by the side of his bed and sing him lullabies and stroke his hair so that he could not keep his eyes open no matter how hard he tried.

He had not thought of those days in a very long time. His mother still tried to hug him and give him kisses, but he always ducked out of her embraces quickly. He had not gone to see her now for over a year. In his mother, he saw his youth, and it made him feel a cynical old man.

And now another woman was conjuring up memories of innocence with soft touches.

Ian stopped speaking and waited for a moment, hoping Olivia was finally asleep. He rolled his eyes. She was his prisoner, and he was acting as if she were a child he was trying to put to sleep. He was going soft, fast.

136

"Did you fix it then?" she asked, and Ian sighed.

"I told the man that Andy loved him, yes. Now, go to sleep." *Christ, I sound like an old grandmother.*

"You love your sister, I can tell," the witch said, her fingers straying from his hair and softly tracing the shell of his ear.

Ian swallowed hard. The memories of his boyhood disappeared like a wisp of smoke up a chimney, and goose bumps prickled his skin.

"I always wished for a big brother to keep me safe. Andy is a lucky woman."

Olivia had turned toward him. He could tell, for he felt the soft caress of her breath against his neck. Her finger slipped down and circled the tender flesh just behind his ear.

He had been about to deny any love lost for his sister, and then interrogate Olivia about her family, but the words choked him. Every single nerve ending in his body was now alert to the fact that a slim finger traced patterns on the skin at the side of his neck.

How very virginal of him. Ian quickly scooted forward and stood, rubbing harshly at his ear. "There now, the rats have been properly scared away, and I must get some sleep." He started toward the stairs.

"Oh, please, Ian, don't leave."

That his footsteps faltered at the woman's small voice made Ian frown deeply. Clenching his fists, he forced himself to take the first few steps and not say anything to his captive.

"I hate this room, Ian. There is no air, and it is so cold. And I'm dreadfully afraid of rats."

He made it up two more steps before stopping. "Fine." He turned around and stomped back to the cot, cursing himself the whole time.

She had sat up, her night rail hanging off one shoulder and displaying an enticing amount of cleavage. Who would have ever thought. Ian closed his eyes tightly and turned on his heel. "Go to sleep," he said gruffly.

"Will you leave when I'm asleep?"

Her shrew's tongue had been silenced by a bunch of rats, for she now sounded like the cowed prisoner he had wished for at first.

"I will stay." He took a lunging step and dropped into the small rickety chair that sat before a desk that held parchment and quills Ian had left for his captive. "Go to sleep." *Just don't touch me*, came the unbidden thought that he fortunately did not say out loud.

He heard the rustling of bed linens as she made herself comfortable, and his manhood hardened almost painfully.

A witch, most definitely. Ian tried to find a comfortable position as he made himself think of numbers. He leaned forward and rested his chin on his hands and counted by twelve. His fingers fell asleep when he reached 240, so he crossed his arms in front of himself and began multiplying.

"Are you cold?"

Ian lost his train of thought completely at the sound of Olivia's low voice. If he had not known better, he could have sworn the woman was a practiced seductress. Her voice in the dark suddenly seemed the very essence of sex, heated and raspy.

"Here."

Ian jumped, for Olivia stood beside him suddenly, holding her blanket toward him. Truly, she could have overpowered him easily in that moment. What on earth was happening to him?

"Take the blanket," she said. "I shall be warm enough." Olivia draped the blanket around his shoulders, but he dared not move. He did not trust himself, for in his mind's eye he could picture perfectly what his body longed to do.

He would take one of her hands in his and pull her down to the floor, and they would both huddle beneath the blanket. He would rid her, finally, of that dratted night rail and kiss her firm breasts. And then he would learn intimately the lean lines of her figure, sliding his hands along her legs and wrapping them around his body as he came into her and relieved the pounding need that hardened him now.

"Oh my God," he muttered, dropping his head into his shaking hands. She must be a witch, and he was under her spell. He had never felt such a need for a woman before in his life.

Of course, no woman he had lusted for had been denied to him. Ian concentrated on breathing as he tumbled this thought about in his mind. That was it, of course. It was not Olivia herself, but rather the knowledge that she was a woman that he could not have.

"Good night," she said finally, and moved away. And Ian still did not move or speak, for he knew that if he did either he would break the tenuous grasp on sanity he now held in his mind.

He knew that if he moved, he would realize that his deductions were convoluted and made no sense.

He knew that if he moved, he would go to Olivia's cot and slide down next to her, and forget who they were and what their circumstances were. He would teach her virginal body how to love.

So Ian kept himself from moving until he heard the soft sound of Olivia's even breathing and knew that she slept. And then he stood quietly and stepped over to the cot.

She was a shadow within shadows, but he could still detect the soft, delicate scent of her. She wore no perfumes, only the clean smell of soap. Ian lifted the blanket from his shoulders and laid it over his captive.

He felt the softness of her hair against the back of his hand and pulled away quickly. And then he went back to the desk, turning his body deliberately away from the sleeping temptress.

Andy was in light spirits as she pranced up the stair. She had a nosegay of flowers in her hands and a smile that she would never be able to wipe off her face. Sir Richard loved her. She did a little pirouette halfway up the stair and laughed. He was going to speak with the Queen this very day.

That thought pulled at the corners of her smile. She said a quick little prayer that the Queen would be in good humor when Richard asked her. It always put Her in a foul mood when one of Her courtiers decided to wed. Especially when he picked one of Her ladies-in-waiting.

Still, it had to work out in the end, it must. Richard loved her. She smiled widely again and pushed open the door to her chambers.

She heard them first and stopped dead in her tracks. A woman was moaning as if in great pain. She could also hear a masculine grunting.

141

What on earth! Andy dropped her flowers and curled her fingers around her eating knife. She moved stealthily toward the sounds. She wanted desperately to turn and find someone else to help her, but the woman's moans were heightening: She *could* be in great danger.

Andy tiptoed to the door of her bedroom, closed her eyes for a moment to find courage, then pushed against the portal.

It creaked open, and Andy flinched. The sounds issuing from within the room did not cease, though, and she clenched her eating knife harder. Another quick prayer, and Andy peeked around the door.

'Twas her maid, Sally. The poor girl stood in front of the window being mauled by some beast of a man. Her blouse was loose and hanging, her breasts painfully clenched within the dark hands of the man.

Andy started forward, knife at the ready, and then stopped suddenly. The man kissed Sally full on the mouth, and it seemed that her maid kissed him back.

Blinking, Andy dropped her knife. It clattered against the floorboards, but the people by the window did not hear it at all. They were clearly in the throes of a very wild passion.

Her face surely an apple red, Andy backed out of the room as quietly as she could. Another grand moan issued from the room she had just left, and Andy turned and fled. Her carefully picked bouquet of flowers scattered beneath her feet as she pushed out the door of her chambers and shut it quickly behind her.

She stood for a moment, her chest heaving with exertion and shock. "Oh my," she whispered finally. Then a smile again curved her mouth, and she began to laugh.

She really ought to dismiss her maid. But how could she possibly begrudge the woman happiness in love when Andy had found it as well. She giggled. And very soon she would be lying over the arm of her beloved, her blouse undone and all of those heretofore taboo feelings ripping moans from her own throat. Andy shivered, the image too fresh in her mind even to think of being with Richard in such a way.

Andy straightened away from the door and shook her head to dislodge such carnal thoughts. And then with a smile and new feelings that caused her stomach to feel terribly fluttery, Andy left Sally to her fun.

Chapter 7

She is not worth what she doth cost, the keeping.
—TROILUS AND CRESSIDA, II, ii, 51

Ian was gone when she awoke, but Olivia could forgive him, for he had left three candles burning and a cat. The cat was curled up next to her, a warm bundle of purring fur against her midsection. Olivia yawned and stretched, then glanced down at the two bright yellow eyes blinking up at her.

"And who would you be, my furry friend?" Olivia laughed. The cat mewed and came up on its front paws. It made Olivia feel funny inside, the fact that Sir Ian Terrance had slept sitting by her bed and then had left this cat with her for protection.

Olivia swallowed against the sudden dryness

in her throat. What a strange man, hard and dark on the outside but with such an obvious softness within.

Olivia shook her head. She could not think of it, for it would soften *her*, and she could not have that.

She must remember that his intentions for her were anything but tender.

Olivia smoothed her hand over the cat's orange head, then pushed herself up and lifted the cat to her lap. "Oh, my!" Olivia laughed when she could barely lift the feline. "Something tells me that Sir Ian has a soft spot in his heart for you as well, my fat friend. Does he feed you whole ham hocks at a time?"

The cat mewed and rubbed its little pink nose against Olivia's hand. She resumed her stroking.

"Well, if we are to be thrust together like this, we really must give you a name. Cat is just so unimaginative, so . . . Sir Ian." She laughed and held the cat up before her. "How about Ham Bone?" The cat made a sound very close to a snarl, and Olivia laughed again.

"All right, then, not Ham Bone. It is a bit on the masculine side." Olivia nuzzled the cat against her chest. "How about Hamlet? Quite a contradiction in terms, but it fits you, darling, it does."

Hamlet meowed and snuggled closer to Olivia.

"I am glad you're here with me, Hamlet. I do hate this little hole in the ground."

It was then that Olivia heard the footsteps overhead. She realized as she jumped from the bed, Hamlet still snuggled to her chest, that the footsteps had been creaking about for a while, and she had not registered the fact that they were footsteps. Now Olivia crept up the stairs and listened.

It was not Sir Ian Stomp-A-Lot, that was very much obvious. The person skulking about upstairs was trying to be stealthy. Olivia held her breath for a moment to hear better.

"Liv?"

She started, then put Hamlet down and scrambled up the rest of the stairs. "Ben?" she called and then banged on the trapdoor. "Ben! I'm here under the rug in the kitchen." She banged a few more times.

And then suddenly there was Ben's dear face peering down at her from above. "I can't believe that I'm doing this, Liv, so come on quickly before we are both put to the rack."

"Oh, Ben!" Olivia ran for the opening and then stopped. "Wait, just a moment." She turned around and took the stairs two at a time. Her fingers shaking, Olivia grabbed the parchment on her desk where she had begun her story of Beatrice again. Rolling it as tightly as she could,

146

Olivia shoved the paper beneath her arm and started up the stair once more. Hamlet followed her through the trapdoor and into the kitchen.

"How did you find me?" Olivia asked as she searched for a suitable treat for Hamlet.

"That great oaf, Sir Ian Terrance, came to your lodgings yesterday, ripped the place apart, and took all of your work. I followed him here, then heard you screaming last night. Scared the piss out of me, Liv, truly it did."

"Not enough to run to my aid *last night*, I see." She scowled at him and dropped a hunk of meat on the ground for her new friend.

"You know I have not one spot of courage in me, Liv. But I did pray for you."

"Well, not to worry. Sir Ian was not torturing me." She shrugged, a bit embarrassed now at her own lack of courage. "I thought I heard a rat."

Ben frowned. "What?"

"Nothing. Come now, Ben, or your heroics will be for naught."

"Ah, yes, 'tis out of this house I want to be as quickly as possible." He stared at her for a moment. "But we must do something about you first."

"What on earth do you mean?"

"You're in your night rail, dearest Liv." He frowned, his forehead a mass of furrows. "And your hair is rather . . . well . . ."

147

Olivia gasped and put her hand to her hair. It was matted on one side and stuck out like the quills of a porcupine on the other. "Oh, my Lord."

"Yes, quite." Ben glanced around and pulled a long cloak from a peg. "Put this on. 'Tis long enough that it will cover most of you up."

Olivia did as she was told, her mind completely taken over by what she must look like. How she had looked to Sir Ian these last few days. And the fact that it bothered her that she had looked like a street urchin aggravated her beyond saying. "It really matters not one whit," she said aloud.

Ben stared at her strangely as he plunked a felt hat on her head. "Pull that down low." He squinted his eyes at her. "And, believe me, it matters. Hurry now, this house makes me nervous." Without waiting for her, he took off out of the kitchen.

Olivia took a moment to stoop down and pat Hamlet's orange fur. "I think I shall miss you, strange as that may seem." And she knew in her heart that she was not speaking to her new feline friend.

With a quick shake of her head, Olivia took off after Ben. The back door stood open, and he gestured for her to hurry. She slipped out, but tripped as Hamlet ran beneath her feet.

148

"Scat!" Ben cried to the poor thing, grabbing for Olivia's arm. She fell anyway, landing face-first on terribly hard cobblestones. She groaned. Of course Sir Ian would live in a house with cobblestones in the back alley, the wretch. She thought longingly of the dirt and trash-filled alley behind the glovemaker's shop as Ben helped her to her feet.

Hamlet curled about her legs and blood dripped from Olivia's nose. "Is it broken?" she asked ruefully, tilting her head back.

"We shall see about that later, Liv. 'Tis definitely not the time to sit about whining over scrapes and bruises."

She scowled. "Scrapes?" she said indignantly. "It hurts like the devil, Ben."

"As will dying at the end of Sir Ian's sword. Now, come on!" He wrapped his hand around her arm and pulled her toward the street just as three men turned the corner and started toward them.

Ben slowed to a more moderate walk. "Act natural," he said.

Olivia made a disgusted sound beneath her breath. Right, natural, clothed in a too-big cloak, an old felt hat with spiky, matted hair peeking out and blood streaming from her nose. Not to mention the two-ton orange cat that threaded himself between her footfalls. She glanced down

149

at Hamlet, only then realizing that she wore no shoes. Oh yes, quite natural.

It did not help at all that her instincts were at full alert and causing each hair on her body to stand on end.

She peeked out at the men from beneath her moth-eaten hat—why *did* Ian keep such a relic hanging on a peg in his kitchen? Olivia shook this thought from her mind quickly and eyed the men. They were striding much too purposefully in a back alley, and the swords at their sides were just a touch too long, a bit too shiny, and much too sharp for her peace of mind.

Ben, it seemed, was oblivious. Olivia shuffled to a halt, though.

"What is wrong with . . ."

Olivia did not wait to hear Ben's lamentations, for the three men had picked up their pace to a trot. She whipped around, tugging Ben with her, and started for the outlet at the other side of the alley.

"Get them!" she heard from behind, and she started to run. She also heard a feline screech and a masculine roar.

"Hamlet!" She glanced over her shoulder to see her new friend clinging to the head of one of her pursuers. The man pranced about the alley, his sword now useless on the ground. Olivia smiled. *Hamlet, her protector.*

And then she screamed as a large beefy arm came around her neck and pulled her backward. She gurgled, unable to breathe, her feet inches from the ground as the tall man behind her held fast. *There had been more men coming from the other side of the alley.*

Stupid. It had been stupid, stupid, *stupid*, to take her eyes off her destination. The pages of her work slipped from beneath her arm and drifted to the ground as Olivia clutched at her captor's arm and tried desperately to pull in her breath.

From the corner of her eye, she saw Ben hurl himself at the man who held her. *Oh, Lord, Ben will die*, she thought. And it was all her fault. Why did he have to pick now to show his courage?

"Halt!" A deep, commanding voice echoed down the alley just as her vision began to blur. She was going to faint again, twice in two days when she had never experienced it before in her life. Well, at least she would know how to describe fainting in her plays, she thought, as a strange buzz began in her ears. It would be awfully nice to breathe, though.

And then the arm about her throat disappeared and suddenly she collapsed once more against those damnably hard cobblestones. Why couldn't the people of London just pave all their roads with hay? Nice, soft hay? The thought skittered through her fogged brain as she dragged precious air into her lungs.

From her vantage point, Olivia saw feet of all sizes scatter. Leather slapped against stone as men dispersed, leaving her completely alone in the alleyway. Alone, until she felt Hamlet's rough nose nudge her shoulder.

She ought to get up. She really should run as everyone else had. Olivia rolled over, and grunted herself up to a standing position. She now had scraped and bloody hands along with a sore throat, and . . . drip, drip, drip . . . yes, her nose was most definitely still bleeding.

She peered about her, noting that all fierce, sword-wielding men seemed to have disappeared. Well, that was something at least. Of course, Ben had taken off as well. Olivia frowned. Now came the question of which way to go.

Out the back was usually what she said in her plays, so she started toward the back outlet of the alley. She would have a very large bruise on her posterior, for it already hurt terribly to walk. Hamlet kept pace with her limping footsteps, and Olivia sliced a glance at the cat. A good protector, but the feline did attract attention . . . bang!

Olivia had walked right into a wall.

On closer inspection, the wall turned out to be a very hard and wide chest covered in a leather doublet that smelled suspiciously of the distinct scent Olivia had come to associate with Sir Ian Terrance.

She tottered back a step and dragged her gaze up. And she was right again, Sir Ian Terrance stood before her, looking terribly dapper in his dark clothing, and windblown hair, but rather unhappy at the moment.

Stupid. Stupid, stupid, *stupid* to take her eyes off her destination.

Without saying a word, Ian curled his fingers around her arm and walked her back the way she came. He bent and picked up her scattered papers from where they lay, and as he rolled them with slow, deliberate movements, Olivia decided it was time to run.

She swiveled about on her heel and took two lunging, painful steps before Sir Ian hooked his arm about her waist.

With a grunt, he picked her up and dropped her midsection against his shoulder so that her torso hung against his back and her feet flailed about at his front. And then he trudged down the alley and out into the street.

She was quickly becoming rather dizzy, and she was leaving a rather consistent trail of blood now, but Olivia had a moment of hope as they came out onto the crowded street.

People.

People were good. She could scream, plead for help. There had to be someone among the throngs of London who would help her. She took a deep breath.

"Do not be such a complete fool, Miss Bea," Ian cut her off before she had time to think of what she would scream. "I am the Queen's number one agent, and everyone in this town knows that fact. There is not a sane man alive who would help you right now."

The hope faded fast, her lungs deflating on a heavy sigh. He was right, of course. Even Ben would keep his distance now.

They walked a few paces, and Olivia did not even bother trying to lever herself up to see where they were going. Instead she pinched her nose closed and found a bit of consolation in the fact that her elbow was banging into Ian's back with each step he took. Her elbow was rather bony—that just could *not* feel good.

Hamlet walked along behind them for a few paces, then stopped, meowed, and scampered back toward the house. Obviously, he did not think it necessary to protect her from his master. Unfortunately, that's exactly who she needed protection from.

And then, suddenly, hope flooded her once more. "Whewe aw you takig be?" she asked.

"You want to die, don't you?" he said.

Olivia scowled.

"You'll be greatly disappointed to know that I'm not taking you to the Queen and your imminent death, which will surely follow that auspicious occasion."

Olivia sighed. And then Ian bent and placed her feet on the ground. She swayed a bit, but he kept his hand under her elbow as he straightened. She blinked into his eyes. They were a beautiful clear green in the sunlight. They made her think of emeralds and deep, hidden, woodland ponds.

"Get in," he said harshly, bringing her back from her short flight of fancy. He pushed her toward a black, unmarked carriage, and she stumbled up the stairs. The shades were drawn, and it was dark inside. Olivia sank onto one of the bench seats.

Ian followed her in, closing the door behind him and banging with his fist on the low ceiling of the conveyance. They jerked forward immediately, Olivia nearly falling over at the quick movement.

"Here." A snowy white handkerchief appeared in front of her face. "Press it against your nose and tilt your head back."

Olivia grabbed the piece of linen without letting go of her nose. "Tank you eber so mut."

"You are welcome," Sir Ian said seriously.

Obviously the man had not heard the sarcasm in her tone. With a glare at the smug man across from her, Olivia tilted her head back and shoved Sir Ian's snowy white handkerchief against the blood still pouring from her nose. They rode in silence for a while as Olivia stared at the ceiling and wondered where they were going.

At one point, Olivia lifted one of the heavy shades to peek out a window, but Sir Ian pushed her hand away and shot her a look of pure distrust.

"Is it so much to ask that you tell me where you are taking me?" she asked.

"Yes."

"Tsk!" Olivia dabbed at her nose. It had stopped bleeding, finally, but it still felt as if she had hit a brick wall. Which, in reality, she had, only it had been a brick street. "Well, the least you can do is ask your men not to be so very physical next time. I am a bloody mess."

"My men?"

"Yes, your bullying, brutish men."

Sir Ian lifted one dark brow. "Those were not my men."

"Then who, pray tell, were they?"

"A question I was just about to ask you, Miss Bea."

Olivia stared at Ian, her jaw slack. "You think those men were helping me escape?"

"It looked just so from my perspective."

"Really? Well then, I shall have to dismiss the brute who nearly choked the life from me as he *helped me*." Olivia flounced back against her seat and crossed her arms before her. "Really! As if I knew one soul in this world who would risk their neck for me."

She thought of Ben, but realized that she could say nothing of him to Sir Ian. Still, it was a bit of consolation that there *was* someone out there worried for her. Although, he did like to run at the first sign of trouble. She scowled.

Ian only stared at her, his eyes once again black, enigmatic pools of darkness. "Calm down, Miss Bea, or you will cause yourself to bleed again."

Olivia glanced up at Ian from beneath her lashes. "Do not tell me to calm myself. I can gauge my own reactions just fine, thank you."

Ian only nodded, settling himself against the back of his seat.

He did not trust her in the least, she could see that clearly enough. And that bothered her. And the fact that it bothered her at all made her even angrier. It was not as if the man had ever trusted

157

her in the first place. And it was not as if she cared that he did!

She turned her face, but, of course, the shades were drawn, so she was left staring at nothing. Contemptible man, it was entirely his fault.

The carriage finally came to a halt after it felt as if they had turned every blasted corner in London. But when Ian handed her down to the street, Olivia realized that they now stood only a few streets away from where they had started.

"Wher . . ." she began to ask, but Ian had taken off down an alley with her in tow. The quick movement caused her mouth to snap shut, and she bit down hard on her tongue. "Ouch!" She tried to dig in her heels, but Sir Ian Terrance was rather strong.

"Come along, and be quiet," he whispered harshly to her.

Oh, she did hate being treated like a woman, Olivia thought, as they practically ran down the alley, then threaded quickly through the masses of people milling about the next street. Some nodcock stepped on her toe, and Olivia wailed again.

"Shush!"

And that did it. Annie had been the last person to shush her some fifteen years before, and she was not about to let this overbearing, bigger than his breeches, Queen's agent get away with it now.

With a good yank, she was free of Sir Ian. Unfortunately, he was a quick one, and grabbed her again before she could blink. Fortunately, he had finally stopped running.

"I will not go another inch unless you tell me where you are taking me."

He growled at her, truly growled, and she flinched a bit. "You, my dear, are my prisoner!" He pulled her close, so that prying ears would not be able to hear their exchange. "It would be wise of you not to forget that."

Olivia pursed her lips together, trying to think of something to say. Ian, himself, said nothing more. But neither did he back away from her. It was as if, among the throngs of Londoners, she and Sir Ian Terrance lived in a huddled moment of their own. And Olivia found herself remembering the odd sensation of safety she had felt with this man before.

She shook her head quickly. She must be hungry. Her mind was obviously weak. Olivia curled her cold toes into the dirt beneath her feet. "You cannot drag me through London with no shoes, Sir Ian. My feet are beginning to hurt, and I refuse to go any farther."

With a frown, Ian glanced down between

159

them. "What on earth are you doing running about without shoes?"

Olivia could only blink in shock. "My shoes are at my lodgings, along with everything else I own, you idiot. I have been living for the last three days in my nightgown! Or has it passed your notice that you *kidnapped* me whilst I was making ready for *bed*?"

"Shh!" Ian glanced around.

"Do not shush me! I will not have it."

Ian cocked his head and glared at her. "Really, Miss Bea, if you act like a child, I must treat you as one."

She opened her mouth to protest, but the man just turned around and started walking again. And, of course, he had his fingers wrapped around her arm, so she was yanked along behind him.

Olivia probed carefully at her aching nose as they went, for she truly feared that it was broken. And then, suddenly, Ian turned and pulled her through the door of a shop, and she bit her tongue . . . again.

She sucked on her tongue as she stumbled behind Ian.

"Shoes," he said, and she glanced up.

They were in a cobbler's shop, oh heaven!

"Sir?" the cobbler asked.

"We need shoes, a pair of women's shoes," he

glanced down at her feet. "Very large women's shoes."

Olivia stuck her elbow in her captor's ribs. "Will you *please* refrain from the comments about my size?"

"Women's shoes, sir?"

The cobbler's question pierced Olivia's disgruntlement. "Women's shoes?" she looked up at Sir Ian.

"Women's shoes," he stated with finality and pushed her into a chair. "And we need them quickly." He glanced out the window of the shop. "Very quickly."

"You want to wear them away?" the little, frazzled cobbler questioned again.

"Yes. Fit them to . . ." Ian frowned at Olivia. "Fit them to *his* feet." He gestured toward her.

Olivia glanced from Ian to the cobbler, then shrugged. With a little laugh, she propped her feet up on the bench before her. "If 'tis free shoes I'll be getting today, who am I to argue?"

She smiled at the cobbler, who turned and took down some felt pieces to size her feet. Olivia knew that she grinned like an idiot, but she could not wipe the smile from her face.

She was about to get a pair of women's shoes. Something so small should not have caused such a stir in her emotions, but it did, oh, how it did.

She had not worn a pair of women's shoes in years.

She had not been a woman in years. Olivia allowed her gaze to slink back to Ian. He stood with his back to her, peering out the window. He wore a cape, black of course, which fell unfashionably low to the middle of his thighs. It accentuated the breadth of his shoulders. And he wore no hat, as usual, his honey-dark curls tossed about by the wind and his own fingers.

Olivia remembered stroking his hair as he told her the amusing story of his sister the night before. How had she dared? Now, in the light of day, Sir Ian was such a different man. She could not imagine going to him, putting her hands in his hair . . . kissing him.

She closed her eyes quickly. Oh, yes, it had been many years since she had been a woman: a lifetime, in fact. For she had been but a girl when she had begun her ruse.

Olivia started as something soft touched her feet, and opened her eyes.

The cobbler held an incredible pair of dark blue velvet shoes up for her regard.

" 'Tis all I have with such short notice. I shall have to charge you double, o' course, they were meant for another, and I shall have to make up

162

another pair in 'alf the time now." The little man glanced over at Ian. "Will they do?"

Olivia blinked.

"They'll do," Ian said from behind her.

"Oh, yes, they'll do," she agreed quickly.

Chapter 8

Good name in man and woman, dear my lord,
is the immediate jewel of their souls. Who steals
my purse steals trash . . . But he that filches from
me my good name robs me of that which not
enriches him, and makes me poor indeed.
                                   —OTHELLO, III, iii, 155

He had locked her up again. Olivia sat staring down at her new shoes, her shoulders slumped forward. After all the excitement of the morning, it was terribly anticlimactic to be locked away once more, and this time without parchment or quill. With a sigh, Olivia looked up and surveyed her new prison.

At least this time she was not in some hole in the ground. There was a rickety old table and chairs and an uninviting cot, and there were windows in this cell, though they were tightly locked and covered with heavy curtains. When she had pulled them aside, Olivia had found herself staring at the back of a building that had no windows at all. A warehouse of some sort, most probably. She was on the first floor of a building, so no one from the alley below would be able to see her unless they craned their necks. And so far nobody had ventured past anyway.

Oh yes, Sir Ian, it seemed, had places to stash prisoners all over London. Lucky her.

The lock at the only door rattled, and Olivia glanced up as Ian walked in. He wore a red hat with a plume that swirled out and around to feather behind his head, and a fashionably short red cape to match. In his hand, he held a large box, which he dropped to the floor before turning to lock the door once more.

Olivia watched him, fighting the totally strange feeling of relief that had washed over her as she laid eyes on her captor. Relief! She must be going crazy. But even knowing how unbelievable such a reaction was, Olivia was honest enough with herself to recognize her emotions.

The sight of Ian's broad shoulders and tall body made her wish to jump up and throw her arms around him. They made her miserable cell so much more bearable, it nearly brought her to tears.

And since it was all this man's fault that she was locked in the depressing room in the first place, Olivia's feelings made absolutely no sense at all.

She was losing her sanity, surely.

"Put this on."

Olivia looked up as Ian shoved the large box toward her with the toe of his boot. She frowned.

"Quickly."

Olivia knelt and opened the box, then she just stared. "Oh."

"Anytime before the next century begins, Miss Bea."

Olivia looked up from the sea of blue silk that lay before her. "Is it a . . . ?"

" 'Tis a dress. We shall disguise you as a woman." His gaze raked her, and then he turned away quickly. "Put it on."

Olivia held her breath when she pulled the delicate garment from the box. The skirt was embroidered with small flowers at the hem, and the blue shade looked as if it would surely match her eyes perfectly. It was the most beautiful disguise Olivia had ever seen.

"I could not bring anyone else here, of course, so I shall help you dress." Ian stopped for a moment, and when he spoke again, his voice sounded strangely strained. "There is a corset, of

166

course, and I do know that women cannot get themselves into the contraptions."

Olivia glanced down to the steel corset that lay at the bottom of the box. She did not look forward to putting the thing on, and she certainly did not look forward to having Ian's assistance in putting it on. But, oh, Olivia pressed the gown in her hands to her lips, for she would consider enduring any torture to wear such a lovely dress.

"May I bathe first?" she asked softly. She knew he would say no, but she could hope.

Ian groaned, a strange animal-like sound that made Olivia look up at him quickly. He still stood with his back toward her, so she could not see his face. He did not make the sound again, in fact he stood quite still and silent for what seemed a long time. Finally, he said, "We have not the time for you to bathe. But . . ." He took a deep breath. "I brought you a new shift."

Olivia looked once more into the box and saw a small bit of lace poking out from behind the corset. Laying the gown carefully beside her, Olivia lifted the heavy corset and then gasped. "Oh my." She pulled her new shift from the box. It was of a very fine material, soft and tightly woven. And the edges were trimmed with lace and ribbons.

It was truly the most beautiful shift Olivia had ever owned. She glanced up sharply at Ian, but the man still stood stiffly facing the door.

"This is quite a disguise," she said.

"Quite. Now put it on, for we need to be away from here."

Olivia just stared for a moment at Sir Ian. The thought flashed through her mind that the fineries before her were meant to be some sort of gift. Whyever would the man buy such beautiful things only to disguise her? He could have spent much less and still made her look like a woman.

What an enigma this man was.

"I hear no movement, Miss Bea. In another ten seconds, I shall turn around and dress you myself."

Olivia jumped up quickly. "I'm changing, I'm changing," she said merrily as she shrugged out of Ian's large coat and dragged the moth-eaten hat from her head. She felt a bit of anxiety as she pulled her old night rail over her head and stood vulnerably naked. But she quickly settled the new shift over her shoulders, the material seeming to float about her like a cloud. It was like goose down against her skin.

"I must say, Sir Ian, you have fine taste in women's clothes."

"Hmmmph."

Olivia laughed as she tied the satin ribbons at her neck. When she looked down at herself, though, she realized that the material was so fine that the shift was nearly transparent.

"Are you ready for the corset?" Ian asked, and began to turn around.

With a great leap, Olivia grabbed the man's shoulders. "Do not turn around," she cried.

Ian stopped, his body stiffening beneath her fingers. "What is the matter?"

"I . . . um . . ." Olivia still held on to Ian, though he had most definitely stopped turning. She dropped her forehead so that it rested between his shoulder blades. "I do not want you to see me."

"Oh, please, I have seen you in your nightclothes for the last two days. Time is truly not our friend now, Miss Bea, we must . . ."

"Fine, I shall change back into my old garment, just do not turn around for a moment." She straightened and let go of Ian.

And the confounded man turned around. Olivia quickly crossed her arms over her chest and backed away. "I said do *not* turn around, Sir Deaf Ears."

Ian blinked once, his gaze going down to her feet and then tracking a hot path back to her face. It was as if he had touched her, for Olivia's legs shook as she stared into Ian's dark eyes.

"You are beautiful," he said.

Olivia did not move. She was sure that she could not have heard right. Her hand went automatically to her hair; even without a mirror she could tell it was a fright. She frowned. "Do not jest, Sir Ian."

"I do not . . ." Ian stopped, took a deep breath, and then he shook his head. "We have no time for this." He went to the box at Olivia's feet and grabbed the corset. "Turn around."

She obeyed instantly, for there was a dark edge to Ian's tone. He reached around her, pulling the corset tight about her torso. Olivia gasped.

"I don't see why this is needed, you're skinny enough as it is. But the woman at the shop insisted."

Olivia frowned. "I am slender."

Ian just yanked harder on the ties.

"Oommph." Olivia fell a bit, her head swaying forward, her chin colliding with soft, fleshy skin. "Sweet Mother of God," she whispered.

"What is it now?"

Olivia quickly put her hands over her new-found breasts. "Nothing!"

Ian made a grunting sound, and then the new gown drifted over her head. Olivia reveled in the feel of the silk against her skin and the lovely sensation of being hidden for a moment, then it settled about her and Ian twirled her around by the shoulders.

His eyes went from her face to her chest and

stayed there. They turned very dark as his thick lashes lowered. He looked a bit like a cat stalking a mouse. Olivia could only guess how she looked, her breasts large white mounds above the low décolletage of her gown. She nervously shied away from the man before her, pulling at the ties of her pannier. "I shall be able to finish by myself," she said quickly, her voice a tad higher than normal.

Ian did not acknowledge her comment at all, his gaze still upon her body. Heat crept up her neck and suffused her face as Olivia turned quickly away. She fumbled with the ties, her fingers shaking nearly as hard as her legs.

She heard nothing from Ian, but she knew that he still stared at her. It was as if his eyes were burning holes into her back. She stopped a moment and took a deep breath, her hands pressed against her abdomen. It was hard to breathe with the corset constricting her lungs, and she had a moment of panic, for her deep breath was not nearly deep enough. She tried to pull more air into her body, but it wouldn't come.

And then large hands curled around her shoulders and Ian's mouth was against her ear. "Relax," he said softly.

Olivia's chest shuddered, and she swayed, her head light. Ian took her weight so that she did not fall. "I am sure you will have to learn how to breathe all over again with this torture device about you." His voice was low, and soothing as if he spoke to a small child. She had never heard him speak so.

She closed her eyes and leaned even harder against his support. His hands moved down her arms and took over the work of her fingers, tying the front of her dress.

"Are you all right?"

She nodded, and he turned her. His eyes were like dark, woodland pools swirling and sucking her deep within them. And then they closed, and his mouth came down upon hers, warm and soft.

Olivia closed her eyes as Ian slipped his hands into her hair, holding her to him. His tongue probed her mouth, opened her lips, and plunged between her teeth. She opened to him, her entire body responding to his kiss.

She curled her fingers into the fabric of his cloak and tilted her head to give him better access to her lips. He groaned, and she answered, slipping her own tongue into his mouth, wanting to taste him as he tasted her.

They kissed forever, the rhythm of their tongues making Olivia's desire carnal and needy. And then he stopped. He pulled back, and she whimpered, blinking up into his dark eyes.

"You are a witch," he said quietly, his thumbs sliding along her brow as his gaze went from her eyes to her mouth and then to her breasts.

Olivia's breath stopped in her lungs, and then began again more quickly than before. His gaze returned to her eyes. "A witch," he murmured.

He leaned forward, nipping at her neck, making a trail to the hollow of her throat. Olivia tipped her head back, keeping her hands wrapped in Ian's cloak for balance.

He kissed the pulse point at her neck, his tongue swirling there and making Olivia's eyes flutter closed in rapture. And then he continued his trail of kisses, wetting the top of her breast and making her shudder.

His hand left her hair and cupped her breast. She could feel the heat of it through every layer, and suddenly wished that she was still gloriously naked. Oh, the thrill to have his hand against her skin. Her nipple tingled, and she made a funny mewling sound like a kitten's cry for milk.

And then Ian's mouth was on hers again, this time his kiss was darkly demanding, one hand still against her breast, the other sliding down to cup her bottom and pull her against his hard maleness.

"I want you," he gasped, and the words made her feel a power she had never experienced.

But they must have been a surprise to Ian as well, for he stopped completely, his hands falling away from her. She nearly fell when he stepped away from her and turned quickly on his heel.

The silence beat around them heavily as Olivia tried to catch her breath.

"There is a wig as well. Put it on. I shall await you in the hall." And he left, his steps measured and deliberate as he closed the door quietly behind him.

But his voice had shook, and that made it just a little easier to handle the man's abrupt departure. He was just as affected as she. She was sure of it.

Her feet felt divine. Of course, that was the only part of her body that had any feeling whatsoever, except for her nose, of course, which ached like the devil. The petticoats beneath her dress weighed a ton at least. Olivia tugged at the stomacher that adorned her chest and fell to a point beneath her waist.

"Stop your fidgeting," Ian said to her under his breath.

"I cannot breathe!" she whispered back as she pulled her wire collar away from her neck. It caught on her wig, which Olivia straightened quickly. "Good God, I am like a prisoner in a cell."

"Just be natural."

Olivia frowned. Again she was admonished to act natural when everything about her situation was completely unnatural. She glanced at Ian, who looked quite jaunty in a new red, short cape and matching hat with a plume that swept around the brim and out behind him.

"You look like a great red peacock, milord," she couldn't help saying before giggling.

He scowled down at her. "And you sound like a simpering ninny."

She gasped. "Did you just call me a ninny?"

"Just walk and quit your fidgeting."

"And where is it we are walking to, Monsieur Peacock?" Of course her companion did not answer. "I begin to think we have no destination. Are you wondering, once again, what to do with me?"

He sliced her a glance, and Olivia laughed. "Ah, yes, 'tis as I thought. You have a woman in your clutches and know not what to do with her." The grip Sir Ian had on her arm tightened. "We do not dare go back to your home, of course. The scoundrels may be lurking. And who do you think those scoundrels were, sir?"

"I am waiting for you to answer that question, Miss Bea."

"Ah, I am such a high-and-mighty person that I have men of arms to do my bidding."

Ian looked out from beneath his red hat at her, his gaze intense, the questions blatant behind his green eyes. Olivia looked away.

She was happy, actually, to be walking about

on the street. It had been too many days cooped up without fresh air for her. And she also wondered at the identity of the men who had thwarted her escape. Truly, she did not wish another meeting with the brute of the thick arms.

"So we walk the streets incognito." She laughed. "Although, I must tell you, Sir Ian, even in your grand plumage, I think you fool no one."

"Ian!"

They both looked up at the cry. A dark-haired woman leaned out the window of a carriage in the street. "Ian," she gestured for him to come to her. "I was just on my way to your house."

Olivia felt as if bile constricted her throat. Jealousy, it was. She was not stupid enough to lie to herself. But it made her livid that she would feel such a completely inane emotion. And for Sir Ian Terrance, at that. "Oh, yes, your disguise is astonishing," she said, and smiled waspishly at Ian.

He did not see her grin, for his eyes were shut as he took deep breaths.

"Ian!"

Olivia transferred her gaze to the woman, and suddenly all traces of jealousy left with recognition. It was Ian's sister, she was sure. She remembered seeing her at the Celebration of the Garter.

Pulling Olivia along with him, Ian finally started toward his sister's carriage. "Do keep your voice down, Andy," he said. "It is not always best that the whole town know where to find me."

"Oh, Ian," Andy said, her hand at her throat. "The most awful thing has happened. I need you desperately."

"Really, Andy, I have not the time at the moment." They had reached the carriage. Ian opened the door quickly and jumped inside without waiting for the footman who stood at the back. Being permanently attached to the man at the wrist, Olivia was dragged inside with him.

"Draw the shades, Andy." Ian banged on the ceiling and yelled for the driver to be off.

"Ian, I am devastated. I shall throw myself from a bridge, surely," Andy lamented as she sat back with a great sigh.

Ian made a low sound of disgust and leaned over Olivia to pull the shades.

"He loved me, and now he does not." Andy began to cry.

"Is this about Sir Richard again?"

Andy snapped her head up and glared at her brother. "Of course 'tis about Sir Richard. Who else has loved me?"

Ian went to run his fingers through his hair, but got his hand caught up in his brand-new hat. It tumbled to the seat.

"Where on earth did you get that hat, Ian?"

Andy had quit her whimpering. "And that cape? 'Tis red!" She squinted at him. "You look different." She stared suddenly at Olivia as if she had just appeared from nowhere. "Marry! Who is this?" Andy was obviously intrigued. She studied Olivia with rounded eyes. "It is a woman!"

"You are quite on your mark today, Andy," Ian said. He turned to look at Olivia as well. "This is, um, Beatrice . . . Miss Beatrice."

Andy smiled suddenly and bowed her head. "Miss Beatrice."

Ian gestured toward his sister. "Miss Beatrice, this is my sister Andromeda."

Olivia nodded. "Miss Andromeda."

"Oh, do call me Andy, everyone does."

"Miss Beatrice is a cousin, some long-lost cousin of mother's come over from, er . . . France. I have just picked her up from the docks."

"France?" Andy asked, and then turned to Olivia. "You do not sound French."

"Oh, she is not," Ian answered for her quickly.

Olivia turned an interested eye upon Sir Ian. "And just what am I?" she asked, intrigued with this little story and where it might go.

Ian gave her quite a look, but Olivia just arched her brow and waited. He turned quickly to Andy. "She is English, of course. But has lived in France for many years."

"How amazing." Andy looked from Ian to Olivia. "I do not remember cousins who lived in France."

"Long-lost, as I said, Andy dear. Now what is this of Sir Richard not loving you?"

But Andy seemed not to be listening to her brother any longer. She leaned forward and peered at Olivia. "Did you fall, Beatrice? There is blood on your nose."

Olivia patted carefully just underneath her nostril with the handkerchief she still carried in her sleeve.

"Faith!" Andy exclaimed staring at the small piece of linen.

Olivia glanced at the bloody material.

"She had a nose bleed aboard ship, I'm afraid," Ian quickly interrupted. "Sea air, it doesn't agree with her."

Andy leaned back again, her brows knit. "Are you taking Miss Beatrice to the country, then, to see Mother?"

"No. Whatever has happened with Sir Richard, Andy?"

"Where will Miss Beatrice be staying?" Andy asked, completely ignoring Ian's change of subject.

"With me. Do tell, Andy, what has happened with Sir Richard."

"She cannot stay with you! 'Tis unseemly, Ian." Andy turned her full attention upon Olivia again. "You may stay with me, Beatrice. I do need female companionship ever so much at the moment."

Ian looked ready to strangle his sister, but he also seemed at a loss for something to say. Olivia found it extremely interesting that he had made up such a story about her. Why on earth could he not tell his sister that Olivia was his prisoner?

Something more was afoot here than the Queen's agent having caught a woman masquerading as a man. Of course, *she* had always known there was more. But now she knew for sure that Ian knew something as well.

What did he know? And why had he not taken her to the Queen?

"Have you ever been in love, Beatrice?"

Andy had been speaking, but Olivia only caught this last question. She blinked and glanced at Ian. "No, actually," she answered his sister.

"Well, try very hard to keep it that way, dearest, for love is a terrible prospect."

"I thought you were very nearly betrothed to Sir Richard," Olivia said. "Ian did help to clear up the misunderstanding with Lord Crandle, did he not?"

Andy looked stunned. "You know of my problems, Miss Beatrice? I thought Ian had just picked you up from the docks?" Andy glanced at her brother, amazement clearly written on her face. "Do I dare believe that you care enough about me to even mention my name in conversation, Ian?"

"Of course I care about you, Andy."

Andy turned back to Olivia. "You see, Beatrice, Ian did help bring Sir Richard and me to an understanding. But that was two days ago, before Sir Richard believed that I dallied with another man."

"What?" Ian roared.

Olivia placed her hand on Ian's sleeve. "What has happened, Andy?"

Andy stared at where Olivia's hand rested on Ian's arm, and then her gaze tracked up to Ian's face for a moment.

Ian had gone mute after his initial outburst. A blessing, that, as his roar would surely give Olivia a terrible headache in such a confined space.

"Has there been another misunderstanding?" she prompted Ian's sister.

"Yes," the girl said slowly, dragging her gaze back to Olivia. "Yes, oh yes, 'tis awful, truly! A rumor has been put about that I am a wanton woman!"

"Whyever would such a rumor be spread?" Olivia asked.

Andy leaned forward conspiratorially. "I must believe that someone saw my maid. She was, um, behaving rather badly with a man directly in front of the windows of my chamber."

"What?" The lion had returned to roar.

Olivia winced. "Really, Ian, yelling will help us not at all." She turned once again to Andy. "You witnessed your maid yourself, then?"

The girl's face went nearly as red as Ian's new hat. "I . . . um, walked in and found them thus, yes. I did not want to interrupt, so I left them."

"You left them?" Ian thundered. "You should dismiss the woman immediately! You ought to have rid yourself of her on the spot."

"But she did not," Olivia interrupted. "And, really, Ian, 'twas no harm meant, I am sure, on the maid's part. But, obviously"—Olivia smiled sympathetically at Andy—"some other vile person mistook the maid for Andy and has decided to make free with his own misguided understanding."

"Yes," Andy wailed. "And Sir Richard was shown the false proof of it as well."

Before Sir Ian could erupt once more, Olivia squeezed his hand. "Sir Richard saw the couple in the window?" she asked calmly.

"Yes. He has refused to speak to me since, and I have heard that he has asked the Queen to send him back to Norway." Here Andy dissolved into tears.

Olivia glanced over at Ian, who sat quietly, a

murderous frown darkening the hard planes of his face.

" 'Tis a tragic twist in the tale," Olivia said quietly.

"Such tragedy, Miss Beatrice, that even Shakespeare himself would not dare relate such an awful tale," Andy cried.

Ian choked.

"Yes, well, 'tis awful, Andy, but, again only a misunderstanding," Olivia said. She turned to look at Ian. "I am sure your brother could fix this little coil as he did your last."

Ian looked as if he would rather chase down a rampaging bull.

"Oh, you must, Ian! I am at my wit's end," Andy wailed. And then she blinked, an idea obviously subduing her distress. "A sonnet, Ian, I shall need one of your sonnets!"

"Andy!" Ian shouted.

"Sonnet?" Olivia asked.

"I know not of what she speaks," Ian said quickly. "Are you quite all right, Andy, I do believe you speak utter nonsense."

Andy fell back against her seat back. "Fine, I speak nonsense, but you must help me to make this right, Ian."

"Of course he will," Olivia said. "We shall go to the palace immediately."

"No we will not." Ian glared at her.

"Then what are we going to do, dearest cousin?" Olivia asked sweetly. "Ride about in this carriage all day?"

"To the palace, anon," Andy said decidedly. She banged on the roof of the carriage and yelled directions.

"I cannot, Andy," Ian said. "I really do not have the . . ."

"Time? Yes, I know, you tell me so often." Andy leaned forward and grabbed Ian's hand. "But I need you, Ian, now. And I know you can woo well in another's name."

"Really, Andy . . ." He glanced over at Olivia. Poor man, what *would* he do now? Olivia just smiled.

"Miss Beatrice cannot possibly go to the palace, Andy. She does not know how to act in such circumstances!"

"Nonsense, good man," Olivia interrupted. "I have been to court often."

"But . . ."

"Not to worry, Ian, I am not showing myself anyway. Beatrice can stay with me and be a boon to me in my upset while you go about your duty as a brother and tidy up the mess my maid has left."

"Yes, Ian, you must." Olivia batted her lashes at her captor.

With the darkest look she had ever seen on the

face of a human, Ian slid back in his seat and folded his arms across his chest. "Fine, then."

"Oh, thank you, Ian, thank you!"

"Do not thank me, sister, until the mess is good and clean." He darted another sinister look at Olivia, then his gaze slashed away from her, and he stared at the blinds for the rest of their journey.

He was living a nightmare. Ian shifted uncomfortably in the small chair that would be his bed that night. It had been too long since he had a full night of sleep in his very soft bed.

He was actually having fantasies of marching into the Queen's chamber, Miss Beatrice Shakespeare in tow. Of course, he would then be dead, but wouldn't that be better than this?

Ian sighed loud and long, and shifted his position once more. Unfortunately, taking Olivia to the Queen *was* a fantasy. The moment the Queen knew that Ian had not done as she had commanded seventeen years before, all of his properties and money would be confiscated, leaving his sister in disgrace and his mother homeless, not to mention the fact that he would be feeding the worms.

Ian leaned his head into his hands. The thought crossed his mind that if he had but done his duty seventeen years before, he would not be in such trouble now. He wondered, though, idly, if he could have killed the defenseless child he had been sent to kill when but a lad himself.

Ian straightened, turning in his chair so that his sister's door lay in his direct line of vision. Now, knowing Olivia Tudor, it was hard to believe she had ever been defenseless, but seventeen years ago he had walked right in the front door of her home and had easily found her hiding behind a portrait.

At the time he had been all of seventeen, a fresh recruit. In those days, Walsingham, the Queen's secretary in charge of the agents, liked to find his men at the universities: young, smart men on scholarship and in need of money. And, as Ian had told Olivia, he had been in need of money.

But he had also been excited. The intrigue of the court was far removed from his studies of literature and very thrilling for a young man from the pastures of Derbyshire.

And he had done well quickly. Given the strict teachings of his father, Ian was quite different from the other young agents. Ian was honest, he had integrity: a characteristic not readily found in the court of Queen Elizabeth.

But his decision to become an agent for the Queen had changed the course of his life completely. Though he still held to his honesty and integrity, Ian was no longer the naive young man who found court life exciting. He now saw the tarnished truth beneath all the glitter. Yet, it was the way he must live, and he was bound to it with no way of escape. Still, it had taken something vital from him.

For he knew without a doubt that the man he was now would not have left the castle in Cornwall without blood on his hands. Ian stared down at his fingers, and then closed his eyes tightly.

"Sir Ian, you are returned!"

Ian glanced up at the interruption of his introspective thoughts. Crandle. Ian stared for a moment at the door to his sister's room, mentally begging Olivia Tudor to stay within its confines, then glanced up at his new companion. "And where is it that I've been, Crandle?"

The man looked completely flummoxed.

"You say I am back," Ian explained. "Where exactly have I been?"

"Well . . . that is, I . . . Fie, man, 'tis been days since you've been at court."

"This morning, actually."

Crandle blinked at this and shifted his weight from one foot to the other. It was interesting to watch a man of obvious strength so nervous and seemingly fearful. It was the effects of so long being at the whim of a powerful female, Ian was sure. Another reason to shun marriage.

Of course, Crandle was not married. The female in the man's life was the same that ruled Ian's.

"You counseled with the Queen this morning, then?" Crandle rolled the hem of his fashionable short cloak between his fingers.

Ian only stared at the earl. "Lord Crandle," Ian asked. "What do you here, in the women's hall?"

Crandle looked around as if he had walked while in slumber and had no idea where he was. "I came looking for you, Sir Ian."

"Yes?"

"Er . . ." Lord Crandle glanced at the door that Ian obviously guarded. "Bad business about your sister, Terrance," he said.

Not a good subject to pick if the man wanted something from him. Ian narrowed his eyes and leaned back in his chair, crossing his arms in front of his chest.

"I . . . that is to say, the Queen is very upset." Crandle looked around. "She has been upset for days, actually." Crandle went to another chair down the hall and dragged it over. "What business bothers her so, Terrance?" The man plopped down casually, yet still his fingers rolled his hem, and now his foot tapped determinedly against the wood floor.

Ian cocked his head and looked at Lord Crandle from beneath his brow. "The Queen has many things which take a toll upon her peace of mind."

"Yes, of course, of course." Lord Crandle cleared his throat. "But, of late, it seems, she has been . . . well, more upset than usual."

"Could it be your little dalliance with Lord Frigburn's wife last fall has stayed more heavily upon her mind than you thought?" Ian asked with a smile.

The man's thin blond mustache twitched. "I am sure that could not be it."

Ian shrugged. "You never know."

The roll of fabric between Lord Crandle's fingers began to tremble. With a sigh, Ian decided that torturing such a lightweight as Crandle was no longer amusing. "It has nothing at all to do with you, Crandle, do not bother yourself about it. Go." He gestured down the hall. "Have merry. You shall be a favorite again soon enough."

This should have soothed the man. Incredibly, it did not. He continued to roll and tap, giving Ian pause. "What, pray tell, do you wish the Queen upset over?"

Lord Crandle jumped in his seat. "Nothing! I would never wish the Queen upset. God forbid."

"Of course, Lord Crandle. But there is something you think she ought to be upset about?"

"No . . . well, I just wondered what has put her in such a foul mood of late."

"She is in a foul mood?" Ian acted surprised. "I have not noticed that."

"You haven't? But"—he frowned—"the entire court has noticed a change in her mood."

And that, of course, put the entire world in a decline. Ian just controlled the roll of his eyes.

"And she has had many intimate meetings with you, Sir Ian. What . . ."

"Ah, ah, ah," Ian interrupted Crandle's query with a wag of his finger. "If I tell you the intimacies of the Queen, I shall then be compelled to kill you."

Lord Crandle's dark eyes widened. Ian nearly laughed. It did help in circumstances such as this to have a rather sinister reputation.

"Can you not at least give me an idea of . . ." Lord Crandle stopped halfway through his pleading and swallowed hard. Obviously, Ian's look of menace was working, he thought. As it did not work at all with Mistress Tudor, it was comforting to know that he had not completely lost his power to make others cower.

"On other matters, Lord Crandle, I think you would find it beneficial to know, and to let others know, also, that my sister has dallied with no one at all."

"But I saw her . . ." Crandle stopped the words

with a hand to his lips. "Does she reside within her chamber now?" the man asked quickly, as if he wished to change the subject.

Ian would not allow that to happen. "You, Lord Crandle?" he said, slowly straightening in his chair. "Are you the one who has perpetuated such a horrible lie through the court?"

Lord Crandle pressed a hand to his chest as if Ian had shamed *his* sister. " 'Twas no lie!" He seemed to gain courage in the false idea that his eyes never lied. "I was standing below your sister's window. I saw her in an embrace with a man not Sir Richard."

"The woman you saw was my sister's maid," Ian said with finality. "And, by the by, Lord Crandle, my sister does not even share the same hair color as her maid. Sally, as I remember, has blond ringlets, whereas Andromeda's hair is black as pitch and straighter than straw."

Lord Crandle huffed a sound of distress.

"You might consider honing your skills of observation. I find your deductive reasoning lacking as well." Ian stood, began to pace, and realized that he could not let Andy's door leave his vision for even a moment. So he stopped.

"I must ask, Crandle, what mission found you standing beneath my sister's window?" The Queen had conveniently placed her ladies-in-waiting on the third floor of the palace just above a patch of rather thorny and painful rosebushes. She always looked to protect her ladies' virginal state. No one lurked beneath the windows of the ladies' hall, except, it seemed, Lord Crandle.

"Um, well . . ."

"Would the Queen find this something to deepen her foul mood, perhaps?"

"Really, Terrance, it has nothing to do with . . . that is to say, we need not speak of this anymore." He stood as well, flattening his palms down the sides of his blue-velvet doublet, and flipping his short cloak over his shoulder. "I shall revise my previous statements about your sister, to be sure."

"And the first person you shall speak to is Sir Richard," Ian said pointedly.

Crandle shoved out his chest and gave Ian a haughty look that showed just how uneasy the man felt. "I only called him out to the window because I hate to see a man cuckolded before his wedding."

"But after the fact is all right?" Ian asked with a smile as Crandle obviously remembered his little rendezvous with another man's wife.

"I shall speak with Sir Richard." Crandle turned on his heel.

"You never explained your presence beneath Andromeda's window, Crandle."

The earl had stomped halfway down the hall.

"I need not explain myself to you!" he yelled over his shoulder, and kept walking. Ian watched as the man disappeared around the corner.

A bit testy and very nervous. Could this all be manifestations of the man's hunger to be back in the Queen's good graces? Or was there something more to Lord Crandle's strange behavior? And what the devil was the man doing lurking beneath his sister's window?

"Good work, Terrance."

Ian turned to find his captive standing in the doorway, her arm linked with his sister's. He wanted to groan. What a coil this had become.

"Oh, yes, Ian. But I thought you had gone to speak with Sir Richard yourself." Andy frowned at him. "What were you doing sitting outside my door this whole time?"

Ian tried to think of something, but his sister thankfully changed the subject herself. "Do you think Lord Crandle will tell Sir Richard that he mistook, truly?"

"If he wants to remain whole, yes."

"I must say, Sir Ian, you can be so commanding." Olivia had taken acting like a woman to heart, it seemed. Ian narrowed his eyes at her. His gaze slipped, though, as it had been doing since she had donned the blasted dress. He found himself staring at the way the candlelight flickered enticingly against her cleavage, which curved above the low décolletage of her gown.

He went hard immediately, his hands clenching as he remembered holding her only hours before. The kiss they had shared when Olivia was dressing had been something akin to a fantasy. He had never before felt such need, such an utter wanting.

And he wanted her again.

He wanted to kiss her.

He wanted to make love to her.

"Will you go and make sure that Lord Crandle informs Sir Richard true, brother dear?"

"Oh yes, Ian, you should go, just to make sure."

Ian closed his eyes for a moment. It was getting more and more difficult to remember that Olivia was a skinny, unattractive woman with the tongue of a shrew. In fact, just the thought of her tongue made his knees weak. Ian opened his eyes with a snap and shook his head. "He will speak true," he said roughly, trying desperately to concentrate on the conversation.

"But I must know, Ian. 'Tis my life, after all, that hangs in the balance."

"Really, Andy, your life is not that dramatic."

"Of course it is, silly man." Olivia pushed passed him, Andy still hooked against her side. "Every life is a drama. 'Tis what makes it such fun. Come now, Ian, we must make sure that Andy's drama ends happily."

Ian stood for a moment staring after Olivia and his sister, shock making his jaw slack. Couldn't the woman see that he was a man to fear, a man of power and darkness? And she blithely started down the hall in her finery as if she were just another woman of the court?

"Halt!" he roared toward the retreating backs of the women. Andy had the grace to stop, and fortunately that stopped his captive. His captive, *dammit*! How in the name of God had he allowed this situation to get so out of hand?

"Is something wrong, Ian?" Olivia Tudor asked haughtily.

That was how. That woman lacked the sense to understand that he could squash her beneath his thumb if he wished. "You are my . . ." He glanced at Andy, and stopped. Ian jammed his fingers through his hair, realizing that he still wore that confounded hat as the ugly red thing dropped to the floor.

"Yes, cousin?" Olivia asked with a taunting tilt to her brow. And in that minute, Ian saw a very strong resemblance in his captive to the Queen. Oh yes, Miss Bea was most definitely the long-lost Olivia Tudor from the top of her regal head to the tips of her too-big feet.

And they would both be the death of him.

But not until he was ready to die.

Chapter 9

What win I, if I gain the thing I seek? A dream, a breath, a froth of fleeting joy.

—RAPE OF LUCRECE, 211

Ian closed the distance between them with two strides. "Bea cannot go into public, Andy." He hooked his own arm through Olivia's and extracted her from his sister's side.

"Whyever not?" Andy asked.

"She is not ready for such things, Andy. She is fragile still."

Olivia glanced at him. "Fragile?"

"Fragile?" Andy echoed her pretend cousin.

"Of course, she has never been quite . . . right. And," he shrugged, "well, after that last incident . . ."

"Incident?" Andy blinked owlishly.

196

Olivia just shook her head.

"Yes." Ian lowered his voice to a whisper, "they found her in the chicken coop, Andy . . . it was most unseemly."

"Oh please," Olivia interrupted him. "Never put your pen to paper with the intent of writing anything other than a dull missive to your mother, Sir Ian."

She turned to Andy. "What Ian is trying to tell you, with no imagination whatsoever, I would add, is that I am rather strange in the head. I never know what is going to happen. One moment I am speaking with all the intelligence of a normal being, and then"—Olivia snapped her fingers together—"poof, I'm rambling and running off to the chicken coop."

She threw a disgusted look at Ian. "Although, truly, I think I could have thought of a better place than the chicken coop to lose control of my wits, but I defer to my cousin on that point."

Andy looked completely confused. "But . . ."

" 'Tis why I am here, Andy dear. I am off to spend some time with your mother in the country, away from prying eyes and situations where I might embarrass myself."

"Exactly!" Ian exclaimed.

Olivia shot him a look of disgust. "Yes, well, except for the chicken coop part."

"But you said you were not taking her to

Mother." Andy furrowed her brow in concentration, and then turned to her brother, and said, "Ian, you should have told me sooner."

His sister really did have a lovely habit of not waiting for him to answer a question.

"He did not want to embarrass me," Olivia answered quickly. "You understand."

Andy looked between them. "No, actually."

"But, really, Ian, we must ensure that Lord Crandle tells the truth to Sir Richard." Olivia switched the subject conveniently. "Perhaps if we lurk in some darkened corner and listen?"

"Oh yes!" Andy agreed. "Beatrice seems in a very good mind at the moment. I'm sure 'twill do no harm."

"Believe me, Andy, Beatrice can do much harm."

"You give me much too much credit, Sir Ian."

"I believe that I give you too little, cousin."

Olivia smiled sweetly. "How flattering." She put her hand over his, which still gripped her arm, and with one touch his anger and frustration melted into lust. "I do believe that is the nicest thing you have ever said to me."

Ian stared at Olivia for a moment, his skin on fire where she touched him. And then he turned, deliberately brushing against the curve of her pushed-up breast. He could not help but smile as he watched the hollow of her throat deepen slightly as her breath caught. "You forget, Miss Bea, I once told you that your feet were not ugly."

She swallowed. He watched the movement in her neck, then watched as her chest shuddered slightly.

"That is right, you did," she said, the small hesitation in her voice so imperceptible only he had caught it.

Ian arched his brow and brushed his finger lightly against her temple, where a swirl of her real hair had escaped the confines of her wig. "I think I even said something nice about your hair as well?"

They were standing close, their eyes nearly on a level since Olivia was so tall, and he wanted to kiss her. It would take only a small movement, and their mouths would touch. He would taste her, feel her tongue glide inexpertly against his lips, drive the thoughts from his mind and the sanity from his body.

"Stop now, cousin," Olivia said in a shaky voice. She took a small step away from him. "Stop before I take your true meaning." Her eyes were round and dark as a night sea. "I also remember the circumstances under which such flattery was given."

"How can you two have had such experiences?" Andy interrupted them. "Have you known each other before?"

Ian nearly laughed aloud. "No," he said instead, and turned sharply away from the fair Olivia. She had addled his brain, truly, for when they touched, when they stood close, he forgot all else but the need to take her body with his.

And that was the last thing that he should be thinking of at the moment. With a determined effort to forget that the arm beneath his fingers was as soft as down, Ian started back toward Andy's room, pulling Olivia with him.

"Now, Andy, I shall go down and make sure that all has been set straight about your pristine reputation. But I must insist that you keep Beatrice in your room." He opened his sister's chamber door. "Do not let anyone in, and most definitely do not let Beatrice out." He shoved Olivia through the portal and grabbed his sister's arm. " 'Tis imperative that you not let her leave, Andy. Promise me. Your tenuous reputation rests upon your obedience to my request."

"Of course, Ian, I shall do my best."

"No, you shall do it. Do not let her leave, and do not let anyone in. I will be back in a moment." He closed the door quickly, and then yelled through the thick wood. "Bolt the door."

As he started down the hall, Ian had doubt hitting him like arrows shot from bows. He should not leave Olivia to the questionable strength of his sister. But he also had to alleviate his sister's fears. And he was quite interested to mingle among the people of court for a moment.

He would like to know what had made Lord Crandle so intensely nervous. And he would like to find the men who had tried to take Olivia that afternoon.

That gave Ian pause, and he glanced back at his sister's door. But whoever had tried to take Olivia today had thought her a man. They would not realize that his cousin Beatrice was that same man.

But why had they tried to take Olivia? Did someone else know who she was?

Ian hurried his steps. The whole mess was a quandary, and he had to get Olivia alone soon, but now he would do his sister's bidding, and quickly. For, in truth, he wanted Andy's name cleared of any dirty gossip just as much as she.

With the thought of Olivia alone with his sister plaguing each step, Ian flew toward the Queen's presence chamber, where he was sure to find Lord Crandle and Sir Richard at this time of night. The Queen might be there as well, although she could also be cloistered in her chamber sifting through the things Ian had brought her that very morning: the things from Olivia's lodgings. He had found nothing of any value or interest, except for manuscript pages.

Ian paused in the guardroom, remembering the pages he picked up off the ground of the alley when he had come back for Olivia. He pulled them out from where he had tucked them under his doublet and rolled them out.

'Twas the beginning of a play, he could tell. Ian squinted and read a few lines. It was the same play that he had found in Olivia's apartment. A few changes had been made to the beginning, but the characters were the same.

Could she truly be the writer of Shakespeare's plays? Ian slowly rolled the pages and stuck them back for safekeeping under his doublet. His mind told him that no woman could pen such genius. His heart told him differently. Ian scowled. His heart and mind had been of one accord until just recently. It was Olivia who had caused the rift which he must repair, and soon. Straightening his shoulders, Ian entered the Queen's presence chamber.

How had the man become one of the Queen's top agents? Olivia nearly laughed out loud as she let herself quietly out the door of Andy's chambers. She felt a tiny prick of conscience when she thought of Andy returning from her nightly ablutions to find her cousin gone. The poor girl would probably run straight for the royal chicken coops.

Olivia flexed her toes within the lovely velvet shoes and pulled at her wig as she quickened her pace down the hall. She had no idea where she was going, but she figured anywhere was better than being in the clutches of Ian Terrance.

The sudden memory of the brute's strangling embrace of that afternoon, and Olivia had to revise her last thought. She would rather be Ian's captive than the brute's. Unless, of course, the brute had been sent to take her to the Queen.

But that would make no sense at all. Sir Ian was the Queen's most trusted agent. No, the brute had been someone else altogether. But who?

Her life had never been simple, but lately it had begun to make even one as intelligent as she wonder. Olivia sighed, but perked up when she heard voices. And then she saw liveried footmen, probably guards actually, standing at the entrance to a large empty room. Beyond the room, though, Olivia saw a door. The door, she thought, had potential, given the guards and the voices.

Warily she started through the guarded door. Fortunately, the men only flicked her an uninterested glance as she went by. How very lovely it was to be a woman. No one gave you a second thought.

She realized then that one of the men had not

looked away, in fact he was staring raptly at her pushed-up bosom. Well, perhaps some gave you a second thought, or a look at least.

It was nice, though, to have the diversion of her bosom. It detracted nicely from her purple nose. Olivia glanced down at herself and felt dizzy at the sight of her small breasts piled so high. It was indecent, surely.

But, of course, she had watched other women adorned thus. She took a deep breath for courage and went through the door at the end of the vacant room.

She entered a world of noise and people with a tangy scent hanging in the air. She was quite used to the odor of unwashed bodies from the playhouses, but here in the Queen's palace there was a cloying smell that intermingled with that of man.

Roses, she realized. The people obviously held possets, wore perfumed gloves, and splashed themselves liberally with rose toilet water.

Too bad they did not just dunk their putrid bodies in scalding hot water. Olivia scrunched her nose, winced at the pain, then skirted the room.

People mingled about, some speaking with each other, some just standing and watching. A quartet played at one end of the room, and some danced to the music. Olivia peered about her, but she did not see Ian, and she did not see the Queen either.

She would not, of course, confront the Queen in such a public place, but she was rather sure that she could get Her Majesty to leave the assembly. More than anything at the moment, though, Olivia just wanted to see her.

It was a burning need within her, actually, to meet her mother. The fire ignited when she had been a small child. And it had never died, only burned hotter with each year of her life.

And she knew that those years were over now that she was about to assuage her need to meet her mother. 'Twas the grossest of ironies, really. Still, it mattered not. Olivia knew that she could never have the things that would make life worth living, the things of which she wrote in order to live them. She would never experience the love of a man, children, family. She could not even allow friends to grow close to her. She had to live her life as another, a fate she would not wish upon her most hated enemy.

Olivia smiled. Her most hated enemy: her mother. But an enemy who had called to her, pulled her in. She searched the room, looking especially for a sight of red hair, a woman of regal bearing and long thin fingers. Olivia glanced down at her own fingers, clenched in the fabric of her gown.

"How could I ever have thought that you would stay where I put you?"

She looked up into the face of her second most hated enemy. Funny how her most hated enemies seemed to draw her to them like a bear to honey. She looked at the curl of hair over Ian's brow, his hat finally gone.

" 'Tis good you defy fashion and do not wear hats, Ian. You have such lovely hair." And she spoke true. It was like dark honey, rich soil, or perhaps chocolate. Oh, yes, chocolate like she had eaten by the pound in Switzerland with dearest Annie.

"I am no woman, Bea, to be flattered out of my pique by honeyed words from your tongue."

"Honeyed words, hmmm." Olivia nodded. " 'Tis a good phrase, Ian."

He only scowled.

"But, again, you do a disservice to my sex by the tart words from *your* tongue."

Ian took a few steps closer, crowding Olivia into a corner. "You will not dissuade me from my purpose with words, Bea."

"And what, then, be your purpose?"

"To remove you from this room immediately."

"Methinks that may be difficult, Sir Ian. I am, after all, not of sound mind."

"You would not dare."

"Oh, yes, I would." She smiled widely at Ian.

206

"You see, I know that you do not want others to know I am your prisoner. Why that should be kept secret, I am still trying to deduce. But, it does give me the..." She placed her hand against Ian's chest. "The upper hand, you might say."

His body was warm to her touch, and it made her shiver. She blinked disconcertedly, but managed to pull her hand away slowly and, hopefully, without alerting Ian to the fact that he caused her distress. She swallowed, wondering a bit at that distress. Not an accurate word in the least for the storm brewing within her body.

She lifted her chin. "Kindly remove yourself from my path, sir."

He did not move. Olivia put all the iciness she could manage into the stare she leveled at Sir Ian, but he met her cold stare equally.

"Why is it, woman, that you harbor such a wish for death?"

"Why is it, Sir Ian, that you have not done your duty and delivered me to the Queen? I am sure that fact will interest her very much, don't you think?"

"My duty is to vouchsafe the Queen's person." Ian closed the small gap between them, putting his mouth so near her ear she could feel his lips move against her skin. "I fear your presence threatens her."

"How would I do that?" she asked a bit breathlessly.

"I do not know. 'Tis the reason I deem to keep the two of you apart."

She could now feel the man's heat against her entire body, not just her hand. The little game of thrust and parry they played suddenly evaporated from Olivia's mind, and she closed her eyes, a soft sigh escaping through her lips.

And then Ian's teeth scraped the lobe of her ear. Olivia gasped, raising her hands and bracing them against his chest. The storm thundered and crackled through her body, wind in her ears, hailstones pounding loudly against her chest, and a whirling vortex sucking the strength from her limbs.

She wanted, suddenly, for this man to kiss her again. Only this time she wanted to feel the heat that spread through her fingers against her mouth, inside of her.

Ian moved, his lips dragging a hot path from her ear to her jaw, and then his mouth left her body, and he stared at her. His eyes were like glittering emeralds above her, and she knew most assuredly that in that moment he felt as she did.

'Twas lust, and Olivia thrilled in it. That she had lived long enough to experience such a thing made her want to sing. She clutched at Ian's doublet and swayed toward him.

The tops of her breasts brushed his chest, and the storm swirled through her bosom and shot lightning bolts toward her abdomen. Her skin no longer protected, but pulled in all the stimuli around her and magnified them.

She glanced up into his eyes again, realizing only then that she had been staring at his mouth. His lids were heavy, his dark lashes thickly hiding the intensity of his gaze, but she could feel it upon her still.

And then he kissed her, finally, the storm whirling to an impossible peak when his tongue skidded against her teeth, pried through and took over her mouth. Her heart thumped with the rhythm of Ian's own as he moved his lips against hers. Oh, yes, it was as she had dreamt. Her entire being caught and thrown into a raging hailstorm by the mouth of a lover.

Such a simple thing to cause such destruction. And to give in to the chaos was such sweet sorrow. Ian kissed her deeply, his face moving over hers, his nose bumping her nose.

She jerked at the contact, pain scattering some of the passion, but not all. She moaned aloud, as Ian broke their kiss. She wanted to beg him to continue. Damn her nose.

Ian kept his face close to hers, but did not move, and Olivia just stared at him, unsure of what was happening. And then Ian's large hand closed around one of hers, still clutched within the folds of his doublet, and he was escorting her toward the door.

And she went most willingly, the only thought in her mind the need to continue what they had started. Of course they must leave, then.

He hurried her out the door, through the vacant room and past the guards. Olivia felt her face heat as they passed the guards, sure they could tell by the urgency in Ian's stride what he was about.

They walked down a hall and through another room without uttering a word to each other. Olivia's ardor began to pale as they went, turning first to disappointment and then, finally, to anger when they reached a door that led outside.

"Where do you take me?"

"Away from here," Ian stated flatly.

Olivia felt as if someone had hit her, hard. She dug in her heels, forcing Ian to stop, and then she wrenched her hand from his grasp. "How dare you," she seethed.

"I dare many things, dear Miss Bea." In the dark, his eyes were deadly black once more, his mien hard and demanding. She stared at the line of his jaw, the strong chin, and wanted to cry for the first time in a very long time.

"You were trying to get me out of the room,"

Olivia said quietly, not daring to look back into his eyes.

"I got you out of the room, and out of the palace. I do not know what stupid game you play, Miss Bea. But 'tis a deadly one."

"You played a worse game, Sir Ian." She turned quickly and began to walk away, but she could not see where she went. The aftermath of the storm within had left traces of fog before her eyes. She blinked hard and broke into a run.

He grabbed her arm before she had taken three steps. "I do not play games."

Olivia tried to pull away from his grasp, but it was impossible, so she whipped around and faced him. "Ha!" she laughed shortly. And suddenly she was in his arms, his strong hands against her back, his mouth upon hers once more. But now she knew that he did not revel in the emotion and feel of it as she, no, her captor was using this weakness within her to control.

And nobody controlled her, ever.

Olivia bit down on Ian's invading tongue, and he pulled away from her with a shout of anguish.

"I do not play that game, Sir Ian."

He blinked at her, his fingers pressed to the wound she had inflicted.

"Whatever it is you need to do with me in the name of Queen Elizabeth you may do." Olivia took a step toward him, putting her face very close to his. "But do not kiss me again."

Ian stared at her for a moment of silence, then he nodded slightly. "Fine," he said around his fingers, and grabbed her arm. "Come." And once again they were on a journey of which Olivia knew not the end.

They were being followed. He could feel it with every step they took. And no matter how many turns he made, or alleys he cut across, he could still feel the hairs prickling on the back of his neck, the echo of footfalls where there should have been none.

If he did not have Olivia with him, he would do as he usually did in this situation, turn around and become the hunter rather than the hunted.

As they crossed another street and started down another alleyway, Ian could not help but berate himself. He had lost his ability to command any and all situations, and it was all Olivia Tudor's fault.

Even now with peril following in their very footsteps, his body sang with the awareness of Olivia's tall, strong form beside him. His mind relived the fleeting fire of their kiss. In that one small moment in the Queen's privy chamber, Ian had felt more passion than in any other sexual encounter of his life. It had shaken him to his soul, the scent of her skin, her swanlike neck against his fingertips, her breasts heaving against his chest.

It had only been a kiss, for God's sake. One kiss.

His grip on Olivia's hand tightened as he heard a step echo behind them. Once again, Olivia had caused his mind to wander. Focusing his attention, Ian lowered his lids and glanced over his shoulder, but saw no one.

It was her fault entirely.

She believed he played a game, and he wished to God that he did. Let her believe it, then. It was better for him that she did.

"Where do you take me?" she asked, her voice tinged with an icy anger he had never heard before. Ian ignored her, as he had the last three times she had asked the same question.

For, in truth, he did not know. He dare not take her back to his house. There could be an ambush.

There was the house he used to immure uncommunicative people with whom he desperately needed to communicate, the one he had used that afternoon. But he could not possibly take her there until he lost the person stalking their every footstep.

And truly, he did not wish to take Olivia back

to that house. In fact, he did not think he would ever be able to be in that house again, for he would now always see Olivia in his mind's eye when he stepped within those walls. He would see her standing before him in a transparent shift, her breasts high, her nipples rigid, the darkness between her legs calling to his very soul.

He would taste her mouth, smell her hair, feel her body.

Ian shook his head sharply. No, he could not go back to the house, and especially not with Olivia. He must avoid such an end since it would help him not at all to add plowing the Queen's daughter to his list of sins. He glanced at the woman as they rounded another corner, her lips pursed in a scowl, her brow furrowed in anger.

Why he desired her was beyond his ken, truly. But he did desire her. When they kissed, he forgot about the Queen, his sister, Lord Crandle. The world ceased to exist when he felt Olivia's lithe body tremble beneath his touch.

"Where do you take me?" she demanded once more.

There really had to be something wrong with him, to desire such a stubborn woman. "I shall drop you into the Thames if you don't leave off the questions."

"Please do, Sir Ian. I swim like a fish."

"Of course you can, and you've a mouth like a fishwife."

"And you've the mind of a pig."

"How now, Olivia, I thought you were going to find another word for me."

His captive quit walking, which forced Ian to come to a stop as well. She stared at him in the gloom of the evening, her eyes round and unblinking.

Ian shot a glance down the street, but whoever followed stayed out of sight.

"What did you call me?" Olivia asked quietly.

Ian could only close his eyes. Truly, he was losing his edge.

"Why did you call me by that name?" she asked, but Ian could say nothing. He could not even look at her.

"You know."

"Yes," he said finally.

"Is this why you . . ."

" 'Tis not the place for questions, lady. We are being followed."

"By whom? And why do you keep me from the Queen? I shall rather kill myself than be part of any plot against her. Think you not in that direction, varlet."

Ian rolled his eyes. "Should I perhaps say that 'tis the time for questions? Then should you close that mouth of yours and keep your silence?" Ian finally looked at her, but had to look away quickly. There was a vulnerability in her blue eyes that made him falter. And he could falter no longer. "Come." He pulled her down the street without another word.

She stumbled along behind him, so he slowed his pace. It made him fiercely angry, though, that he showed the woman such a concession. In faith, he was becoming soft.

This thought made Ian stomp loudly around a corner, thus masking the footsteps of those in front of him, and thus causing his demise. For when he turned the corner, hands fell on him and his captive, and they were well and truly caught.

And, of course, it was all Olivia's fault, Ian fumed as he suffered the humiliation of being bound and gagged and dropped in the back of a pony cart.

Chapter 10

More should I question thee, and more I must,
Though more to know could not be more to
trust.

—ALL'S WELL THAT ENDS WELL, II, I, 207

"**M**y man heard Sir Ian call the girl Olivia. He sent a messenger with the news this very night."

"Olivia!" Essex's eyes widened in excitement. "Oh, yes, we were right to pursue this, Crandle. I know exactly whom we have within our clutches, and it's one who could ultimately be the downfall of our monarch."

"How now, Lord Essex, you speak of the girl? But can she be the key to our deceit?"

"Oh yes, and how, Lord Crandle." Essex lowered his voice dramatically. "What I tell you now is a secret from my father's deathbed."

Crandle edged closer to his friend. "A secret that shall be mine alone, Essex, I promise you!"

"This woman within our clutches is the daughter of our Virgin Queen. She, whom we hold bound, is verily my half sister."

Crandle gasped. "It is true, then, our Queen was with child?"

"Aye, truth that serves our purposes."

"I had heard the rumors, but softly spoken, for anyone who breathes such slander shall meet with the gallows."

"Do you not wonder why the Queen is so sensitive upon the subject?" Essex asked with a laugh.

"Ah-ha!" Crandle rubbed his hands together in glee, but then he sobered. "Is there proof of who she is, though?"

"She is in possession of a ring my father had made, a family crest with her name, along with the Queen's and my father's."

"What fortune for us!"

"And that is not all. I feel certain that the girl will wish to unite with us in our endeavor. She has been ill-used by our Queen as well."

"Perfect! How could it get more perfect?"

"Yes, the girl, I was told, was killed in a fire when she was ten. But upon his deathbed, my father voiced his fears that Elizabeth, the power of her position taking all the humanity from her actions, had sent someone to kill the girl, my half sister."

"She is vile, truly."

"I must agree with you, Crandle. And to think that I had not made this conclusion some years ago, with all of the things that I know."

"But she has flattered you and me, both, Lord Essex. Do not berate yourself so."

Essex took his friend's hand in his. "Of course she does, it is how she controls us. But, now, I think, we control her."

"Yes, yes, I shall send a messenger posthaste to tell my men exactly what they must find out from the girl."

"And Sir Ian," Essex said quickly. "Tell them to find out what he knows."

"Of course. And I shall make sure that they are diligent in finding out. The more pain involved the better for that farmer's son who thinks himself a man of breeding."

Sir Ian had been a most wonderful jailer, Olivia decided in retrospect as she sat bound, blindfolded, and gagged in some vile filth that smelled of cow dung. Making it worse was the sure knowledge that her true identity was no longer a secret. If Sir Ian knew of her existence, knew also that the man named Shakespeare fulfilled that existence, her plight had become much more urgent.

For no longer was it only her safety in question. Now, the safety of her mother fell subject, as well as her monarchy. And Olivia would not linger to see Queen Elizabeth brought low. If it came to such a conclusion, she would put a knife to her own breast.

And the reason had nothing to do with any love lost for her mother, for she believed that nothing of that emotion existed for her. Rather, Olivia would never again let her life be in the hands of another.

She heard the rumble of voices and straightened her back against the rough wall of her prison. But the sounds came no nearer. She strained to hear what they said, but could not make out the words. The voices ended on a high note, as if in question, and Olivia heard another answer.

She recognized the voice even as she could not hear the words: It was Sir Ian. Did he plot with these men? Or did he suffer her fate of prisoner as well?

And then she heard the distinctive thud of flesh hitting flesh. Olivia flinched. The sound came again and again. Olivia closed her eyes even though blindfolded and prayed for the blows to stop.

When they finally ceased, Olivia let out a long-held breath. Again, the mumbled voices, and then Ian's, the muted sound of his baritone made Olivia feel sick to her stomach. They interrogated him, she was sure. What would he tell them?

And then came a sound that made Olivia's blood run cold: a crack, and then a scream. "Oh, dear Lord in Heaven," Olivia whispered urgently.

The beating continued for what seemed hours, but must only have been a half hour at most. And Olivia prayed the entire length of it, trying desperately to spirit strength through the walls of wherever she was toward Ian.

When she finally heard only silence, Olivia dropped her forehead against her knees. And then with the dark and quiet lying upon her like a tomb, Olivia wept. No wrenching sobs for her first experience at the sport, but silent tears that wet her blindfold and slipped down her cheeks in silence.

Ian was dead, she was sure.

He wished he were dead, and then knew that he could not think such a thing. He had to gather strength, find Olivia, escape. He knew that at least two of his fingers were broken, for when he tried to work his way out of the bonds that held his hands behind him the pain was almost unbearable. He felt with his tongue the bloody space at the back of his mouth where his tooth had once been.

Much worse than the pain, though, was the knowledge that he had been outsmarted. And it was all Olivia Tudor's fault. If the kiss they had shared had not set his mind spinning off into fantasies of having her naked in his bed, he would not be here.

He suddenly felt a gentle touch on his shoulder and went rigid.

"Ian?"

It was she. He could not see because of the blindfold his captors had never taken off, but he would know her touch and voice in the darkest of hells.

And this was the darkest he had ever experienced.

"Ian, you live!" she whispered.

He was lying facedown in what must have been horseshit, his fingers were broken, and his head ached like the very devil, but he breathed, so, yes, he must be alive.

"What have they done to you?" Her hands ran lightly over his back. "Can you move?"

Ian tried to roll onto his back.

"Wait." He felt her hands at the bonds around his wrists, and then they were free. "Here." She helped him move onto his back, so that he no longer breathed dung into his lungs.

"Will you live?" she asked.

He could only grunt.

"Ian, you must tell me how you know who I am. Who else knows?"

He wanted to yell at her to help him up, help him escape now before the men returned, but his words came out garbled. He relaxed his head back for a moment to regroup his strength.

Her hands bracketed his chin lightly, and he let himself take another moment to relax. Ah, but it felt good to have the woman's hands against his skin. More fool he, to find succor from a woman, this woman.

"You are truly a beautiful man, Sir Ian. I hope they have not scarred such beauty for life."

Her words frustrated him, and he tried to entreat her to hurry once more.

"My lady!"

The shocked statement seared through Ian's fuzzy brain as Olivia's touch left his face.

He heard nothing more from Olivia, but another man said quietly, "You mustn't come to him, my lady. He is the enemy."

And then rough hands turned him over once more, but before they could rebind him, Ian's world went black.

Where was Ian? Andy paced her room as she had paced the entire night. Both Beatrice and Ian had disappeared, and no one knew where they had gone.

Added upon that terrible thing was the fact that her reputation still lay in tatters about her feet. Lord Crandle had not cleared her name, nor, it seemed, did he have any intention of doing such a thing.

She had seen him that morning, nearly begged at his feet that he tell Sir Richard that it had not been her in the window. But Lord Crandle only stared at her as if she had run mad.

Andy wailed and threw herself upon a chair. She had been abandoned!

A knock at the door had Andy jumping up from her prostrated grief and flying to the portal. "Ian!" she cried as she threw the heavy door open. She stared instead into the eyes of her only love.

"Sir Richard?" Andy took a step forward. Perhaps all was right. Perhaps Ian had done as he promised.

But, no, Sir Richard stepped back as if she might infect him with the plague. He frowned fiercely at her. "The Queen bade me come to you," he said flatly.

Andy blinked.

"You are to leave the palace this instant."

Andy bit on her lower lip, trying desperately not to cry. How could the Queen send Sir Richard to give her such news? She must know the hurt that would wrench her heart to look upon the love of her life and receive the words she feared most.

"My brother?"

"Has disgraced himself in public this yester-night."

"But . . ."

"The name of Terrance will no longer be spoken in the hallowed halls of the Queen's palace. You are to take yourself away from here this instant."

"It was a mistake," Andy cried. "Lord Crandle mistook. He saw my maid, not me!"

"You dare to question the word of an earl?" Sir Richard's lovely face was set in the harsh lines of an ugly grimace.

Andy held her hands out to him. "You said, once, that you loved me. Do you not believe your love?"

"I believe you have betrayed my love." Sir Richard turned quickly on his heel and left Andy staring after him.

For a moment she stood as still as a statue, and then she clutched her chest with both hands and fell to the hard, unforgiving floor.

Oh, yes, he was a coxcomb of the worst kind, to entertain even the hardest of tender feelings for such a person as a woman. Ian berated himself as he had for the last two days. He sat in the filth of an abandoned barn, his hands and feet bound, his head covered by a sack and a gag within his mouth. And all because he had allowed himself taken in by a woman. O fortune's fool, indeed!

His captors had let him be these last two days, at least. There had been no more beatings. There had been no more questions about what the Queen knew, or where some mysterious ring resided. But they had not let him free, either.

And he had heard nothing more of Olivia.

Ian rolled his eyes, but sat still. He did not want to expend any energy, for he needed it all to strengthen his body enough for escape.

And escape he very well would.

There was a timid knock at the door, and Ian heard the portal open. It would be the maid who fed him. Why she knocked as if he were a guest in her home baffled him. She pulled the rough-woven bag from his head, but all he saw was the small, dark girl in the weak circle of light that sputtered from the candle upon her tray. As usual, the girl said nothing to him, but eyed him warily as she set the tray of gruel before him.

She circled around and untied the gag from his mouth, then crouched before him and moved the slop that she was going to feed him about with a wooden spoon. She held the utensil to his lips.

With a dark scowl, Ian took the bite of food into his mouth. The girl's dull gray eyes rounded with fear and she dunked the spoon quickly in the bowl of gruel once more. She was a mouse, this one, but though he had cajoled she would not speak to him at all, much less help him escape.

Since he had not seen his captors since they had beaten him to a bloody pulp, Ian was very anxious to escape soon, for it seemed they had left him altogether. Again, Ian's thoughts threatened to move toward the fact that Olivia was probably with them, but he forced himself to think of something else.

"Where is this place?" he asked the girl, but she just looked intently at the bowl between them.

He asked her the same questions each day and received no answers, so Ian did not truly think he would get an answer now. He put his mouth around another spoonful of the dry gruel and worked at swallowing the stuff down.

"You obviously know nothing of cooking," Ian said tersely, and the girl glanced up at him quickly. He gave her a little smirk, and she went back to working some of the heavy stuff in the bowl onto the spoon. Oh yes, there were times he felt like he might be beside his wits . . . all this silence.

Finally, the meal over, mouse-girl left with the empty bowl. Ian sat, his stomach noisily trying to digest the meal of gruel, and awaited the humiliation that would come next. There were no windows in his converted barn, so even with the bag off his head, Ian sat in utter darkness. Still, he knew that it was night when his new best friend came pounding into the room.

He was one of the largest men Ian had ever encountered, an ape, surely, with dark hair hanging in his eyes and curling on his hamlike arms and knuckles. He never spoke, but grunted, a blessing, actually from the perpetual silence. The man lumbered into Ian's room this night and went straight for the chamber pot and then began the now familiar chore of helping Ian use said pot. For his captors would not untie his hands or feet to allow him the dignity of taking care of himself. He had to be glad, at least, that they did not force him to defecate upon himself.

His humiliation complete, Ian was left alone for another uncomfortable night of dozing on the stinking dung heap that was his bed.

There were times when he wished they would just kill him and get this ordeal over with.

Again, during one of his short sleeps, Ian dreamt of Olivia. He often experienced their ardent kiss in the Queen's chambers over and over during the night, and found himself hard and needing when ape-boy came to help him with his morning ablutions. His life had truly deteriorated.

This night, however, the soft hands against his body seemed headily real. Ian groaned lowly and tried to move his arms, tried to pull Olivia's body to him.

"Sh!" someone whispered harshly, and Ian was instantly awake. It was dark, as always, but he knew who knelt above him.

She untied his hands. "How are your injuries?"

He blinked at her dark shadow, but said nothing for ape-boy had replaced his gag, like the good-working fellow he was.

And then suddenly the gag slid free. "Can you walk?"

Ian swallowed, his throat painfully dry.

"We must hurry this time, Ian. I do not want to be caught again."

He did not trust her in the least, but if their plan was to let him escape, far be it from him to protest. If he were forced to stay in this room another day, he would probably turn into a caterwauling freak.

"I think my ankle is wrenched, but if you support me, I can walk, I think," he managed to say.

229

" 'Tis better than nothing."

" 'Tis good of you to say so."

Olivia sat back on her heels for a moment. "I have missed you, Sir Wit."

He said nothing to this, as he had to use all of his strength to gain his feet. Once there, Ian took a deep breath.

"Lean upon me," Olivia whispered, hooking her arm around his waist.

He did as he was told, wondering if he were walking into a trap but not sure if he cared any longer. When Olivia pushed open the door, though, no one waited for them on the other side. A dark farmhouse sat across a small field.

Olivia helped him to the side of an old cart, and they encountered no one. Very suspicious, that. Someone was making this escape too easy. If they wanted him to believe Olivia was his ally, they should have made a bit more fuss of his attempt to vacate his home of the last two days.

Noisily, Olivia helped Ian heft himself into the back of the cart, the bottom of which was covered with a layer of straw and a blanket. Oh yes, this escape was far too easy. When Ian finally fell to the straw with a grunt, and Olivia covered him with another blanket, he just closed his eyes and decided that he would not fight her in the least. Five seconds later he was deeper asleep than he had been in a week.

* * *

Olivia had never been more afraid in her life. If those men caught up to her, they would kill Ian. They had kept her apart from Ian since they found her trying to escape the first time. Unfortunately, she had shown her weakness, for they used Ian to try and get her cooperation with their plot. She had spent the last two days knowing that they were allowing Ian to heal so they could hurt him all over again, unless, of course, she would tell them where the ring was and agree to be their accomplice in their plot to dethrone the Queen.

She had told them, finally, this morning. And, while one man had run off to London for the ring, the other two had made merry. They were now lying facedown in their own vomit, and she hoped they stayed that way at least until morning.

They had not tied her up since that first day, so it was an easy thing for her to escape her room and head out to the barn where she knew Ian was being held. The husband and wife who were taking care of Ian only came during the day. Usually one of the men who had questioned her so consistently sat outside the barn guarding Ian. But not tonight.

Olivia clicked the reins against the backs of the horses, wishing they would go a little faster.

They were probably older than death.

She checked over her shoulder once more, knowing that she would not be found out until morning, but still feeling terribly jittery.

She could hear Ian behind her, the soft sound of his breathing, and it made her want to cry. She had lain alone in her bed the two days, missing Ian's breathing. There had been mice, too. She had never seen them, but she could hear their tiny squeaks and scrabblings in the rafters, and she had longed for Ian's presence.

Once her enemy, now a longed-for . . . Olivia sighed heavily when her mind wandered to these thoughts. What was Ian? She knew that she cared for him enough to do anything possible to make sure that he was not beaten again. Even her captors had realized that.

But why?

Ian had been her captor as well. He had taken her from her home and held her hostage. He was one of the Queen's men.

Olivia glanced back once more, then let her gaze travel down and caress the man asleep in the cart. He lay on his back, one arm out, the other across his chest, his fingers splayed over his heart.

He had the beginnings of a beard, a dark one with gray scattered about. She definitely liked him better without hair upon his face. He had a good strong jaw that shouldn't be obscured.

With a funny flutter in her stomach, Olivia turned and faced front once more. One of the horses stumbled, and Olivia's fingers tightened around the reins. She sent another prayer heavenward that the horses would not drop dead before they reached London.

And then she prayed that she rode in the right direction. For, in truth, she had absolutely no idea where they were.

"Where are we?" Ian asked the sky. He could tell that it was a lovely spring day. Warm with just a slight breeze. He lay looking at a beautiful expanse of blue sky with scattered puffy white clouds.

The sky reminded him, actually, of Olivia's eyes. "Where are we?" he asked again, but still nobody answered.

With a groan, he propped himself on his elbows and glanced over the side of the cart. He expected to see Olivia standing there with his still-unknown captors.

Instead he saw a peaceful stand of trees, and two decrepit horses chomping away at a bunch of clover. Ian frowned and looked about. He found nothing but a bucolic scene of trees and wildflowers and the tiniest sound of water, a small stream no doubt that wound its way through this too-perfect portrait.

Was he dead?

He could not imagine still feeling such pain if he were dead. Of course, he could be in Hell. Hell *could* be a beautiful place in which you could not move without pain slicing through your body.

And then he saw her. She lay in a splash of sunlight at what had to be the bank of the stream. Her eyes were closed and her chest moved slowly and rhythmically in sleep.

Yes, he was in Hell. Ian shoved himself up, and then painfully maneuvered himself out of the cart and off his lovely bed of hay. He wondered shortly if he would ever again see his beautiful feather tick. Ah, such a lovely bed it was.

He limped over to where Olivia lay, his bare feet tender and his ankle aching. "Where are we?" he asked again. Still, she did not stir.

Ian gained her side and looked down on the sleeping beauty. Her skin was nearly translucent in the sunlight, the spattering of freckles across her nose making her look like an imp.

Still, she had a regal bearing even in sleep, her nose rather perfect, long and straight, her lips full. She wore the gown he had bought her, but it no longer had a rich or elegant air. She seemed thinner, if that were at all possible. Her collarbones looked as if they might pierce her fragile skin.

Fragile. Ian glanced away from Olivia quickly, squinting into the sun as the light burned his eyes. He could not imagine thinking of the overly large Olivia as fragile. But there she was . . . asleep and most definitely fragile.

Ian sat, taking pains not to look at Olivia's face again, and prodded her shoulder.

"What?" she gasped, pushing up quickly and nearly rising to her feet in her panic. Ian held her down with a hand to her shoulder.

He could see her turn toward him out of the corner of his eye, but he kept his gaze away from her still. "Where are we?" he asked again.

"You scared me!" she cried, and took in several deep breaths. Ian remained silent as she composed herself. And finally, she said, "I do not know where we are."

He turned a disbelieving glare upon her.

"Truly, I just know that we should not be on a main road in the daylight, so I found this spot."

"Why should we not be on a main road in the daylight?"

Her nose wrinkled, and she stared at him as if he were daft. "If those men catch us again, they will kill you, Ian."

"Those men?" He lifted one eyebrow with the

question. "And who exactly would 'those men' be?"

She shook her head, looking truly perplexed. She really must have acted as well as written. "I still do not know," she said. "I think they are someone's lackeys, and I believe that someone is a man of the court. Perhaps, even, a peer."

"Really?" The sarcasm in his reply was rather thick, and Olivia peered at him strangely.

"You do not think so?"

"Olivia, dear, I do not care."

"But, Ian, they plot to overthrow the Queen." She moved closer to him, tucking her legs beneath her so that she knelt beside him. "They know who I am."

"And why should they not?"

She blinked. "How many people know the Queen has a daughter?"

Ian shrugged and looked away. "The Queen, obviously, me, and anyone whom you have deemed to take into your confidence."

He picked a long thin blade of grass from the ground beside him and placed the end of it in his mouth. Olivia stayed silent for a few tense moments.

"You think I have conspired with those men who tried to kill you?"

"No." He turned his darkest look upon her. "I know you have."

She frowned and then shook her head and glanced away. "Did they tell you this?"

He laughed harshly. "They haven't spoken to me since they tried to make gruel out of my bones. No, Olivia, you told me when you came to me after the beating."

"You speak nonsense, Ian. I was trying to help you escape."

Ian spit the blade of grass out of his mouth and grabbed Olivia's arm. "Then why didn't you help me escape? Why did you waste precious moments interrogating me, *milady*?" He yanked her close, so their faces were only a breath apart. "I am the enemy, remember?"

She blinked, the innocence in her eyes unnerving in its sincerity. "They came up behind me, Ian. One of them held my mouth so I could say nothing more, and another said those things."

"You are quite an actress, Olivia."

Her eyes widened, then narrowed, and he suddenly felt the sting of her palm against his cheek. He let go of her and sat back reeling.

"Why would I help you escape now if I were one of them?" she asked, her voice sounding very far away.

His strength was obviously at a low ebb, if a mere slap from a woman hurt him so. Of course, he must take into account the fact that it had been Olivia who hit him. Obviously, the woman was far from fragile.

Ian finally managed to shake his head. "I'm rather interested in knowing the reason myself," he said.

"Oh!" She stood, turned her back to him, and stomped away.

Ian wanted to jump up and shake her, but of course he hadn't the energy. And in such a condition he would have to find his way to the Queen. Quite a task he had ahead of him.

Ian edged forward and stuck his sore foot in the icy stream that babbled over rocks. He did not even want to think of what his enemies had told the Queen of his disappearance. Add to that the fact that the last time he had been seen, he had nearly seduced a woman in the Queen's presence chamber.

Things were not good. Ian dropped back into the grass and once again stared up at the clear blue sky. A bird twittered not far from him, and a bee buzzed across his line of vision.

The water numbed his ankle so that the throbbing and ache finally died away. He ought to move so that he could put his swollen fingers into the icy stream, but he was just too damned comfortable to move at the moment.

If only manna would fall from the sky to feed

his shrinking belly, he might actually be close to happy at this very second in time.

Olivia suddenly towered above him. "Here," she said, and dropped a loaf of crusty bread on his chest. Ian blinked at the manna he had just wished for, then squinted up at Olivia.

"There is cheese as well, but I could not find meat." She sank down beside him, unwrapping a foul-smelling cheese as she did. "Of course, another mile or so and I think the horses will give up the ghost. Perhaps we shall have roasted horse flank this night."

Ian still did not move.

"Go on, suspicious one, I shall not poison you to death, I can promise you that upon my honor." She grabbed the bread off his chest and tore it in half. "If I wanted you dead, I would make sure that it was a painful death." She handed over half the bread, and then lifted her skirts and whipped out a knife from a holder about her ankle. With a quick flick of her wrist, Olivia sliced off a hunk of cheese and held it upon the point of the knife just under Ian's nose. "Cheese?" she asked prettily.

Ian glanced from the proffered food to her face, and then back to the bread in his hand. He, of course, hated this woman for conspiring against the Queen, but he still could not shake the feeling of admiration he had for her. Strong, courageous, and rather feisty: all qualities he had never thought a female ought to have, but in this female they were definitely admirable.

With another glance at Olivia, Ian took the cheese and sat up. "How did you get the knife?" he asked taking a big bite of bread.

"I took it from one of the men."

"Hmm."

"He was passed out drunk at the time, and I wanted a weapon."

"Hmm."

"Oh, do shut up."

Ian took another bite of bread as he cocked his brow at her in question.

But she kept her tongue, turned away from him, and kept eating her small meal of bread and cheese.

"So, my lady, where do you take me now?"

She shot him a look of displeasure over her shoulder. "Do not call me that."

He shook his head innocently. "Whyever not?"

" 'Tis what *they* called me."

"Yes, so what is the problem, then? If your friends call you that, why can't I?"

She took a deep breath, her chest rising, her breasts pushing up out of the low décolletage of her dress. "They are not friends, and neither are you."

Ian blinked, realized that he stared at her

chest, and angrily brought his gaze to her face. "Methinks the lady doth protest too much."

She stared at him, blue eyes icy, and then turned away once more. "Sarcasm rides ill upon your shoulders, Sir Ian."

"And treason shall take your head from yours, Princess."

"Cease your babbling." She took a vicious bite from her hunk of bread and chewed.

"Are you not going to answer my question then?" he asked, rather enjoying watching Olivia in a pique.

She swallowed. "Which question is that, Sir Babble?"

"Where do you take me?"

She smiled and glanced at him with a sly look in her eye. "Well, now, this is quite a circle we have made, is it not?"

He frowned.

"I seem to remember being yanked about London by my arm as I asked you the same question." She batted her lashes and pressed her hand against her chest. "Perhaps I shall do as you did to me?"

He tried to remember, hoping that he had not done anything too awful.

"I shall ignore you, sir, until you go stark raving mad."

Ah, yes, now he remembered. "Hmm," he said

thoughtfully. "That would mean, of course, that you have achieved such an end and are, at this very moment, stark raving mad, yes?"

She threw her cheese at him, and it caught him square on the nose. "I am not mad."

"Are you very sure?" he asked, taking the cheese from where it fell and popping it into his mouth. "You seem a bit beside your wits, I must say." He chewed slowly, savoring the tangy cheese.

She smiled, a bit too sweetly for Ian's peace of mind, actually, and pushed up from her sitting position. "Would you like some water with your cheese, sir?" she asked and squatted beside the stream.

He frowned at her tone, and then sputtered as a great wash of icy-cold water splashed in his face.

"Why you!"

"I thought, perhaps, you needed some cooling off."

Ian blinked the water out of his eyes. "I would have to say 'tis you who needs cooling, Lady Hypocrite." And he took his bad foot from the icy stream and shoved against Olivia's bottom. She swirled her arms for a suspended moment, then toppled headfirst into the shallow stream.

His foot now throbbed, but it was well worth it, he thought, and bit off another great mouthful of soggy bread.

Chapter 11

We should be wooed, and were not made to woo.

—A MIDSUMMER NIGHT'S DREAM, II, i, 141

Olivia lay for a moment, stunned, the cold water seeping through her pores so that she burned. Slowly, she pushed herself up onto her knees and wiped the water from her eyes. Her skirts and bodice were soaked and freezing against her skin.

She smiled sweetly at Ian. "That was very stupid," she said.

He frowned, then scooted back quickly, but not fast enough. Olivia took hold of the front of his dirty tunic and yanked him forward.

Unfortunately, she miscalculated, and he landed upon her. She fell, her back now just as wet as her front, and Ian still relatively dry.

He laughed down at her. "A bit chilly, isn't it?" He scooped a handful of the cold water and splashed it in her face.

Again, Ian laughed and tried to move away. But Olivia quickly looped her arms around his neck and pulled him toward her, knocking him off-balance, and making it easy to turn and pin him beneath her.

" 'Tis *very* chilly, Sir Ian."

He howled and thrashed, but Olivia just laughed and held on. She was already soaked through, so it only mattered now how wet she could get Ian.

When her strength ran out, she let go and plopped back into the water. It swirled about her head and ran over her neck.

"I am wounded," Ian said from beside her. "You took advantage of a wounded man."

"You stank, good sir. I did you a favor."

"Oh, yes, and you smelled of roses."

Olivia winced. Would this man ever see her when she did not stink, or her hair was combed? Of course, at that very moment, she rather suspected her nose to be the size and color of a plum.

And why on earth did it matter how she looked to Sir Ian Terrance?

She reached up behind her head and dug a

handful of sand from the bottom of the stream. "Do not speak to me so, Sir Ian. You shall hurt my delicate woman-feelings," she said, trying to cover the fact that he had done that very thing.

Olivia sat up, turned away from Ian, and rubbed the sand into her hair.

Ian made a snorting sound. "Delicate? There is not a delicate bone in your body, Olivia Tudor."

She turned quickly to glare at him. "Would you leave off with the comments on my size, Sir Hateful?"

Ian made a sound of disgust and began to wash his hair as well. "I do not make a comment on your Amazon-like body, my lady. I just commented that you are not of a delicate nature. You take after your mother in that way."

Olivia bit her lip and turned away once more. She cupped her hands under the water of the stream and splashed herself with the icy cold liquid.

"Is she so harsh, then?" she asked, glancing at Ian once more when she was finished.

Ian rubbed another handful of sand into his scalp and then dunked his head. "No," he said flipping his hair back away from his face when he sat up again. "But strong, yes. She has a certain way that she wants things, and she does not tolerate anything else. When she is happy, she can be very funny." He stopped for a moment, as if in thought. "She is actually enjoyable company." Ian glanced at her. "When things are going as she wishes."

"They do not go that way at the moment," Olivia said on a sigh.

"No, they do not." He watched her for a moment. "In truth, I can see why you plot against her. She did plot against you when you were all of ten."

Olivia huffed a small breath of frustration and ran her fingers through her short hair. She could still feel small bits of gritty sand, and so she lay back in the water. "I do not plot against her. I do not care enough about her to expend the energy."

"Right."

Olivia sat up, the icy water streaming in small rivulets down her face. "I speak the truth."

"You speak a lie, Olivia." Ian took her chin in his large, warm hand. "You do care of her. Why else would you ask questions about her."

Olivia pulled her chin from Ian's grasp. "I do not wish to talk of this." They stared at each other for a moment, their faces very close to one another. Olivia watched as a crystal-clear bead of water dropped from the end of one curling lock of brown hair over Ian's forehead and with a *plink* found its way back home to the stream.

246

It did not seem to matter that the man believed her to be treacherous enough to have him kidnapped and beaten near unto death, she still wanted to kiss him. It did not matter, even, that the last time he had kissed her, he had done so only to manipulate her out of the Queen's chambers. It was completely without reason, this need she felt for Ian Terrance deep within her soul. He was everything her heroes had never been.

Sweet Romeo, whom she had worshiped as she wrote of him, was the complete opposite of this brash, rude man who thought so much of himself.

She could not imagine Sir Ian ever dying for her, or professing his love to her. And, yet, she looked upon his face, and butterflies flitted about within her stomach. She gazed upon his lips, and her legs became weak. Lust was obviously a far thing from love, surely.

"God above, do not look upon me so," Ian muttered.

Olivia blinked, and looked up from his mouth to his eyes. They were like a bottomless pool, so dark and endless. "Your eyes change color, Ian, did you know that?" she asked without thought.

"They change as my body changes, innocent one." He cupped the back of her head and brought their lips together. He was cold, and then hot when his mouth opened against hers.

She inched forward, excited at the prospect of reawakening the lust she had felt for Ian in the Queen's chambers. His other arm circled her, pulling her close to his body, as his mouth claimed hers with a hunger that made her tremble.

His tongue breached her lips, tantalized, and then retreated, and Olivia moaned. She touched her own tongue to his teeth, and quickly realized that she held the power to enthrall as well.

Ian groaned beneath her onslaught, his hand moving from the nape of her neck, to her cheek, and then down to her breasts pressed against the drenched material of her tightly laced pannier. Olivia threaded her hands into Ian's wet hair as their kiss continued, and her body was thrown back into the storm that had begun days before.

With a low grumble of sound like swelling thunder, Ian licked her lips, and then descended the column of her neck with hot kisses. She shivered, her body like ice except where Ian's tongue caressed her skin.

She leaned her head back as he stopped at the sensitive spot between her collarbones. "Mmm," she heard herself mumble as if the sound came from another being. And then he continued down, his mouth warm against the top of her breast. Her nipple beaded painfully, and she writhed, wishing suddenly that she were free of clothes and confinement.

Ian gentled her with a hand against her cheek. She felt the bandages that tied his fingers, and she turned her head to kiss them. With a dark sound of need, Ian pulled at the pointed bottom of the busk that covered her from chest to stomach.

The silk fabric scraped the overly sensitized skin of her nipples, and she felt her most secret woman's place contract. "Faith," she whispered harshly, her eyelids fluttering and her fingers clenching within the mass of Ian's wet, heavy hair.

"Yes," he said darkly against her skin as he tongued the skin of her breast that had emerged above her gown. It was as if she could not bring enough air into her lungs as she reached up to rip at the bodice of her dress.

Ian laughed, his warm hand trailing up to hold hers still, and then he slipped his fingers between her gown and skin and lifted one breast free.

Olivia gasped, her lids slipping closed as she leaned her head back on her neck. The chaotic storm circled about in her stomach, causing her center to convulse again. And then, finally, Ian's mouth was hot against her nipple, sucking it into his mouth and flicking at it with his tongue. But rather than dissipate, the raging feelings within her escalated.

She gasped for breath, her knees shaking like saplings in a harsh wind. And suddenly Ian forsook her breast. She whimpered, raising her head, but he crooned softly to her as he took her mouth once more with his. She opened to him in hunger as his hand cupped her breast, his thumb razing her nipple and his breath stealing hers until she thought she might die from the sweet agony.

"Do something," she managed to gasp against his lips. "My body needs something, and I know not what."

"By my troth, you would tempt a monk," Ian rasped, and kissed her deeply, lifting her as he did. She gasped, her arms sliding about his neck as he stood.

"Ian, you should not do this with your injuries."

"I should not do this, 'tis truth." He limped to the bank of the stream and set her down.

She ached as his arms left her, and then pulled desperately at the top of her gown as she realized where he gazed upon her. Once again, he had roused her to a screaming pitch, and then dropped her. She absolutely despised this feeling.

But then he came down beside her, his large,

strong hand calming her own with a gentle touch. "I should not do this, but lately I have made a habit of doing that which I shouldn't," he said, his voice like velvet against her upset.

" 'Tis a bad habit," she said.

"Very bad."

She looked up into his dark eyes. And then, as his face came near, she closed her eyes again, knowing that he would show her what she wanted to know. His lips were soft and gentle, warm against hers as she slipped her arms around his neck once more and leaned back on the ground.

He leaned with her, his body hard above hers, but his arms against the grass taking most of his weight. They kissed long and deep, and Olivia wondered if she would ever again feel as wonderful as she did at that very moment.

Strange, that she feel such contentment at a time of misery. But, it seemed with Ian's large body above her own, his mouth against hers, and his fingers in her hair, she would never again know such security. He leaned closer, his rough doublet abrading her naked breast, his arousal hard against her stomach, and the storm once more began to churn within.

She reached for the painted buttons of his doublet, pulling at them. Again, his hand covered hers, and she allowed him to undo the front of his wet clothes as she found the string about his waist and untied it.

He broke away to shuck his soggy clothing, and Olivia sat up quickly. She pulled on the ties at her back, finally freeing herself of the boned pannier, steel corset, and heavy skirts of her gown. With only a sodden chemise covering her body, she glanced up at Ian.

He knelt beside her, his body uncovered except for the dark golden hair that swirled about his navel and dipped toward his groin. Olivia felt her face heat and her breath grow shallow as she followed the path of hair to the hard shaft that stood against his belly.

"We are mad," he said.

She dragged her gaze back up his muscled chest to his bearded face. "We have caused the malady in each other, I think."

Ian chuckled. "Thee and I are too wise to woo peaceably."

Olivia raised her brows as she pulled at the string that held her chemise together at her breast. "Is that what we do, Ian? Woo?"

He pulled the hem of her chemise from under her knees and lifted it to her hips. "In truth, my lady, I know not what we do, for it is without reason." His hands skimmed her body sending tremors through her nerve endings as he pulled her chemise over her head.

She knelt before her nemesis naked, but she could see nothing of the man who had stolen her away from her life in this man before her. His eyes burnt like those of a tiger as he looked at her.

She covered herself with her arms, suddenly sure in the knowledge that he would find her wanting. She had none of the curves of the street-side lightskirts that filled London.

And her hair—she reached up and smoothed her short locks.

"Sweet, Olivia," Ian said. "You blush."

"I . . ." She stopped, her mind blank: a new experience for her. She blinked and tried to flatten her hair against her head. "I look a fright."

"In faith, I do not love thee with mine eyes." And he leaned over her, bending her over his arm.

Olivia felt as if she had been slapped. She placed her hands flat against Ian's chest and stiffened her arms. "Excuse me?"

Ian frowned. "What?"

"You do not love me with your eyes?" She shoved with all of her might, but he did not budge, so she whacked him with a fist.

"Ow!"

"In other words, you *cannot* love me with your eyes? I am that sore to look upon?" She gave him another good smack. "Get off of me, you oaf!"

253

" 'Tis not what I meant at all!"

"Oh!" She shoved again, and this time he rolled away from her. And then she just lay there staring up at the sky. All the need she had felt only moments before was gone, completely . . . vanished. In its place stewed frustration and heartache. And humiliation. She grabbed at her gown and pulled it over her body. It was freezing against her skin, but she just gasped and then bit her lip.

"I never thought you to be a vain woman."

She wanted to cry. Romeo he was most definitely not. "I am not vain, you fool. But sweet words would be nice as you bed me!"

He sat up quickly. "I was trying at sweet words!"

Olivia pushed herself up on her elbows. "Well, you obviously try in vain." She found herself staring at Ian's muscled chest and whipped her gaze back to his face. "You called me ugly."

"I did not."

"You did."

He turned away, shaking his head.

They sat in stony silence, Olivia staring at Ian's back, he staring at the stream.

"You ought to have praised me," she finally said quietly.

Ian said nothing.

She rolled her eyes. "You could have said that

my eyes were like the sun, my lips like red coral, my hair . . ." she shrugged, "my hair like golden wires . . ."

"Wires?" He glanced at her in disbelief, and then quickly looked away. "Anyway, 'tis not golden, 'tis red."

"It is *not* red." Olivia glared at Ian's back. "Why can you not say pretty things to me? Compare my cheeks to roses?" She was sounding pathetic now, but she wanted so desperately to hear the honeyed words of her own heroes come from Ian's lips. How could he make her feel so . . . so amazing with only a touch, but be such a . . .

"My mistress's eyes are *nothing* like the sun," Ian said in his deep baritone, turning to look at her.

Olivia caught her breath, for his beauty was clear in that moment, the sun in his hair, his eyes like emeralds, and his man's body called to the woman within her.

"Coral is far more red than her lips' red." He crawled toward her.

She frowned at his words. "You obviously misunderst . . ."

"If snow be white, why then her breasts are dun."

Olivia's jaw dropped and she made a sound of disbelief, but Ian crept toward her still.

"If hairs be wires, red . . ."

Olivia frowned harshly at this, and Ian's full mouth quirked up in a smile. "*Black* wires grow on her head."

"If you think . . ."

"I have seen roses damasked, red and white, but no such roses see I in her cheeks." He came close, but Olivia looked away.

"And in some perfumes is there more delight than in the breath that from my mistress reeks."

"All right, I have had enough." Olivia went to move backward, but Ian grabbed her, one hand supporting her back, the other whipping the soaked gown from between them and flinging it away.

"I love to hear her speak; yet well I know that music hath a far more pleasing sound." He held her close now, warming her skin.

Olivia blinked at the word love.

"I grant I never saw a goddess go; my mistress, when she walks, treads on the ground."

She swallowed as she watched Ian's mouth form his words, and she realized suddenly that they were beautiful: that he praised her.

"And yet . . ." He kissed her softly, his lips hovering a moment over hers as he said, "By heaven, I think my love as rare as any she belied with false compare."

Olivia could only stare into Ian's eyes. "That

was lovely," she finally managed to say.

"Only as lovely as my inspiration." And he kissed her.

Olivia closed her eyes on a sigh and surrendered. How could she not, for though his words were not exactly as she had wanted, the sentiment was far beyond. And what skill the man had with his words! And his hands.

A low sound of pleasure crossed her lips as Ian found her breast once more. His hands warm against her skin, cupping her femininity gently, she felt as beautiful and cherished as any woman the world over.

No wonder people enjoyed this so much.

She giggled a bit, and Ian lifted his face from hers. "You find this amusing?"

"Fun t'would be a better word, dear sir." She smiled. " 'Tis lovely to disport so, don't you think?"

"Hmm." He leaned down and touched his lips to her neck, and she shivered.

"You are very good, Ian."

"I know." He kissed the lobe of her ear, taking the sensitive flesh softly between his teeth.

"No, I mean you are very good with words. I would never have thought."

"Good idea, Liv, cease thinking." His mouth trailed hotly down her neck.

"But you really ought to write that down. It was lovely, truly."

"Hmm." He tongued the top of one breast.

"To speak such splendid verse and with such genius without even spending more than a moment of thought . . ."

"If you would close that mouth of yours, I could show you genius." His lovely warm mouth closed over her nipple, and she lost all breath to speak. She relaxed against the ground and gave in once more.

This time the storm was gentler, less hurried. As a light breeze rustled the leaves above her head and brought a chill upon her skin, Ian's mouth worked warm magic. She could feel his large, strong hand upon her knee. He slid his fingers upward, and a tremor followed in their wake.

Ian caressed her thigh, and suddenly her entire being centered upon his hand as it inched closer to her woman's center. Olivia spread her fingers in his hair, cold against her palm.

And then he lifted from her breast, his body hard against her length as his mouth found hers once more. She groaned against his mouth, and arched against his hand that covered her moist center. And then he touched her most private place, his finger swirling wetly inside of her.

Olivia's stomach spasmed, the muscles of her

legs clenching as she cried out. But Ian took the cry within his mouth and kissed her still, long and hard.

His finger touched a spot that surely fed every nerve in her body. Olivia moaned with pure pleasure, her hands cupping Ian's chin and holding his mouth against hers, his beard rough against her fingers.

His touch against the center of her being roused the storm once more. The swirling vortex began again within her, and it was heaven to let it take her with it: every part of her alive to the sensation of touch, every muscle within her quivering with anticipation.

Ian left her mouth once more, taking a turgid nipple between his lips, laving its peak with his tongue. Olivia cried out again, her back arching off the ground as lightning streaked through her, splitting and arcing in its ferocity.

She writhed beneath the onslaught of Ian's fingers, his mouth, his tongue. And then the earth moved, worlds collided, and the raging storm within her peaked in a silent wail of thunder and wind as her woman's center clenched around Ian's finger. She pulsed, the most wonderful, incredible feeling of satisfaction radiating out from within her to every nerve ending and feeling center in her body.

She sighed, the wind receding, the thunder

rumbling off to other lands, and then she relaxed. It was as if she had turned to liquid, her
whole body suddenly able to seep into the
ground as she lay there.

"By my troth," she whispered in awe.

Chapter 12

. . . these fellows of infinite tongue, that can
rhyme themselves into ladies' favors, they do always reason themselves out again.

—HENRY V, V, II, 160

He throbbed, still, with need, his entire
body tense with the desire to roll over on
top of Olivia and slake his lust. But he could not,
would not, do that.

'Twas bad enough that he had allowed their
mutual desire to go thus far.

"You are not finished."

Ian opened his eyes to see Olivia above him.
If someone had told him that first night he had
seen her as a woman that he would someday
find Miss Bea beautiful, he would have fallen
over laughing.

261

He did not laugh now as her soft, auburn hair lifted off her patrician forehead on a waft of spring breeze. Her eyes were not like the sun, rather the sky it hung upon. They were as he pictured the crystal blue waters of the Mediterranean. And as he remembered her lithe, long body under his fingertips, Ian knew that he would never be able to look upon her again without needing to touch her . . . like now.

He turned his head away. "The dusk comes."

"Why did you not come into me?"

Ian sat up and reached for his hose. "I can think of nothing worse at this point, then my babe in your belly," he said, gingerly pulling one pant leg over his injured foot.

She said nothing, and Ian could feel her hurt: 'Twas palpable.

"Such discipline in the face of lust."

He knew exactly what she thought, and ought to have let her go on thinking it. But Ian reached over, grabbed Olivia's hand, and pressed it against his hard phallus. " 'Twas a lust I felt as well, my lady, I promise you that."

She stared into his eyes unblinking, and then her long, thin fingers curled about him. He sucked in a breath of air, and pulled her hand away.

"I did not get to feel you," she said. "I want to feel everything."

Ian tied his breeches carefully, his injured fingers making him wince as he kept his gaze away from Olivia's nakedness. "Dress yourself."

"Tsk!" She put her face directly in front of his. "If you did not want to finish, why did you start?"

"Faith, you are like the plague." Ian reached over and grabbed Olivia's gown. "Put this on." He pushed it toward her.

"Ian." She plucked the sodden gown from his fingers and threw it aside. "I want to know all there is to know. Please," she took a hold of his hand. "Show me."

He should receive a medal for the strength he showed, Ian thought, as he pulled his hand from Olivia's grasp and stood up, never once looking at the naked nymph at his feet. In truth, no medal awaited him, rather he would probably swing at the end of a rope.

"Put your clothes on," he said, and, swiping his dirty linen undershirt from the ground, limped away toward the stream. Since his clothes were already wet, he might as well clean them as best he could.

He found a large flat rock at the edge of the small stream and knelt. As he took another rock and tried fruitlessly to rub his shirt clean, Ian thought of all the things he missed desperately. First of all, of course, was his bed. It had cost him a fortune, but was well worth it, for he was a big man and anything less felt like sleeping on the floor.

Which he had been doing for the past few days, Ian thought with a scowl. Would his bed be there for him when he got back to London, for that must be where they were going? And, if not, that's where they *would* be going. For now that Ian knew that Olivia plotted against the Queen, he would do as the girl had pleaded, and take her to the monarch.

He would have to beg for the Queen's mercy on behalf of his mother and sister, and then he would probably die.

Ian stopped his pounding for a moment and stared off at the horizon. The sky had darkened, the breeze had cooled; it would be night soon.

He suddenly, fiercely, wanted to live to be old. He wanted to see his sister's children. He wanted to make sure they grew up far away from the intrigues of court.

He wanted them to live as he had on the farm, and then stay that simple: souls intact.

"Ian."

He nearly groaned aloud when he heard Olivia's voice behind him. Now, even the sound of her husky whisper made him ache with need. He was doomed.

Her arms came about him from behind, her

hands cool against the top of his. "Come into me, Ian."

Ian just closed his eyes and resisted when she tried to turn him around.

"Are you afraid of Her?"

"More afraid of you at the moment."

"Why can we not have this? Our bodies know each other, and yearn for the comfort they can obtain from each other. It will change nothing."

"Olivia." He turned quickly and cupped her chin in his hands. "I will not take you now or ever. You are untried. I have never had a maid, for that is a precious experience that should be saved for a husband."

She blinked up at him, and then frowned. "But you have bedded whores?"

He jerked at the word.

"Of course you have. Someone, not their husband, took their maidenhood. 'Tis a hypocrite you are, Ian."

He groaned. "Why do I try to reason with you?"

" 'Tis a mystery to me, sir, for you have no reason at all."

"I will not take a maid and then not marry, and I shall never marry, so I will never take a maid."

Olivia rolled her eyes at this statement of integrity. "Some rise by sin, Ian, and some by virtue fall."

"Rise or fall, it makes no difference to me, for I shall be dead soon anyway."

She scowled at him. "Why do you speak such nonsense?"

"I never speak nonsense." He succumbed to a small temptation and skimmed her cheek with a finger.

So soft.

He wanted her, no matter that she was sick of spirit, that she had him beaten and plotted against the Queen as well as him. She was right, his body ached for hers as if it had known her since the beginning of time.

"What is this you say then when you speak of death?"

"You take me to London, do you not?"

"I thought to warn the Queen."

He huffed a sigh of disbelief and took his hands from her face. "Yes, well, I am sure it never occurred to you to implicate me? Cause my downfall so that the Queen would be left vulnerable?"

"Of course it has not!"

Ian nodded and turned away from Olivia's shadowed, naked form. "When she knows that you yet live, I will surely die for my duty undone so long ago."

The moment the words crossed his lips, Ian wanted to snatch them back. He winced, knowing that he had just made a crucial mistake.

She did not know it had been him sent to kill her that morning seventeen years ago. Now she would.

Ian closed his eyes in disgust. Lust was a debilitating emotion.

"Oh no," Olivia whispered, a stark sound of grief in the night.

Ian turned, and then stared. Olivia stood before him, in her tall, slender glory, her hands to her face as she wept.

He looked around, wondering what had happened to her. Had she seen something that so horrified her it caused a torrent of tears?

"Uh . . ." Ian looked back at Olivia and shifted his weight from one foot to the other. God, he would do anything to make her stop crying.

She looked up at him then, and he took a step back, his bare foot splashing into the icy stream.

"You," she gasped, the tears still wetting her cheeks liberally.

He frowned.

"You are my angel," she finally managed to say.

"Excuse me?" Ian sputtered.

"My beautiful guardian angel!" she cried, and

267

rushed into his arms. He managed to stay on his feet by some miracle.

Olivia leaned her head back on her neck and looked up at him. "I sensed goodness within you, truly I did, even when you acted like such a pig."

Ian blinked, and then realized that his hands had slid down to cup Olivia's bottom. "I am no angel." He lifted his arms quickly, trying not to touch the woman at all. Unfortunately, his man-root was not listening, for it bulged at the front of his breeches and lay cuddled against Olivia's stomach.

This was not a good situation. He could not stand within the arms of the Queen's naked, virgin daughter; it was just a very bad thing to do.

Ian placed his hands gently on Olivia's shoulders. She had lovely shoulders, broad and strong, yet feminine, still.

Ian squeezed his eyes shut and pushed Olivia away from him. When he dared to open his eyes, though, he knew he was in trouble. The wench looked at him as if he had just descended from heaven on the wings of a dove.

"I am swine, remember?" he asked. "You called me that a score of times, at least."

"Oh, Ian." She moved as if to plaster her lithe body against his once more, but he quickly jumped backward across the stream. A torrent of ice-cold water now ran between them; that would help.

"Your hair is darker, is it not? I remember watching you from my hiding place and you were like the angel Gabriel, your head wreathed in gold. And now I have found you again, my angel." She shook her head. "Sir Ian Terrance you are a good man, not at all as you seem!"

And she walked right through his deterrent for closeness. Damn.

"I am all that I seem!" Ian took a deep breath, and staid Olivia with a hand to one of her delectable shoulders. Damn, damn, damn.

She had detected the softness that he, himself, had sensed with the reawakening of his conscience. Well, he would put that behind him now. Olivia would not be his downfall. He had no soul, and if she took away his hardness, he would have nothing.

With another great breath, Ian frowned and used all of his willpower to turn back time and become the feared man he had been before Olivia had written her way into his life.

He glared harshly at the woman before him, disregarding her tears completely, and grabbed her other shoulder. He shook her, his fingers biting into her tender flesh.

"Listen, woman, I am all that I seem! Seventeen years ago, I was but a green youth, not even nineteen. I was a boy that knew nothing of the harsh realities of the world.

"Today, I am a man. If the Queen were to send me out on the same mission she gave me seventeen years ago . . ." Ian hesitated. And then he narrowed his eyes and said with all the conviction he could muster, "If Queen Elizabeth sent me to kill a ten-year-old girl today, I would do it."

"I do not believe you," Olivia said, but her voice shook.

"I have sold my soul to evil. I have rich clothes, and servants, because I *would*, and *do*, kill anyone who crosses the path of the Queen."

The light was dying quickly, but Ian felt Olivia tense beneath his touch, and he saw one brow arch above her eye. "Then why do you not kill me now, Sir Ian? For you truly believe that I plot against our Queen."

He waited for a full minute before replying. She was right, of course. He ought to kill her. She was a threat to the Queen, as he had believed from the start. If he killed her now, he might even be able to save himself—might. But he would not know with whom she conspired.

"The Queen shall have you, Olivia. And she will pry from your treasonous mouth the names of those you plot amongst."

Olivia laughed, but the sound held no amusement. "Then perhaps we shall hang from the same gallows, Sir Ian."

"Perhaps."

Olivia reached up suddenly, placing her hands at the back of Ian's neck and pulling him toward her. And then she kissed him, hard and with no passion but anger.

She pushed him away. "You could have just taken me to her. You did not have to make it so personal, Sir Virtue. Did it amuse you?" She cocked her chin at a haughty angle. "Did you find it funny to watch my virgin body writhe beneath your touch?"

Ian swallowed hard. Somewhere, deep within him, a voice cried out to stop this madness. He could not hurt her so.

But then Ian closed his eyes and squelched the voice. He would do his duty, as he did with everyone and in all other circumstances, and he would leave nothing undone, as he had seventeen years ago in his careless compassionate youth.

This time he would act as Sir Ian Terrance, the Queen's agent ought.

"Yes," he said, his voice a flat, emotionless sound as the last light left, and they were left in utter darkness.

It would be full morning soon. Olivia lay in the back of the jolting cart, staring up at the lightening sky. She had not spoken one word more to Ian Terrance, and did not plan to for the rest of her shortened life.

He was not her Romeo at all.

For one small moment when her mind had processed the fact that he was the man of her memories: the golden angel of mercy who had allowed a child to live, Olivia had thought that she loved him. She had believed him good and merciful, with kindness hidden within his heart.

She had thought wrong.

Olivia turned over onto her stomach, her face against the spun-wool cloak that covered the hay. He took her now to her death. He would die too, most probably, and she did not care.

Her mind drifted, and visions of her most sturdy heroines came into view. Portia, standing so tall and wise cloaked as the manly judge in *The Merchant of Venice*. Oh, how she loved that heroine who, while dressed as a man, had power to grant life and death to the Jew Shylock, but who also held her lover's fate in her own hands. Then, in the person of Kate, the beloved shrew so tamed. Olivia thought of her heroine's mettle and how no one, neither villain or suitor, could demean her. Her heroines were of a stock not seen before in all of England. How she longed for the love that befell many of those wonderful women.

She had dreamt of true love, written of it, lived it through her characters, but was it real? Now, with reality so harsh upon her, Olivia closed her eyes and tried to think of anytime in her life she had ever witnessed true love in the context of life rather than plays.

She thought of her mother, and quickly shook her head. Ben came to her mind, abandoning his wife because she smothered him, he said. Was love some sort of fallacy, a lie she had never seen but believed with some feeling part of her heart?

Well, she would think with her heart no longer. Olivia flipped onto her back and sat up, ready to be as everyone else around her, cruel and heartless. And then she saw dust.

It rose just above the small hill behind them on the road. "They come," she said loudly, and Ian turned quickly on his planked bench. Without looking at him, Olivia pointed at the brown dust dissipating into the morning air.

"They mustn't find us," Ian said.

"They will not use me, I shall die first." Olivia stood quickly and jumped from the moving cart. She hit the dusty ground hard and fell, rolling into a stand of weeds at the side of the road. For a moment she could not breathe, and then, finally, she pulled oxygen into her body and pushed herself up.

Ian was there, the horse's reins in his hands.

"You are a pea-brained fool. You could have broken your leg, and then we most definitely would be caught."

She just scowled at him, remembering clearly why she had decided never to talk to the lout again.

"Help me unhitch the horses, quickly!"

Olivia shot him a hate-filled glance, but went to unhitch the horses. They worked on different sides, and she finished first.

"Put them out to field. Hurry!"

She led the horses down the side of a steep ditch and up the other side, then walked along a low stone wall, looking for somewhere to put the horses through.

"Make them go over!"

Olivia glanced over to scowl once more at her partner just in time to see him heave the small cart into the ditch. The sound of splintering wood etched against Olivia's ears, and she winced. He had probably just broken the axle, and he called her a fool.

Olivia then looked back at her own problem. Four rheumy, baleful eyes stared back at her. These two old things were never going to be able to make it over the low-lying stone fence. Most probably they would get caught on their bellies, and that would certainly make everything for naught. The men behind them were sure to stop if they saw two tired old nags drooped over a stone wall.

The picture conjured in her head actually made Olivia giggle.

"I see nothing to laugh about."

She whipped around and glared down at Ian. He was pulling up grass and throwing it on top of the cart.

"But then you probably have this all planned, don't you?" he asked, suspicion clear in his tone.

Olivia looked away from the despicable man and across the road, noticing that the field there was bordered with trees not fence.

She yanked on the horses' reins. They didn't even protest, just swayed around and plodded along behind her, struggling down and then up the side of the ditch. She had just guided them through a stand of trees and out into the field when Ian grabbed her from behind.

She cried out, but the sound was muffled as Ian clamped his hand over her mouth and then fell on top of her. She could not breathe with Ian's great weight against her back, his hand smothering her airway and her face shoved against the ground, and so she struggled.

"Be still!" he hissed into her ear.

She heard the thundering hooves of horses then, and went immediately quiet. They waited for a few minutes in silence, Ian still holding his hand over her mouth as if she might call the men back. And then he pushed up and away from her, leaving her where she lay.

Olivia took in great gulps of air, then glanced up at Ian, wondering if he were even going to offer to help her up, odious man. He stood staring after the horsemen, his hands on his hips and an intense look upon his face.

Looking away quickly, Olivia helped herself off the ground. Ian struck an imposing figure, and it did her no good to look upon him overlong. It made her heart ache, truly.

She made her way, now, out onto the road and back to the overturned cart. "I do not think we will be able to use the cart anymore," she said.

Ian did not answer, and she looked back at him. He had not moved. "Ian!" Olivia shouted. "Did you hear me?"

Finally, the man turned toward her, his forehead creased with concentration.

"Did you recognize them?" she asked suddenly.

His eyes focused on her then, and he nodded. "I think . . . I mean, no, no I did not recognize anyone."

She frowned. "I do not understand you in the least, sir. You seem a rather smart man, at least you must be in light of what you have accomplished in your life. How can you think that I plot with these men? I know them not. And I am helping you to escape from them."

"I am smart enough to know that things are not always as they seem."

"Exactly!" Olivia said triumphantly.

His scowl deepened, and he did not answer her. Instead, Sir Ian Terrance turned and began walking down the road.

"Are you going to walk all the way to London?" Olivia asked.

"Yes," he said without turning around.

Olivia watched him for a long moment. She spared a look at the horses, but knew that neither of them would ever be able to hold her weight. And, anyway, she was not the best of horsewomen. Riding bareback all the way to London would probably be much worse than walking there.

With a shrug and a longing glance toward the cart, Olivia followed after the tall, stubborn, bull-headed, manipulative swine of a man that still made her heart flutter when he turned his emerald eyes upon her.

Chapter 13

This is the night that either makes me or fordoes me quite.

—OTHELLO, V, i, 128

"Things go not well, Essex!" Crandle whispered in his friend's ear.

Essex snorted and thrashed, then opened his eyes. He stared at Crandle. "What do you here, in my bedchamber?"

"I try to warn you, fool. We are in a coil; 'tis the Queen's affair."

"But I thought your man had procured the ring?"

"No, he thought he knew where it was hidden. He was mistaken."

Essex sat fully upright. "We have not the ring?"

"Worse, my friend, we have not the girl or Sir Ian. They have both escaped."

"You mean Sir Ian has kidnapped her."

"No, it seems she has tender feelings for the uppity Sir Ian," Crandle said with a sneer.

"Tender feelings?"

"Yes, my man said that he has been trying to use it to force her hand. 'Tis why he believed so fully that he had the ring's location from her lips."

"But she led him wrong?" Essex asked.

"Indeed," Crandle answered. "And now they have escaped together."

"Well, find them!"

"I've sent my men upon the road to search. I cannot believe but that they will find them."

Essex scowled and threw back the bedclothes. "Your men! Ha! They resemble a pack of simpletons."

"I did not see you offering up any of your lackeys, Lord Essex!"

"And I very well should have, for then we would not be in this mess you have put us in."

"I have put us in? Me? 'Twas you that moaned nearly the entire winter of the Queen's betrayal."

Lord Essex shoved Crandle away from him and stood. "And it was you who dallied with another's wife and caused the Queen's most famous upset of the year."

"But 'tis you that wants to usurp the Queen's power and place yourself upon her throne."

"And it is you who wants me there!"

Crandle shook his head quickly. "Listen to us, will you? One tangle in our plans and we sound like schoolchildren. Let us calm ourselves, Essex. Even if Sir Ian and the girl find their way back to London, we are in no way connected with their kidnapping. I have made sure of that."

"Good thinking, Crandle."

"Thank you, Essex. I should say I know better than to leave anything to connect us with a wrongdoing that could land us in the Tower."

Essex shuddered. "Just the thought turns my blood cold."

"And well it should. But, not to worry. My men still look for Sir Ian and the girl, and if they find them, I shall have them force the information from them both."

"Perfect." Essex clapped his hands.

"And if we do not get to them before they reach the Queen, we know that they can in no way connect us with this perfidy."

"A good plan, Lord Crandle."

"Thank you, Lord Essex."

They came into London on the milk cart the next morning. Ian felt as if he had been the dog in a bear-baiting, and Olivia looked no better. He dared not take the time to get cleaned up, though.

He grabbed Olivia's wrist, and they jumped from the cart a few streets from the palace. He could only hope the Queen was still in residence and had not removed to Hampton. She was scheduled to be here at Whitehall, but with the Queen things could change upon the instant. Especially when she was angry or upset.

And he would guess that she was both at the moment.

"Can we not go to your home and get better prepared, Ian?" Olivia asked.

"No," Ian said shortly, pulling her along behind him. Olivia said nothing more, a miracle from heaven, Ian thought as they reached the palace.

The men-at-arms who flanked the entrance stared at Ian in shock as he walked up to them.

"Sir Ian," said one in obvious disbelief, "you are thought dead."

"You will wish yourself dead if you enter here," another stated.

Ian stared darkly at the lad. "Send a messenger to the Queen. I request a private conference in her chambers."

The soldier blinked. "I am not a servant!"

"Go now, man, or you shall wish *yourself* dead."

He looked from Ian to Olivia, narrowed his eyes, and nodded quickly. "Very well." He turned and strode before Ian into the palace.

Ian made his way through the maze of corridors to the rooms outside the Queen's private chambers and then stood silently, waiting for Her Majesty to send someone bid him enter.

Olivia stayed uncharacteristically silent at his side, and he noticed suddenly that her hand shook within his. He glanced at her suspiciously, wondering if she planned something. Perhaps he had walked right into some sort of trap, or worse.

Olivia took a deep breath and let it out slowly as he watched.

"Is there something to happen here that I should know?" Ian asked sharply.

Olivia jumped and then glared up at him. "I am to meet my mother for the first time in my life."

Ian felt something very close to shame skitter about his conscience. He looked away from Olivia quickly and said nothing more.

When the doors opened, though, and they were ushered in, Ian squeezed Olivia's hand. An awkward attempt at comfort, to be sure. And he wondered why he even tried.

Olivia yanked her hand from his grasp, and then she stood very straight, her chin lifted and walked ahead of him through the doors of the Queen's, her mother's, private chambers.

She saw her back first, as the great lady stood staring out a window. Olivia twined her fingers together before her and stopped a good distance from the Queen.

She had, of course, dreamt of this moment her entire life. Sometimes she had imagined herself angry and haughty, and other times she had thought that she would just be silent and cold. But more often, she had imagined how it might feel to go into her mother's arms and have them close around her.

Now she stood staring at the back of the Queen's white-velvet gown in awe and fear, and she could do nothing at all. Her feet were planted, and they had surely taken root, for she would never be able to make herself move again. A buzz sounded in her ears, and the morning sun streaming through the windows went suddenly, terrifyingly white, nearly as white as her mother's gown.

She swayed on her feet as she stared at the dark outline of the Queen against the harsh glare of the white windows.

And then Ian's arm slid about her waist. He held her gently against the side of his strong, warm body. Olivia closed her eyes for a moment, storing up strength, borrowing it, really, from the man at her side.

When she opened her eyes again, the light had gone back to normal, and her legs were strong beneath her. She took a step forward, away from Ian's arm, and he let her go without saying anything.

The thought crossed her mind that he had probably wanted to show her that she was weak, that she could not do this alone. Olivia knew that she could no longer read good intentions in any of Ian's actions. Still, whatever his reason, Olivia did feel better, and she was glad for that as the Queen slowly turned.

She was tall, but not quite as tall as Olivia. Her eyes were an icy, piercing blue, her skin painted white and her hair a wig of bright red. Olivia found her gaze wandering down to the woman's hands. And they were as Annie had said so long ago. Olivia clenched her own fingers, which so resembled her mother's, looked back up at the woman's face, and blinked to find her mother staring directly at her.

Elizabeth frowned slightly and then with a flick of her hand, she dismissed Olivia completely and looked beyond her to Ian.

"You have caused us much distress, Sir Ian. We are not amused."

Ian stepped forward so that he stood beside her once more. He bowed.

She had forgotten to curtsy. Olivia dropped quickly into a shaky obeisance, but when she glanced up she realized the Queen still took no notice of her.

"I am sorry, Your Majesty, for your concern."

"You shall be more than sorry, I think, Sir Ian." The woman turned away from them and paced to the window again. "We still await Shakespeare's arrival in the Tower, and we have been made to wait your presence for these three days. You have shirked your duties."

"I was waylaid by men who then beat and bound me. I have been a prisoner for these past days."

The Queen stopped, but did not turn around. "And the woman is your attacker? Or perhaps she plays the part of your rescuer?" The Queen turned around. "Do enlighten us on her identity, Sir Ian."

Ian's chest lifted with the breath that he took in and held for a moment. He looked over at her on his sigh.

Olivia could feel herself shaking and folded her hands in the front of her skirts. And then she determinedly smoothed the front of her gown. She could not allow the Queen to see her nervousness.

"*This* is Shakespeare," Ian said finally, never taking his gaze from her face.

Olivia nodded slightly, then looked to the Queen.

She arched her brows and turned her head slowly toward Olivia. "Do not patronize us, Sir Ian."

"He speaks true," Olivia said quickly. "I am the writer of the plays attributed to the man named Shakespeare."

The Queen stared at her. "Know ye not that 'tis contrary to the law to impersonate a man."

"Yes."

They looked at each other in silence. And then the Queen closed the space between them with a few short steps. "You are the writer of Shakespeare's plays, truly?"

Olivia nodded, trying desperately to keep her legs from buckling beneath her.

"You wrote The *Merry Wives of Windsor*?"

"Yes, Your Majesty."

"We have wondered, since seeing your play, how you come up with the names of your characters?"

Olivia moved her hands in a careless gesture. "I do not know. Sometimes I just pick from the air, other times I use names at irony to their persons."

"Do you ever, perhaps, use the names of people you know?

Olivia smiled slightly as she knew what the woman asked. "Yes, Your Majesty. Actually, I do."

The woman stood very close. Olivia could smell the scent of roses on her skin. She could see the slight creases in her makeup where lines bracketed her mouth. She saw the moment her mother recognized her.

Chapter 14

I think the King is but a man, as I am: the violet
smells to him as it doth to me.

—HENRY V, IV, I, 106

"**L**eave us," The Queen said to Ian without
looking away from Olivia.

"I . . ."

Elizabeth jerked her head to glare at her agent.
Ian quit his objection mid-sentence. "I will be
right outside when you need me." The Queen
returned her gaze to Olivia.

Olivia heard the great door to the room click
shut, but she could not look away from her
mother's intense stare. Power radiated from the
Queen like the rays of a hot summer sun. And
in that moment, no matter everything her mother
had done to her, Olivia felt a surge of pride run
through her.

"It seems we have both taken to positions more often filled by men, have we not?" her mother said then, her tone giving no hint to her mood.

Olivia nodded. "And done rather well."

"Better than any man could."

"You have accomplished this, yes. But I . . . well there was Marlowe . . ."

"He had half the talent of you."

Olivia could not help the smile that turned her mouth. "If you insist."

The Queen quirked a brow, and then one side of her mouth lifted in a half smile as well. "Of course I do, dear girl, I always insist."

Dear girl. The endearment made Olivia wish she could cry. She knew that the Queen had not meant it to be anything close to an endearment, but Olivia realized that she would take the smallest of offerings from this woman and savor them.

She could not hate her mother. She could not hate her even though the woman wished her dead, had tried her best to make her dead, actually.

It was pathetic of her, in truth. But Olivia had learned early in her life to accept the weaknesses that she could not change and strengthen only those which could be.

The Queen was staring at her again, and Olivia stared right back. Her trembling had ceased, and she now stood straight and tall without fidgeting in the least.

Elizabeth reached out, then, carefully touching the back of Olivia's hand with her own. "You have my hands," the woman whispered.

Her mother's soft touch made her take in a sharp breath. "Annie always told me that I did."

Her mother looked back into Olivia's face. "And my eyes."

Olivia felt Elizabeth's fingers curl about hers. And another simple childhood dream came true as her mother held Olivia's hand.

Elizabeth closed her eyes suddenly. "Oh, I did fear for you," she said, her voice wavering slightly over the last word. And then a single, crystal-like tear appeared from under her lashes and tracked through the white makeup on Elizabeth's cheek.

Olivia watched the bead's straight path down her mother's cheek, and wished she could stop it with a kiss. But she held herself in check, and then closed her own eyes against her heart's weakness.

Finally, she found the strength to pull her hand out of her mother's grasp and open her eyes. "You mean you feared me, don't you, Mother?"

Elizabeth opened her eyes as well. She carefully blotted at her single tear with a handkerchief from her sleeve. "Do not call me that, girl, 'tis dangerous."

Olivia nodded stiffly, then kept her chin at a haughty, upward angle. "I am no girl, Your Majesty, but a woman grown. My name is Olivia."

"I know. I named you."

They stared at each other once more as the silence beat around them like the tattoo of a drum.

"Indeed," Olivia finally said. "You birthed me, you named me, and you had me killed. You are all-powerful."

"You look very much alive to me."

"Thanks be given to a secret missive warning Annie of your intent, and to . . ." Olivia stopped suddenly. If she said nothing, the Queen would never have to know of Ian's role in her salvation. She could save Ian now as he had saved her seventeen years before. It did not matter that the man he had become deserved not to be saved. Olivia pressed her lips together and said no more.

"If I had wished you dead, Olivia Tudor, you would not breathe the air of mortality."

Olivia frowned.

"My secretary sent an agent to rid me of my one weakness, for it scared him that you lived." Elizabeth folded her arms in front of her and arched her brows delicately. "And I warned Annie of her impending doom. We had spoken secretly of what she would do if the need arise."

Olivia shook her head. "But Annie never . . ."

"Because I bade her not to."

Her legs once again threatened to forsake her, and Olivia turned away, searching for support. She found a resting place in a gilt-covered chair and sank onto the hard seat.

The truths of her life were lies.

"You did not send Ia . . . the agent to kill me?" she asked, needing to know in clear words that what she had believed her entire life was not true.

"No, I sent a note warning Annie to run."

Olivia folded her fingers carefully around the intricately carved arm of the chair on which she sat. She stared at her hand as if it belonged to someone else. "Why did you never come to see me?"

"I will tell you true, Olivia. I wished you had never been born. You were a grave mistake, and Walsingham wished to kill you at birth."

Olivia nodded but did not look at her mother.

"I will admit to you now, for you should know the reality of it, I contemplated the idea."

With her thumbnail, Olivia traced one of the delicate carvings beneath her hand.

"It was Annie who promised to take you away, to her father's home of Cornwall, and never bring you back."

"Why did you not have her take me away from England as a babe?" Olivia finally looked up into her mother's eyes. "You could have given her another name, had her raise me as her very own from the very beginning."

"You would rather, then, not know who you are?" the Queen asked.

Olivia looked back to the work of her thumbnail once more. "I wish the child I was had not known."

The Queen turned and walked away from her. Olivia could hear the tap of the woman's heeled shoes against the marble floor. "I cannot turn back time, no matter my power. But I can tell you this, Olivia. I selfishly kept you in England after your birth, for I . . ." she hesitated, and Olivia glanced up.

"My heart pined for you."

As mine did for you, Olivia thought. But she said nothing.

"We planned for Annie to take you to the Continent if there was any sign of danger to your life, but we also thought it best that I not know exactly where she went. I have spent many long nights since Annie took you away from this country wondering where you were, wondering if you were well."

With a shaking hand, Olivia covered her eyes for a moment, for her head ached terribly. "We went to Italy at first," she said finally. "Annie took me many places, though. She wanted me to learn through traveling. And she kept me well. She loved me like a mother ought."

There was silence for a moment, and then her mother asked quietly, "Do you have the ring?"

Olivia nodded, her mind still trying to grasp what she had just learned. "Yes, 'tis safe."

"It was folly that Robert made it, and greater folly that I had Annie give it to you. But I needed you to have something of us."

"Did you love him then?" Olivia asked, once again looking up at the imposing figure of her mother. She had always wondered at the union that had brought her into the world. She had seen her father, Robert Dudley, once, an old man walking through the streets of London with his entourage. He had the look of a handsome man. He had the look of a kind man.

The Queen smiled slightly, sadly. "Of that I should not speak. My love, my husband is England."

And her children were the people. As the true blood child of Elizabeth, Queen of England, Olivia had no place in the world.

Olivia took a deep breath and held it for a moment. She had no place here, but neither had her mother set out to kill her. She let out her breath slowly and deliberately.

Her mother seemed to know what she thought, for she nodded, then turned away and strode to the window. "Annie was supposed to make sure that you did not return to England."

"Annie is dead," Olivia said.

Elizabeth said nothing for a moment. "You must have known, though, the danger of returning to England."

"I knew, but I could not hide any longer, always afraid of being found out."

"So you come back to England?" The Queen glanced over her shoulder. "That is how you assuage your fear?"

Olivia could tell by the look in her mother's eye that the woman understood. They were both of the same courage and mind. "Even under another name, I could not live, truly. I would not bring another into the danger that plagued my life. I certainly would not bring children into a life such as mine." Olivia shrugged, belying the hurt that knowledge had always given her. "Annie's money did not stretch as far as she thought it would, and I was penniless upon her death. To make money, I wrote. And a writer of plays can only make money here in England. And so I returned."

"Still, it is dangerous for you to be here. There are those who would use the fact that you live to their advantage."

295

"And to your detriment."

The Queen turned and looked at her for a moment, her expression guarded, her stance wary. "And yours as well."

Olivia knew that her mother feared her then, and she took no thrill in the knowledge. "No one shall ever use my life to further their own agendas," Olivia soothed her mother. "I have never plotted against you, nor do I support those who do."

"But there are those who do."

"Indeed." Olivia gave a quick, short nod of her head. "They took Sir Ian and me hostage. I did not ever see their faces, but they tried to charm me with talk of riches and power. They wanted the ring. I gave them false information that they would leave me and allow me time to escape."

"Who are they?"

"I do not know."

The Queen tapped one of her fingers against her gown. "Tell Sir Ian to return," she ordered.

Olivia stood, realizing that the reunion of mother and daughter was at an end. The Queen would never again acknowledge their relationship. Olivia knew that as she knew her own name.

Olivia went to the door, but it burst open before she placed her hand upon the knob.

"She is dead!" Sir Ian roared, going straight to the Queen.

Olivia quickly closed the door behind Ian so that no prying ears would hear the confidences of the Queen.

"She is dead to *us*," the Queen stated concisely. "Do not thunder about so, Sir Ian, you will upset us more than we already are, and that would not bode well with you now."

"I care not about myself."

"Obviously, for you smell of a dung heap."

Ian stood staring at the Queen, his jaw slack in obvious shock. "I will never understand you."

"Of course you will not, *you* are common, Sir Ian. *We* are the Queen."

"How dare . . ."

"Stop now, Sir Ian, before you say something stupid. Your sister lives not with God, but your mother. She wished herself thought dead, and we happily obliged. She disgraced herself and then you added upon her humiliation by disappearing."

"Did not the earl of Crandle tell the truth of the matter and publish my sister's virtue?" demanded Ian.

The Queen frowned. "What does Crandle know of this?"

"He reported false the downfall of my sister's reputation."

"Well, he has yet to report true."

Ian slammed a fist into his open palm and turned on his heel. He stopped quickly when he saw Olivia, obviously having forgotten the true problem at hand in the furor brought on by the false rumor of his sister's death.

Olivia wiggled her fingers at him in a mock wave. Ian glared at her.

"Since the well-being of your sister has been established, Sir Ian, shall we move on to more pressing problems?" the Queen asked.

Ian drew a deep breath and turned back to the Queen. "There are men that wish you harm, Your Majesty, and this woman conspires with them, be aware of that. I shall go to my death easily. All that I ask is that you clear the name of my sister."

"How very valiant of you, Sir Ian." The Queen glanced at Olivia. "But We do not understand why your death is required."

"Ian," Olivia tried to stop him. He would admit to his perfidy when it was now of no consequence. Still, he had disobeyed, and Olivia was afraid the Queen would take only this to heart.

Ian glanced at her, and then shook his head, and turned his gaze back to the Queen. "You know the identity of this woman?"

She went to stop him physically, but the Queen stayed her with only a look. Olivia swallowed and glanced at Ian. She did not want him to die.

"Be still, girl," the Queen said, then nodded for Ian to continue.

"It was I that Walsingham sent to . . ." Ian hesitated, and then cleared his throat. "Seventeen years ago," he began again, but the Queen stopped him with a wave of her hand. Ian immediately became silent as the Queen walked over to a dais and went slowly up the two stairs to the chair that sat at the top.

"We shall tell you this once, and then we will never speak of it again, Sir Ian. Do you understand?"

Ian frowned as the Queen turned around and fluffed out her skirts so that she could sit. "We asked you a question, sir."

"I understand that we speak of this only once."

"Good." She gestured toward the chair Olivia had recently vacated. "Do sit, Sir Ian, you make Us nervous when you pace about."

Ian glanced behind him, avoiding eye contact with Olivia, she noticed, and sat upon the uncomfortable gilt chair. The Queen tapped one of her rings against the arm of her own chair as she spoke. "Sir Walsingham sent you on a rather grisly errand many years ago, when you were but a boy yourself, is this what you are trying to tell Us?"

Ian nodded.

"We knew of this errand, though Walsingham thought he acted without Our knowledge. In fact"—Here the Queen stopped and then huffed a small laugh. "In fact, *I* myself warned your quarry of your intentions."

Ian went very still.

"You shall not be punished for not fulfilling your duty in this instance, Sir Ian."

Olivia watched Ian as he learned that something he had feared for the last seventeen years had no sting at all. Yet, even still, the man gave none of his emotions outlet upon his face.

"But, it shall not happen again." The Queen's ring *pinged* against the arm of her chair a few more times; then silence reigned. "And We have asked you to bring Shakespeare to the Tower," she finally said.

It was as if her heart stopped in that moment, for Olivia felt sure she had quit breathing. She transferred her gaze from Ian to her mother.

Was she to die then, after all?

"We hear from both you"—the Queen nodded at Ian—"and Shakespeare himself that men plot against us. For the protection of all, Shakespeare will take up residence in the Tower." Elizabeth glanced at Olivia. "A warm and comfortable chamber, we promise you."

Olivia only nodded, wondering if perhaps her

mother did not trust her completely. But, truly, whom could Elizabeth trust? Her own secretary had secretly tried to kill her child. Olivia had to admit that she did not blame her mother in the least for acting on the side of caution.

"Go now, Sir Ian, dress Shakespeare appropriately and take him to the Tower." The Queen flicked her hand at Ian and rose.

"May I be allowed paper and a quill?" Olivia asked quickly.

The Queen stopped in her tracks, her gaze skipping over Ian and coming to rest upon Olivia. "Shakespeare's wish, Sir Ian, is your command. Make sure that the lad is content."

When Ian did not respond the Queen turned on him. "Do you understand, Sir Ian?"

"Indeed, Your Majesty."

"Return posthaste when you are done." She wrinkled her nose in distaste. "Do bathe first, though. You stink."

A large table in the middle of Olivia's new quarters groaned under the weight of a meal fit for royalty. Ian surveyed the cell quickly, noting that the bed had a fat feather tick and a velvet coverlet. The rug beneath his feet was also a sumptuous change from the last time he had brought someone to this very room.

Olivia stood at a large desk piled high with

parchment and quills. She reached out and took up a bottle of sand, weighing it in her palm in silence.

She had not spoken to him as they left the palace in the Queen's own conveyance and went to his house to bathe and change.

The Queen had sent over some clothes for Olivia, a doublet of velvet, embroidered with golden thread as well as silk stockings and velvet breeches. An ensemble the Shakespeare he had met the week before would never have been able to afford.

Olivia seemed not at all impressed as she transformed herself back into a man. Her hair had grown a bit, now covering her ears and actually lying straight rather than sticking about her head like straw.

She had beautiful hair, truly, soft as the belly of a chick, and Ian wished that he might see it long and curling. He could imagine her dark red hair twisted about her lithe, pale body as she lay naked upon his bed.

But, again, he allowed this woman to distract him from his duty. Ian had to remember the humiliation of being captured. That would surely keep his thoughts on business. "Would you tell me now who plots against the Queen?" he asked her abruptly, trying to dislodge the thoughts from his mind.

Olivia sank into the chair before the desk and did not turn around. "Go away, Sir Ian, you tax my patience."

"She did not wish you dead."

"I know. And I have told her what I know. The men who held me these past two days wanted proof of my birth. They wish to undermine the Queen's authority and bring another to power. A noble, I suspect, someone close to the Queen, for when I told them where the ring was, one of the men went rushing off to London saying that he would get the ring and inform their man of their success. Their man, I would suspect from that, is in London."

"Ring?"

Olivia took up a quill and began paring it with the knife at its side. "The Queen shall tell you of the ring, if she wishes."

"But they have this ring then? You told them where it was?"

"I told them where it could have been found a fortnight ago; 'tis there no longer."

Olivia finished preparing her quill and pulled one of the parchment pieces forward. "I moved the ring when I heard that you asked questions about me. I hid it in a safer place." She dipped her quill in the inkpot and set about scratching at the paper.

Ian watched her for a moment. His heart

wanted to believe her, but that only made his mind stronger against such a thing. She had softened him from the beginning, and he winced to think of how he had bungled this assignment. It was lust, that was all. And it was an easy thing to slake elsewhere and so make it have no power.

Ian turned quickly on his heel and stalked to the door.

"Are you not going to try harder, Sir Ian, to get the truth from me?"

He placed his hand upon the door latch and glanced over his shoulder at her.

She had turned in her chair and sat, one arm hooked over its high back, her delicate brows arched above her blue eyes. Even from across the room he could make out their bright color, so large were her eyes.

"You say I have the truth," he countered, wishing with all of his being that she did not carry such power over him. For even now, as he contemplated finding some soft, curvaceous woman to use his body until he would not feel anything but the need to sleep, he wanted the thin, tall girl who sat staring at him with hatred in her eyes.

"But you do not believe me. I expected another gallant attempt at getting the truth from me. A quick roll upon the mattress, perhaps. Or—" She rocked the chair. "The chair is sturdy enough."

He wanted to deny her charge; with all the breath in his body, he wanted to deny it. And that he cared so deeply that she hurt scared him more than anything had in his entire life.

He could not care. If he desired her, so be it. That would end with distance. But he could not care. Without another word, Ian pushed through the door and left her.

"Who intrigues to take the throne, Sir Ian?"

Ian stood once more in the Queen's private chambers. Now, though, he felt more his old self in black, unadorned clothing and a sword at his side. "I saw a man the last night that I was in the palace. He was with Lord Crandle in the presence chamber."

"Yes, We heard of the spectacle which you caused, Sir Ian. 'Twas the night you disappeared? Rumors had you absconding with a lovely maid to Europe."

Ian swallowed hard. "I had Olivia with me, I was trying to keep her from harming you."

"You mean Shakespeare, do you not?"

"Yes, of course, Shakespeare."

"And why is it, Sir Ian, you could not inform Us of your mission then?"

Ian said nothing for a moment, trying to find the right words to explain. Perhaps he would hang after all.

"Oh." The Queen shook her head in disgust and began to pace the room once more. "Do not get the look of the doomed upon your pretty face, Sir Ian. We care not that you feared for your life. 'Tis a good thing, actually, for We had worried that you were not human, so perfect you were. Now, you saw a man with Crandle?"

Ian had to spend a moment digesting the Queen's last speech. She had never called him pretty before, and she seemed rather less perturbed with him than usual. This was all bad. He had lost stature in her eyes. He had obviously become more like the bumbling fools who swarmed about her, dipping and bowing and flattering.

Ian scowled with distaste. He would have to recapture his persona of old, for he would not be one of the Queen's many pretty men.

"Crandle was with a man in the presence chamber. I think I recognized the man as one of my abductors," Ian said shortly.

"Hmm." The Queen took another turn about the room, stopping at a large window for a moment, and then moving on. "Crandle, you say?"

"Indeed." Crandle, of course, was a crony of Essex. Essex was the son of Robert Dudley, the late earl of Leicester. "It would help for me to know . . ." Ian cleared his throat. "If I could be privy to . . ."

"You wish to know Shakespeare's parentage," the Queen cut off Ian's stuttering.

"Yes."

The Queen nodded, and went to sit upon the chair that rested on the dais. She placed herself neatly, moving her skirts out of the way and carefully smoothing them, doing all the things her ladies of the bedchamber usually did when they attended her. With such delicate subjects of which they must speak, though, the Queen had dismissed everyone and had instructed that no one be sent in. She picked daintily at a piece of lint. And then, finally, settled against the high back of her chair.

"After the fire, her father believed her dead. He believed this unto his death, We are sure."

Ian nodded. "I beg your understanding at my questioning you, Your Majesty, but I remember you mentioning something about Essex during one of our conferences where we spoke of Shakespeare. You said he knew something?"

The Queen's gaze upon him was sharp. "You are quite good, Sir Ian, at what you do. We are glad that you find yourself always on Our side."

Ian bowed slightly.

"Essex is the only left living, besides myself . . ." the Queen hesitated for a moment. "And you, now, who knows that Olivia existed. His father took him into his confidence against Our better judgment."

Ian now knew for a certainty that Robert Dudley, Essex's father, was Olivia's father as well. The thought that Olivia shared blood with Essex made Ian grimace. "But he thinks her dead."

"Her guardian was the only one that knew she lived still. Even *We* were not sure if they made it through the fire." Again the Queen stopped and stared at him. "Except, it seems now, that you knew as well."

Ian carefully placed his hands behind his back, clasping them together tightly. They trembled. He wished, suddenly, that he had thought to send a messenger to his mother and sister. He would do it immediately upon leaving the Queen's chamber. They ought to be off to Europe, he thought, a grand tour with all of their possessions and all of his money along for the ride.

"How do you think Lord Essex learned of Oliv . . . Shakespeare's survival?" the Queen asked now.

Ian shook his head. "I know not." He cleared his throat softly and began to pace. "I took Shakespeare from his lodgings late at night and saw no one about." Of course, he had been rather preoccupied by the fact that Shakespeare had breasts. "I then kept her at my house for three days interrogating her . . . er him."

"Interrogating, you say?"

"Yes."

"Hmmm."

"I do have reason to believe that Crandle has been keeping my goings and comings under a watchful eye. My sister mentioned that the man asked her questions about me, and he seemed to pay attendance upon her suddenly after I captured Shakespeare."

"You say that it was Crandle who saw your sister in the embrace of a man at her bedroom window."

"It was not my sister, but her maid."

They both went silent for a moment. Ian thought back to the night he had captured Olivia for the first time. Someone could have been watching him without his knowledge. He had been completely preoccupied from the moment he realized Olivia's true gender. And then there was this whole thing with Crandle constantly causing his sister woe. Perhaps none of the incidents was coincidental. Perhaps the man had intentionally besmirched his sister's name.

He was just going to offer this information to his monarch when Elizabeth said, "We do believe you, Sir Ian. You have always been a man to stand aside of the intrigues of this court and put your integrity and faithfulness to Us first."

Ian had reason to thank his father this time, for the lessons of his youth.

"Do you think," she continued, "that Crandle seeks to bring your name asunder, using your sister's vulnerability at this time?"

Ian nodded slowly. "I thought that very thing, Your Majesty."

"Yes, well, you have always been intelligent, Sir Ian. 'Tis the reason for your success."

He would still send his sister and mother on a little voyage. As the Queen had said, he was not an idiot.

"We believe," the Queen interrupted his thoughts, "that Essex has allowed this knave, Crandle, to pull him into a plot of which he did not understand the graveness."

Ian wanted to object. Essex was not an idiot, either. And Crandle was no genius. But neither was Essex smart nor Crandle stupid. It seemed to him they would have to have come up with their ideas together. But Essex was a particular favorite of the Queen, and she obviously did not want to think that he would knowingly go against her. Ian, being intelligent, of course, said nothing, but knew that he would keep a keen eye on the Queen's favorite from now on.

"Essex has angered Us mightily, for the boy

speaks aloud a secret that was to be kept within his heart for the rest of his days."

His days hopefully being cut short now that the Queen knew of his perfidy, Ian hoped.

"Let us bring out this knave with a funeral, Sir Ian."

Ian glanced up at the Queen, wondering whom they would mourn, and still jittery enough to think it could be his funeral she planned to attend.

"Your sister is believed dead, Sir Ian. We will honor her memory this time on the morrow. We shall see what they do when they see you at Our side and Shakespeare reading your sister's eulogy."

Ian blinked. "Shakespeare?"

"He is the writer of the greatest plays of this century. Surely you would be honored to have him pray over your sister's spirit?"

"Of course, Your Majesty."

"He is of obvious genius, a testament to good breeding, We must say." Elizabeth's smile was of unadulterated joy. Something he had not seen in her mien before this moment. "Now, go to him, Sir Ian, and advise him of this new honor." She stood. "No more interrogating, though, Sir Ian. We shall not have such a thing of you."

Ian bowed low. "Never, Your Majesty."

Chapter 15

Where love is great, the littlest doubts are fear;
Where little fears grown great, great love grows
there.

—Hamlet, III, ii, 177

Suzette of the Boar's Head Inn had the largest breasts Ian had ever seen. So round and full, they were, that her nipples protruded above the tightly laced bodice of her wool gown. Her hips were of the same proportions as her breasts, and nary a bone could be seen poking from under her skin. Her hair was long and whitely blond, and her skin the color of milk. Suzette of the Boar's Head Inn was everything that Ian enjoyed in a woman.

And he tried desperately to remind himself of this as he paced about the walk under Olivia's bedroom window. Only one hour before, Ian had been sitting beneath the lovely weight of Suzette in the Boar's Head Inn. He had felt only soft flesh as her plump buttocks rode his knee and her bounteous breasts strained the bodice of her gown just beneath his nose.

The other patrons of the tavern had looked upon him with envy. But his manroot had lain between his legs without any interest whatsoever. It was a travesty, truly.

And now, of course, as he paced about beneath Olivia's cell, garnering strange looks from the guards that stood their posts at the Tower, Ian's phallus was as hard as a rock in his breeches.

God save him, he was possessed of an evil spirit.

"I wonder, Sir Ian, how much longer you will march about beneath my window?"

Ian stopped in his tracks and glanced above him to where Olivia pressed her face against the bars of her window. He scowled at her.

"Do you protect me, or protect the world from my evilness, I wonder as well?"

"I protect the world from your vile tongue."

He heard the sound of her laughter. "Oh, yes, I speak with the viperous tongue of a snake, do I not?"

Ian huffed an exasperated sigh.

"Is there some reason you lurk about in the

darkness beneath my window, then, Sir Ian? Do you play at Romeo, perhaps?"

"That would make you the fair Juliet?" Ian asked sarcastically. "I think not, for that woman was as a woman ought to be, her tongue giving forth pleasant words, her being one of sweetness and love. Would she ever scream shrewish words at her Romeo? Would she ever beat him with constant sarcasm and cutting wit? I think not! Would she not trust his judgment in all things? Would she not acquiesce to his higher knowledge? I think so!"

"You know nothing of Juliet, then."

Ian kept his silence, for he had said too much in his frustration. Why this woman caused such furor within his body angered him no end. He was not used to feeling thus, as if he would throw all caution to his enemies and run pell-mell up the stairs of the Tower to bed the virgin daughter of the Queen: a thin, gangly woman who should not spike his need to such heights.

Ian readjusted his breeches with a grunt. His penis had finally become a most loathsome part of his body, which he would never trust again. Damn Olivia Tudor for that injustice.

"And, truth be told, Sir Ian, you are most definitely *not* Romeo. So we shall quit with that comparison."

314

Ian scowled. "And who would want to be like that sniveling excuse for a man?"

"At least Romeo would not use a woman's inexperience at love to his advantage. He would never play so with a woman's..." Olivia stopped abruptly.

Ian's breath hitched in his throat. Had she been about to say heart? Did she care enough for him that her heart had been hurt?

Did he want her to care so?

"Do tell, Sir Ian, the reason you march beneath my window like a man angered beyond reason and keep me from my sleep."

No, of course he did not. And that was enough thinking along those lines. Ian folded his arms across his chest and huffed a great breath of disgust.

Still, he had the problem of telling Olivia the Queen's plan. He would have to go into her room, for he could not yell his message for all to hear. But he trusted himself not to enter her chamber.

He ought to have plowed Suzette. He could have done the deed if he had but tried.

As if God found his thoughts ludicrous, a loud clap of thunder rumbled in the still of the night.

"Well, now you shall be all wet, Sir Ian." Olivia laughed from above him.

Ian opened his mouth to retort, only to be

nearly drowned as the heavens opened and dropped upon him a deluge.

He ran for the tower leading to Olivia's chamber, shaking water from him like a dog when he finally reached shelter. God surely laughed so hard he cried, Ian thought, as he nodded to the guards on the stair, and then, with his hand upon the hilt of his sword, entered Olivia's cell.

He entered with his hand upon his sword as if he feared she would attack. Idiot man, she would never touch him again. He stared at her for a long moment, water beading and rolling down his face. Olivia folded her arms across her chest and sat back against the pillows piled against her headboard.

She had spent the day writing, and her hands ached. They were out of practice at the sport. Fortunately, her mind had taken back to it with a vengeance. If only she could figure out whether she wrote a comedy or a tragedy. She had written two acts already, and she still was unsure of which direction she went.

"You must write a eulogy for my sister."

Olivia blinked up at Ian. "A eulogy?"

"The Queen has a plan that we will put into motion upon the morn: a funeral in which all the suspects are gathered together. The Queen will gauge their reactions to my presence as well as yours."

"An interesting plan."

"Indeed."

"And then?" Olivia asked.

"And then the knaves will be taken off in chains, I would say."

"And the prisoner?" She held her arms out to bring attention to her cell.

"I should hope that we will both return to our lives before, with not another thought to what is happened here."

Olivia stared at Ian for a full minute of silence. "I think that is rather impossible."

"Perhaps you are right." Ian turned away from her as if to leave. Olivia felt the ache within her heart, and wished she had more strength over her emotions. She hated Sir Ian, she truly did. But so close was hate to love, she thought as she looked upon Ian, that she could not tell which she now felt.

He had been awful to her. She *must* remember that! Of course she hated him!

She closed her eyes with that thought. If only she could dwell on the way he had kept her prisoner, used her virginal attraction to him to further his own goals.

But confusing the issue was the fact that, in her heart, Olivia knew what led Ian to do the things he had done. His duty to the Queen, his integrity, his innate goodness had taken Ian down the road of his decisions. And those things she could not hate about the man in her bedchamber. Those things made him one of the best men of her acquaintance.

He had protected her from the rats.

"I will not be allowed my life back," she whispered, opening her eyes to watch Ian's back as he left her.

He stopped with his hand upon the latch of her door.

"I will either be imprisoned for the rest of it, or it shall be taken from me."

"She will not kill you."

Olivia shrugged. "It does not matter, does it? My freedom is not mine. Of course, it never has been. I was not born to a life, but to threaten another's. And so I have always known that I should not have those things of which I write."

"You could have stayed away and had those things," Ian said without turning around.

"You know that I could not. What if I had married? What if I had children? I would fear for them always. What life would that be?"

"What life is it without them?" Ian asked harshly, and swung about to face her. "You deserve to have them!"

"And you do not?" Olivia asked with interest.

He blinked, his face showing his true bafflement.

"Why do you keep yourself from love and family, Sir Ian? You have no reason to, but you put on the cloak of an emotionless, hard man and say that love interests you not. But it does."

He scowled. "I have no interest in the folly of marriage and children."

"You lie."

"I do not."

"All right, then you do not."

Ian squinted at her with mistrust.

"You swear you are made of truth, and I shall believe you though I know you lie," she said.

Ian took a step away from her, though she had not advanced upon him at all. "That is a game of lovers, I think."

Olivia shrugged. "To your cynical mind, perhaps." She cocked her head to the side, for the scent of a cheap woman had wafted from Ian's direction. "Have you tarried, once again, in the back of a pub, Sir Ian?"

His face grew dark. "What does that matter? I am my own man."

"Of course." Olivia nearly laughed aloud at the man's upset, but she kept her visage straight. Still, a tiny bite of jealousy plagued her. "I merely wished to advise that you bathe before the morn. The Queen seems to have a keen sense of smell, and she would not appreciate the scent that lingers on your body this night."

319

" 'Tis the scent of sweet Suzette you smell upon me!" Ian announced. "I have just come from her well-rounded bosom."

Olivia's jealousy speared through her heart, but she showed none of her disquiet. "Very good, Sir Ian," she said softly.

He glared at her, and then pulled his sword from its scabbard and shoved its tip into the wooden floorboards. " 'Twas not good!"

Olivia jumped at Ian's yell.

"You," he pointed at her. "It is all your fault. I cannot find pleasure where before it was my only solace."

Olivia waited, her heart still sore that he had taken another woman, but her soul glad that he found no pleasure in the act.

"She sat upon my lap as I drank my ale, and the others were ripe with envy. And what do you think I did?" Ian stomped over to her, and then he leaned his fists upon her bed. "What do you think I did, fair Olivia? Faced with a woman whose charms were evident and given without rancor?"

"You left her?" she asked hopefully.

"I left her," he affirmed as he walked his hands along the bed. "I paid for my ale, and I left, for what I oft desired before now seems empty."

Olivia bit her lip for a moment. And then she

glanced downward at Ian's breeches. " 'Tis not empty at all, sir. You mistook."

"No, 'tis hard as your tongue, Lady Viper."

"Take my tongue, then," she said. "Take it and make it soft and sweet."

He groaned and leaned toward her, taking her mouth in a bruising kiss. "You are like a poison which I crave, Olivia, 'tis sure."

She slid her arms around his neck to keep him near. "Partake of the poison, dear sir, and we shall die together."

"Marry, if I but could." He kissed her again, but kept his body levered away from hers. "My duty to the Queen . . ."

"Your duty is the Queen's, but your soul is your own," she said against his mouth.

"You are wrong, for I have no soul." Ian pulled away from her, breathing heavily. "But I shall not take your virtue."

"What of virtue? Who shall ever partake of it?"

"But . . ."

"No." She pulled him off-balance so that he lay on top of her. "Earthlier happy is the rose distilled, than that which, withering on the virgin thorn, grows, lives, and dies in single blessedness."

He stared down at her for a moment, and then, suddenly a smile curved his lips and lit his glorious eyes. A smile that Olivia would remember the rest of her days, for it was a thing of great beauty that she had naught seen before.

"I should hate to see you wither," he said, his voice rough and edged with need.

"Pluck me now, sir, and I shall never wither but live forever in this moment."

His kiss upon her lips then took her soul, and she threaded her fingers in Ian's hair, settling back against the pillows, sure in the knowledge that he would take her and that she would know physical love in her lifetime.

He kissed her long and hard until her entire body craved the touch that her mouth took so greedily. Keeping one hand at the back of Ian's head, so that he would not leave her, Olivia opened her doublet with the other. Ian's fingers stopped hers, and then took over the chore. She sighed against her lover's mouth, and began to free him of his own clothes.

The storm she had known before eddied about on the tide of her need as the cool air kissed her breasts and Ian's touch, like the softest velvet, caressed her throat.

Around them beat the staccato of raindrops from Heaven, making it seem that they lived in a world unto themselves. And it was perfect, for beyond this small room was a world that would not let her love or be loved. But now, within the warm cocoon of Ian's arms, Olivia could have anything she wished for.

Free, finally, from the confines of their clothes, Ian's strong, hard form lay against hers, their bodies heating each other. He kissed her again, his hand sliding down her side and then back up to cup her face to his. She arched against him, yearning to feel his touch upon her breasts.

"We are fools," he whispered, but she pressed her mouth to his lips.

"Olivia"—Ian put his hands on either side of her face—"what if we make a babe? 'Twould be folly."

Olivia hesitated. It would be folly. But, suddenly, the thought of having Ian's child made her keen with longing. If only they were different people in a different lifetime.

"There are ways," Olivia said finally. "I have been among the men of this world long enough to know that there are ways to avoid such a thing."

He stared at her for a moment, his eyes sad. "You shall not feel everything as you wish, then, Olivia."

She wondered in that moment what he thought. Did he hunger for their child as well? But it did not matter. They had this night, and that was all.

Olivia slid her own hand down to curl around

323

Ian's hard manhood once again. "I shall feel you inside of me. That is enough."

But it wasn't. Olivia closed her eyes against the pain, though, and pressed her mouth to Ian's. He groaned, and she explored him with her hand as all thoughts of folly and fools fled. Olivia kissed him again, mimicking the way that he kissed her. She touched her tongue to his teeth, and then plunged into his mouth.

He groaned beneath her, his hands sliding down to cup her breasts. But Olivia had tasted the power of her womanhood, and she pushed against Ian's shoulder until he rolled onto his back.

She followed him, lying atop Ian as she allowed her hands to feel every part of him that she had ever thought to touch: his shoulders, so wide and strong, so different from her own, his chest, his stomach, and again his arousal.

Olivia kissed him, and touched him and felt her own need heighten as Ian cupped her buttocks, pulling her against his hardness. Her knees slipped down around Ian's hips so that her wet woman's center was open against his hard manhood.

Ian groaned. "Let me come over you, Olivia. I shall hurt you."

"You will not hurt me, Ian." She reached between them and held him in her hand, touching the tip of him to her center.

"Lord have mercy," Ian ground out between his teeth.

Olivia giggled. "I shall have no mercy, Ian, I tell you now. I have waited for this too long to have mercy upon you now."

He smiled at her again, and her heart fluttered lightly in her chest. "I have asked no mercy from you, my lady." His voice, the dark treble of it, brought chills down Olivia's back. She closed her eyes and pushed her woman's center upon Ian's manhood.

He took hold of her hips, guiding her and holding her as her legs quivered and her arms trembled. And then she lowered herself, impaling herself with one swift move, crying out at the pain, but reveling in it as well.

Ian pulled her close, taking her cries into his mouth, as they turned from pain to urgency. They kissed as she lay still across Ian's chest. And when he moved his hips beneath her, there was no pain.

His hands, curved about her bottom, rocking her forward and back, until her entire being centered at one spot, at the core of her woman's entrance. She groaned, closing her eyes and picking up the rhythm of Ian's motion, a motion that seemed ingrained in her and a part of her even though she had learned it not in this lifetime.

Ian pulled her down to him, his mouth against her neck, hot and seeking. Olivia writhed at the intensity of so much feeling, and rocked against Ian's hardness. His lips trailed kisses to her breasts, against her nipples, biting with a lover's softness but with enough force that lightning arced within her.

The storm again within her raged, fed by Ian's mouth, his hands, his hardness inside of her. And then the elements rushed about her, coming finally to a sweeping standstill as her center convulsed around Ian. Olivia closed her eyes and stayed very still savoring each pounding heartbeat and quivering pulse of their entwined bodies.

Ian moved within her on the tide of her small death, and she knew that he needed more. She slid her body up and then down against his hardness, her center still in the throes of her climax.

He called out her name, pushing her off and rolling over just as his seed spewed forth onto the coverlet. Olivia closed her eyes, wishing that he had given himself to her fully. Wishing that she could bear a child. Wishing that her life was her own.

When she gazed again at her lover, she saw that his back glistened with a sheen of sweat.

Curving her body against Ian's, Olivia opened her mouth and took his essence upon her tongue. It was as if she could not and would never get enough of this man. And she knew then with all the conviction of her being that she loved Sir Ian Terrance with her heart as well as her body.

She had found the man she would love until the last breath of life left her body.

It was a most wondrous feeling, but one tinged with utter heartache, for she could never share her feelings with Ian. She would never burden him with that, for she knew that he did not feel the same for her. And because of that she was glad, actually, that they could never be together.

"Do not regret our actions this night," she said as he turned over to face her. She cupped his face in her hands. "For I do not, nor will I ever. I longed for the knowledge of love, and you have given it to me."

"And I will wish to give it to you again, lest I leave you now."

"Do not leave then."

"I must." He kissed her gently. "I do not regret, but no matter our precautions, I worry that we make a child. And I shall not make the chance higher by slaking my need upon you again."

"You would not be slaking, for I partake in that need."

327

He chuckled. "All words of no consequence, unless a child is born, and then we shall regret even though you say we should not."

"Sleep with me, Ian, this night. Please."

He frowned.

"I beg you, stay. I wish not to sleep in this cell alone with the tears of God as my only company."

With a deep sigh, Ian slipped his arms around her and pulled her close. "I will stay." And he kissed her.

Olivia closed her eyes, her arms around her lover, her forehead against his neck. She remembered the feeling she had discovered with this man, many nights before when she first lay within the circle of his arms. And she felt it still, the utter security at a time of great upheaval. A gift from Ian, which she did not think he knew he gave.

Chapter 16

∽○○∼

. . . they have committed false report; moreover,
they have spoken untruths; secondarily, they are
slander; sixth and lastly, they have belied a lady;
thirdly, they have verified unjust things; and to
conclude, they are lying knaves.
—MUCH ADO ABOUT NOTHING, V, i, 214

They were assembled in the Queen's own
chapel. Ian stood in a corner watching as
the guests entered to take their seats behind the
Queen. Crandle came with Essex, though neither
of them laid an eye on him as he stood in a
shadow. Sir Richard also attended the service,
his eyes rimmed in red. Ian did not spare a moment of sorrow for the man, who was so easily
tricked into thinking his love dead. He had
falsely believed her fallen, he deserved a few
days of sadness for such folly.

The service began, and there was no commotion until it was announced that Shakespeare would read the eulogy. Ian watched quietly as Crandle turned rounded eyes upon his friend the earl of Essex. They conferred silently, but heatedly, as Olivia entered the room and walked regally up the center aisle. And then from the corner of his eye, Crandle saw Ian. The man whipped his head around and stared straight at him.

Ian smiled and nodded to the man in silent understanding.

"Death lies on her like an untimely frost," Olivia began the eulogy quoting her own play, *Romeo and Juliet*, if Ian was not mistaken. "Upon the sweetest flower of all the field." Her voice was clear and sweet, and she did not deepen it at all as she had when they first met.

Ian glanced again at Crandle and Essex, they were both staring back at him now. He smiled again and waved two fingers at them, just as Olivia had done to him when they had been in the Queen's private chamber the day before. They turned around in their pew quickly, and Ian wished he could laugh aloud. They were well and truly caught, for they had the look of conspirators.

Ian returned his attention to Olivia, not hearing her any longer, but just watching her. She

330

had such a feminine bearing, it was amazing that he had ever thought her a man. And she was truly the most beautiful woman in the world. How could none of these people see that?

As he watched, Olivia reached into a pocket at the front of her doublet and pulled out a small, gold ring that she held up before her.

Ian straightened away from the wall, all of his senses alert to a danger that lurked now at the surface. She would betray them. He had worried, of course, but after last night . . .

"I would like to take this moment to bestow a special memento . . ."

"Stop!" Crandle stood from his seat and pointed out across the small audience to the ring in Olivia's hand. "That ring is proof of our Queen's betrayal to us, her people!"

Essex looked as if he wanted to vomit up his breakfast, but Crandle stood tall and proud. Ian moved quickly toward Olivia, ready to whip the ring away from her.

The Queen stood slowly, regally, and turned upon Crandle. The man's pointing finger wavered slightly, but he said, "Read the inscription aloud! I demand that this assembly know the truth of what this piece of jewelry entails."

"You demand?" the Queen asked haughtily. "We find that rather forward of you, Lord Crandle."

"I shall read it," Olivia offered.

"No!" Ian shouted.

"No!" Crandle also denied her to go on.

"Perhaps you should read it, Lord Crandle," the Queen said.

"I think that would be ..." Ian stopped mid-sentence when the Queen shot him a scathing look.

"Master Shakespeare, bestow your gift upon Lord Crandle, that we all may know the words inscribed upon this ring."

Lord Crandle pushed past Lord Essex, puffed out his chest, and trotted up to Olivia. He seemed very happy with Olivia, and this made Ian inch closer, for he would not have Lord Crandle read anything that might hurt the Queen.

" 'Tis a crest of arms!" Crandle cried, holding the ring aloft. And then he brought it down and read the inscription. "For giving this generation a season of words from the pens of writers, I thank you." Crandle's voice had lowered dramatically in volume, and he said the last two words nearly in whisper, "Master Shakespeare."

"We thank you for the thought, Master Shakespeare," the Queen said. "Lord Crandle." She nodded at the man, and then turned sad eyes upon Lord Essex. "Lord Essex, you will follow Us now to Our private chambers."

"He is a woman!" Crandle cried out in obvious desperation. "Shakespeare is a woman!" He reached over and grabbed the hat from Olivia's head. Her hair sprang forth, newly shorn that morning and poking about her head. Crandle grabbed at her hair and pulled.

"Ow!" Olivia yowled, and kicked the man in the groin.

Ian could attest to how that hurt. He ran toward the two and grabbed Crandle by the arm.

"I shall prove it!" Crandle reached for the front of Olivia's doublet, but Ian latched on to his other arm and held them fast behind him.

"That is quite enough, Lord Crandle!" The entire assembly went quiet at the Queen's yell. "This man, Master Shakespeare, is one of the most gifted writers of our day. You will not besmirch his name as you have tried so vainly to do that of poor Andromeda Terrance."

A rush of whispering moved over the crowd. "That is right. This man, Lord Crandle, has told lies about Andromeda Terrance in order to bring her and her brother low in your regard. For he thought, in this way, to put another on the throne of England." The Queen gestured about her with a regal hand.

A gasp rose from those around them. "Andromeda lives still, have no fear, and shall yet marry Sir Richard Avery." There was shocked silence, and then the entire assembly applauded. All except Essex and Crandle. "Shall we adjourn to Our chambers, my lords?" The Queen looked pointedly from Crandle to Essex. Without another word they followed her quietly through the throng while Ian took up the rear.

The Queen wished Olivia to run away once more; to live in another land and bother Her no longer. Olivia knew that was why she was left alone for so long. But she stayed.

She sat down on one of the pews at the front of the small chapel and waited as the room slowly became deserted. She watched as the candles burnt themselves down to the quick, and then she knew that Ian came into the room.

Ian, her Ian whom she hated and loved with such intensity. She could admit to herself now that she loved him, for she could look back and see the valiant man that he was, truly. He tried to hide behind his gruff exterior, but there was a soul beneath. He had not sold it to anyone, though he believed it so.

She hated him, too, though, for not trusting her, for not trusting himself.

No Romeo strode up the aisle toward her now, rather a real man whom she loved beyond reason.

"She wanted you to vanish," he said as he came up behind her.

Olivia only nodded.

"She ordered me to take you back to the Tower if you were still here." He stopped beside her. "I think we both hoped that you would be gone."

"I tend to cause that reaction."

Ian said nothing to that, and Olivia decided she could feel as sorry for herself as she wished.

" 'Tis your own fault," Ian said. "You should never have come back to England. And you should have run from here, now, when you had the chance."

"Would you run, Ian?" She looked up at him suddenly. "Would you go with me now to a far-off land that lives under the sun's warm rays all the year round?"

No emotion played across Ian's stern face as he stood staring down at her, and she sighed, returning her gaze to the flickering, dying candles.

"But no, you are, again, the Queen's agent. You change personas just as the color of your eyes change."

"I do not change, Olivia, I am one man."

"Tell me, though, for my mind is curious. How did you know 'twas me?"

Ian took a breath, his broad shoulders rising and then falling. "You sneezed," he said.

And she laughed. "Oh, dear Annie." Olivia turned back to face the altar. "Did you hear, Annie? The sneeze! It was my downfall after all."

Olivia stood and turned to Ian. "Her hand upon my shoulder when I sneezed was like a death grip, I tell you. She thought the end had arrived, I am sure. And then you let us go, and it was our salvation." Olivia shrugged. "But, in truth my sneeze has caught me in a foul trap after all."

"May I ask my own question now, Oliv . . . Master Shakespeare?"

She nodded as she stamped her bottom lip with her teeth. That he would never again call her Olivia suddenly made her wish to cry. She would never again wear velvet women's shoes, or make love while the rain pelted the roof above her head.

"Where is the ring?"

"Ah, the ring!" Olivia's sadness washed away with the force of her sarcasm. "That ring will haunt you, will it not, Ian?"

"I wish it destroyed, yes."

"Did not the Queen tell you?"

"She said that you sanded away the true inscription and wrote your own."

Olivia stared into Ian's dark eyes. "And you believe her not?"

"I believe *you* not."

"Ah." She reached out and touched the dark silk of Ian's doublet, so warm. " 'Tis too bad that

336

you must live your life without trust, Sir Ian. You shall deny yourself much happiness, I fear."

"As you deny yourself?" he asked, and she heard the emotion finally, deep and rooted and so within him that it would never come to the surface.

"But I do not, Sir Ian, for all the world's a stage. And I get to live my life through the players."

"Then 'tis too bad for you as well, Master Shakespeare, that you do not live your life true."

"But I was never given the opportunity, by way of birth." She took her hand from his person. "You were."

"So you think."

"So I know." She took a step closer to him. "You say you have no soul, and I know you believe that, with the job you do for the Queen, it must be gone. But it is not, Ian, 'tis there, strong and true, yet fighting to breathe. In so many ways I have seen the true man that you are. Let him live."

He blinked, and his lids fluttered a bit as if he might actually break, but then he tilted his chin. "Come now, Master Shakespeare, your room awaits." He moved aside to allow Olivia to pass before him.

She stood still a moment. "I shall need more parchment, Sir Ian."

"Of course," he said flatly.

"I have a comedy to write, I think. Something light and happy and full of love."

Ian swallowed, and Olivia could see that his throat worked a bit harder at the action than it ought. "I'm sure it will be a fine play, Master Shakespeare."

"If anyone is allowed to see it, yes."

Sir Richard accosted him as Ian walked, head down, through the presence chamber on his way to confer with the Queen.

"I must still ask you, Sir Ian, for the hand of your sister!"

Reluctantly, Ian halted, glancing up at the beaming man. It had been a fortnight since Crandle had been sent to his death. Essex, unfortunately, had only been sent to Ireland. That man, it seemed, would have to do far worse than treason to meet his just end. Ian had meanwhile put his household back in order, and his sister had returned to court.

Shakespeare had been spirited away without even Ian's knowledge of where "he" now abided. And that was a very good thing, for the writer of plays had caused him to become someone unable to be the hard man he ought.

He glanced down at Sir Richard now, for the man was not on par with Ian's height. The man was probably even shorter than Olivia, Ian thought, and then quickly shut his mind to that.

"It has taken you rather a long time to come to me, Sir Richard," he said shortly.

Sir Richard's face lost some of its joviality. "But, of course, Ian. There have been other things taking up your time."

"You took another's word before hers, Sir Richard. Is this a testament to true love?" He could feel the silence that came over the room, as the milling people turned and stared. He looked up and caught his sister's eye, but looked quickly away.

Sir Richard blinked, and then became deadly serious. " 'Tis true love, what I feel for your sister."

"What if, some years hence, another varlet speaks badly of her? What shall you do then, Sir Richard? Will you be off to Norway and break my sister's heart?"

"Ian!" Andy interrupted him with her cry as she came to stand near Sir Richard. "Why do you speak thus at the time of my happiness?" She glared at her brother and put her hand upon Sir Richard's arm. "Give unto Richard my hand in marriage this very instant."

"No, Andy." Sir Richard put his hand over hers. "Your brother is right. Even though our misunderstanding has been found to be much

ado about nothing, I did not show trust in thee."
He turned back to Ian. "But, I promise you, Sir
Ian, 'twill never be so again."

Sir Richard stepped back, projecting his voice
so that the entire assembly could hear him. "I
here now state my troth to this woman before
all. I shall never doubt, again, her pureness of
nature, her trueness of self." He took both of
Andy's hands within his own and looked into
her eyes. "Though I be no poet, I shall use what
words I can put together now to tell the world
of my love for thee, dear Andromeda.

"I died a thousand deaths when I thought you
lived no more in this world. And I knew that I
could go no more upon this earth without the
knowledge that you would be always at my side.
I am now the happiest of men, to find that you
have cheated death. Know this, sweet Andromeda, even if we do not always agree, I will always listen to your arguments. Even if you find
reason to be angry with me, I shall always beg
forgiveness at your feet. And even as we grow
old together, I shall always find you the most
beautiful of women."

Tears streamed down Andy's cheeks as a great
chorus of hurrahs went up from the people
around them.

Ian could only stare as the great hole that had
become his heart seemed to constrict and fall in

340

upon itself. "Have her then," he said quickly, and turned on his heel.

He could not see the Queen. He ate the ground with strides twice the length as usual, not seeing where he went, but needing to be away. He burst finally through a door to find silence and peace, and staggered out through a hedge-lined walk.

A bench appeared at his right, and he dropped upon it, his elbows against his knees and his face in his hands.

He had fought against it, but even though she no longer plagued his physical life, Olivia plagued his very existence. He was no longer a man, but a whimpering fool who could not see a rose, but be reminded of her fair complexion; who could not feel the rain on his face, but think of her touch against his skin.

It had been days since he had slept, though he dropped each night into his bed weary and exhausted. Ian leaned against the back of the hard bench and stared at the bright blue sky. "Is it thy will, thine image should keep open my heavy eyelids to the weary night?"

"Not at all, Sir Ian, though you do flatter Us when you say so."

Ian jumped, and then looked around at the ugly sound of women giggling. The Queen stood among a few of her ladies, her mouth curved in a smile, but her eyes far from amused.

"Go," she commanded the women. "Return to the privy chamber anon. We wish to speak with Sir Ian in confidence."

Ian wished to groan, but he kept his silence as the ladies threw him sly glances and hurried away. He was a fool in their eyes. Where before they had run from him, now they laughed at him. And it was all Olivia Tudor's fault.

" 'Tis beyond Our understanding, Sir Ian, how you can write so prettily of love, yet not understand it at all."

Ian went very still. He would kill Andy for telling.

The Queen sat beside him. "You did not bow, Sir Ian. Do so now."

Feeling as if he were in a trance, Ian stood and bowed deeply before the Queen.

"Very good, you may sit beside Us now."

Ian did as she asked.

"Now, you wonder how we know that you are the writer of the sonnets which circulate among the court and cause young girls to sigh and women to ache? Not to mention the boys, do you not?"

Ian had a fleeting memory of how these conferences had gone before Olivia caused such havoc in his life. He had always felt as if he controlled the situation. And now the Queen had it just the way She liked. He was as Her other minions, a cowering fool, and She was triumphantly superior.

"Andromeda has rather a hard time keeping a secret, I think."

"It was not from your sister that I learned of your coy pen, Sir Ian. I know of everything that happens within my realm. 'Tis why I am Queen." The Queen flicked a nonexistent piece of dirt from the red skirt of her gown. "Now, then, you have found love, but it cannot be. And so you mope about the palace like a whipped dog."

Ian scowled at the rosebushes that grew across from where he sat. First of all, he had found nothing as idiotic as love. Secondly, he acted nothing like a whipped dog.

"We can not have you so distracted, Sir Ian; it does not bode well for our own well-being since you are the sole reason for that well-being."

"I am not distracted."

"You love her, admit it now."

Ian knew exactly of whom the Queen spoke. He thought of Sir Richard's pretty speech. "I love her not. I do not agree with her when we argue, and I would never beg at her feet for anything."

"We do not believe you."

"I would never beg."

"Yes, you would."

Ian went stonily silent, wondering if he could

set the roses ablaze with the fire he knew roared from his ears. "I would not."

"Fine, then, until you do, you shall have her not."

Ian frowned at this, and then he turned to face his Queen. "I cannot love, Your Majesty. I have given all that is myself unto you."

The Queen sat a bit straighter, but did not take her gaze from his.

"As a boy I loved, I felt, I agonized even. And then I became an agent to my Queen, and the being that was my soul withered and died. For if it had stayed, it would have killed my body as well." He looked away then.

"I cannot love. I am Sir Ian Terrance, your principal agent. I am the blackness that steals into your palace while all other souls revel, and commits those crimes that must happen to save you."

Elizabeth stayed silent for a very long time, and Ian followed suit. What he said was true, and it was good for his mind to hear it aloud. He would mope no longer like a whipped dog. What of him was left to mope?

"You are right," the Queen interrupted his depressed musings. "And with all that you have sacrificed, I could not possibly ask more of you."

Ian glanced at his monarch. "Excuse me?"

"We do not know what We shall do without

you, my lord." She studied her fingertips for a moment. "But, of course, there are other young men We have yet to destroy."

"I never . . ." Ian stopped mid-sentence. "Why did you address me as a lord?"

The Queen shrugged. " 'Tis the least We can do, after ruining your life." She turned to him, her pencil-thin brows arched above her sea blue eyes. "Do you enjoy Suffolk, Ian, or perhaps that is too close to London for your peace of mind? Actually, I do have just the place for you. A large estate just north of a small hamlet called Upper Tidbury." She waved her hand airily. "Oh, yes, I know, it sounds like a veritable hole, but 'tis a lovely place, truly. A nice earldom for you, my dear man. And you can fill your days checking on your tenants and figuring out which fields yield the best wheat." She smiled and stood. "Perhaps you shall find your lost soul there?" The Queen turned and pranced away, her pointed, heeled shoes crunching the gravel as she went.

Ian watched her leave, his mouth open in shock.

Chapter 17

Langston Abbey
One year later

> When I said I would die a bachelor, I did not
> think I should live till I were married.
> —Much Ado About Nothing, II, iii, 222

"**M**y Lord?"
Ian looked up from the account
books, stuck his quill in the inkpot, and rubbed
at his temples. "Yes, Weston?"

The butler snapped his heels together and held
out a silver platter with a crisp, white, folded
note sitting upon it. "For you, my lord; it has just
arrived."

Ian frowned at the youngish Weston. The man
was just too perky. At first Ian had thought the

butler would mellow with time, but it had been a year, and he still bustled about the abbey as if dogs nipped at his heels.

"Well, then, bring it here."

"Of course, my lord." Another snap of his heeled shoes, and the butler rushed over to flourish the silver platter beneath Ian's nose.

Ian plucked the note from the platter and unfolded it as Weston waited. "No need to wait, Weston, this missive does not require an answer."

"As you wish, my lord."

Ian just nodded, though he was rather sure that someday all the "my lording" would probably make him batty. With a shake of his head he turned his attention back to the parchment in his hands. His sister had given birth to a boy.

A smile curved Ian's lips. He could remember a time when he had believed that he would never live to see his sister's children. He folded the note again and pushed it into the inside pocket of his jacket. His fingers felt the well-worn edges of another parchment, and he hesitated.

Slowly, Ian transferred his sister's missive to another pocket and then extracted the paper from his inside pocket. He had put it there just that morning, as he did every morning. He did not like to think why he did it, but still, Ian kept the paper over his heart each day of his life.

He had not opened it, though, in over seventeen years. Ian fingered the worn parchment now yellow with age. He had never told her that he had kept it, and she would never know. The man he had been had not wanted to admit that he still owned it.

And what of the man he was now? Who was he? Ian was not sure; nor was he certain he wanted to know. But he did know that he kept this paper folded and close to his heart, though he had not read it since he had found it in the book of a doomed child.

Ian brought the parchment to his lips for a moment, his gaze setting on the cluttered desk before him. There sat his life now, the accounts and workings of his estate. In the last year he had begun to feel a deeper respect for his father, the farmer. To bring life from the ground was an incredible feat.

He tucked the parchment back in his pocket and sighed just as someone knocked on his door. Ian glanced up as a maid poked her head around the massive wooden door to his study.

"Would ye like a fire, milord?"

Ian smiled slowly. "I would, Ruth." He patted his pocket. "I'm an uncle," he said, as the young girl hustled into the room, the tin bucket on her arm clattering against her hip.

The maid blinked, obviously surprised that he had addressed her. "Excuse me, milord?"

Ian sat forward in his chair and plucked his quill from the inkpot. "Nothing, Ruth, nothing."

The girl frowned, nodded, and knelt before the fireplace.

Ian tapped his quill against the blotter on his desk. He had no one to share his news with, and so, of course, he thought of Olivia as he did nearly a hundred times a day. He wondered where she was, what she was doing, if she ever thought of him. And then he stood and left, the quill still held tightly in his hand.

He felt the thrill in the air as he entered. People whispered behind their hands, and he knew that he had caused quite a stir. He did not get out much, and it always excited the townspeople when he came to one of their functions.

Ian smiled politely and moved to find his seat. He was celebrating the birth of his nephew, alone. It was not often that a group of players came to Upper Tidbury, and it was quite a happy coincidence that they should be there on a day when he wished desperately to do something besides drink a glass of port and retire to bed. The whispers around him softened and then died, as a man stalked out onto the makeshift stage. Ian glanced down at the program in his hands, then blinked.

His heart stumbled, and his breathing stopped in the silence, and then it *whooshed* from his chest, and black spots danced before his eyes. *Much Ado About Nothing*, Ian read again, by William Shakespeare.

That name, it made his fingers clutch the paper he held. It made his head snap up when he heard the man on the stage begin to speak. And then a player came on stage, a young boy dressed as a girl, and through a haze Ian heard another player address her as Beatrice.

Ian closed his eyes for a moment. Miss Bea, oh, it seemed a million years since he had thought of that name. The players were still saying their lines, and Ian opened his eyes and listened, his mouth quirking into a sad smile when he recognized the opening lines of the play. For he had read them before, a lifetime ago.

But now, as he listened, Ian heard much more than he had when he'd read them. Ian leaned forward in his chair so that he missed not one word from the players' mouths.

"I need to speak with the Queen," Ian announced as he stood outside the Queen's private chambers.

The guard at the door nodded. "Of course, Lord Langston, she awaits your presence."

Ian grinned hugely and darted through the

opening as three women hurried past him.

"Lord Langston," the Queen greeted him from her perch atop her chair on the dais. "I do hope all is well?"

"Yes, yes, Your Majesty, all is more than well!" Ian smiled.

"I have cleared the room. You implied that your need to see Us immediately is of a delicate nature?" The Queen arched her brows at him.

"Yes," Ian said and then walked right up to the Queen's chair and kneeled at her feet. "I am here to beg."

The Queen cocked her head to the side. "Really? Whatever for, Lord Langston?"

"You told me once that I might have her if I begged. Here kneel I, ready."

"Ah." The Queen stood and carefully picked her way around Ian. "But are We ready to hear your supplication? That is a much graver topic, We believe."

Ian stared for a moment at the empty chair. And then he swallowed hard and stood. When he had realized, through the words of the play she had written, that she loved him, he had not given any thought to the fact that he might fail to claim her. She loved him. She had seen his worst, and yet still she loved him. The Queen would not keep her from him now, would she?

"I love her," he said urgently.

"Do you? But I could swear, Lord Langston, that you believed such a pithy emotion below you. In fact, I believe, you said 'twas impossible for you to love."

Ian turned to face his Queen. "It was above me, in all truth. As Olivia was and is."

The Queen nodded, her face showing her surprise. "Well, it does seem that you beg. And prettily, at that." She turned away from him again and went to the window. "And so this year spent alone in the country has urged you to believe that you love this person of whom you speak?"

Ian took a deep breath. "My heart knew that I loved her from the beginning. But it has just been lately that I have found the connection between my heart and my mind."

"But you did not trust her. Even as she swore herself true, you did not trust her. How can you love without trust?"

Ian stayed silent for a moment. "I trusted her not, 'tis true. I put your safety above all. Will you begrudge me that?"

He watched the Queen's shoulders lift slightly. "For her, We begrudge you that."

Ian shook his head confused. "I do not understand."

"When the men of the court decide to wed, We mourn, Sir Ian. For they will never again put loyalty to Us ahead of another woman."

"But . . ."

"It is the truth of it, though they protest," she cut him off. And then she turned to face him, her heavy makeup a mask to her emotions. "So you come here to beg, and We must ask you. Will you put your trust in her? For if you do not, you will only hurt her again."

The Queen arched a painted brow. "And *I* will not have her hurt."

"She has my heart, my life, my trust," Ian said quickly.

"Will she accept it, We wonder?"

Ian stiffened.

"She is a stubborn woman, Lord Langston." The Queen actually grinned. " 'Tis in her blood to be so."

"Will you at least tell me where to find her that I might put that question to her?"

The Queen did not move, but her smile faded, and her gaze jumped to his. Ian bowed his head quickly and dropped to his knee once more. "I beg of you."

There was a long silence, but Ian kept his submissive pose, his heart praying through each agonizing moment.

"My, my, We do believe no one would recognize you at this moment, Lord Langston. The great agent of the Queen, Sir Ian, would never kneel before Us for so long, his head bowed in such supplication."

Twelve months before, the Queen's words would have scraped along Ian's nerves. Now he cared not what the woman said, just as long as he left this room knowing where to find Olivia.

"We would say, dear man, that even if she does not accept you, she has given you a great gift."

Ian allowed himself to look up.

The Queen blinked a few times, her visage so sad that Ian believed she might be fighting tears. "You have a soul, do you not, Lord Langston?"

He glanced down at the marble floor beneath his knee, then back up at his liege. "I do," he said simply.

The Queen watched him for a moment, then turned away quickly and went to a desk tucked against one of the long walls. She dipped a quill, wrote, and then held the parchment toward Ian. "Go, Lord Langston, you have another to whom you must beg upon bended knee."

The knock on her door pulled her from her work. Olivia stood, stretched, and took a deep breath before she went to allow her visitor entry. It would be Ben, she was sure, for he had said that he would be by today. And so her gaze alighted upon a broad chest when she opened the door, for Ben was a touch shorter than the man who stood before her.

With a little gasp, Olivia stepped back.

He entered her apartments, his hand upon his heart. "I have need of thee," he said, then dropped to his knees at her feet.

Olivia let out a sigh of disbelief, as her hand fell upon his shoulder. She had to make sure that he was not a ghost.

His hand covered hers, and it trembled.

"Ian?" she finally managed to ask.

He did not raise his eyes to hers, but stayed before her, head bowed. "I love you," he said simply.

Olivia stood mute, wondering, perhaps if she dreamed.

"I was angry for a while after you left, because you softened me." He finally tilted his head back to look up at her, his dear eyes the color of spring grass. "The Queen sent me off to the country, with a title, and I knew it was because you had changed me so completely that I could no longer be the man I was before you came. I could no longer be the Queen's agent. I had to be one of her simpering, manless men."

Olivia frowned, her mind trying to understand what Ian said at the same time as she tried to believe that he knelt before her, truly. He loved her? Had he said that he loved her?

"I lost what I had worked for, and I resented that."

Olivia brushed the brown curl that hung over Ian's forehead, and then caressed his face. It felt so good to touch him again and have him strong and real beneath her fingertips, not some figment of her imagination. "Are you still upset with me, Ian?"

He smiled that beautiful smile Olivia had thought she would never see again, a full, boyish smile that showed his straight white teeth.

"How can I be angry with you, Olivia? You have revived the boy I was before, that boy I should never have lost, but had to in order to live. And now I can be that boy in my manhood, and I love you. With all that I am, I love you." He curled his hand around hers and brought it to his lips. "Be with me, Olivia, make our lives true."

She slipped down to kneel with him upon the floor, her entire body shaking. His lips were soft against her fingers, and she stared at where his mouth touched her skin. And she envied her hand. "I want with all my heart to be with you, Ian, but . . ."

He looked into her eyes. "Do you love me?" he asked.

Olivia took a deep breath, her throat closing in on the sharp sting of tears. "Oh, yes," she managed to say, and then opened her arms and clutched Ian to her bosom. "I do love nothing in the world so well as you. Is not that strange?"

Ian held her tightly, his mouth against her ear. "You wrote that in your play, and I heard it with my heart. Only you had Benedick say it, I think."

"Does Benedick believe it?"

Ian pulled back from her embrace and cupped her face in his large, strong hands. "I do love nothing in the world so well as you," he said roughly. "But it is not at all strange, only the most wondrous thing. I must object, though, to the title of your play."

"*Much Ado About Nothing*? I thought it rather clever."

"Could I suggest another?"

Olivia leaned back slightly and smiled. "What suggestion have you?"

"*Much Ado About Love*."

Olivia laughed lightly and kissed him. "You speak as a poet, dear Ian. But it is hard for me to reconcile your cynic's soul with the man who sits before me."

"My poet's soul has lived within me for as long as I can remember, dearest Olivia. But I closed it away, and it searched in vain for another to release it."

"And it has found that person?"

"Ah yes." Ian reached into his pocket and

brought out a folded yellow parchment. "It found her many years ago, and then lost her." He handed her the piece of tattered paper.

Olivia took it from him, and she knew what it was. "You kept it?"

"It is a beautiful sonnet, full of innocence and the need of a child to feel the love of her mother. It touched me."

She laughed softly. "It saved my life then."

Ian ran his fingers through her short hair. "I could not be the person to snuff out such genius."

Olivia rolled her eyes. "I have never been so good at poetry."

" 'Twas good enough to keep the flame of my soul alive within the shell that became my body, though I thought it long extinguished."

Olivia leaned forward and touched her lips to Ian's. They were hard, yet so soft, and she shuddered with a longing she had only allowed herself to remember in the very darkest of nights when rain pelted the roof above her and the emptiness beside her seemed like it would swallow her whole. "You have found her again, then, the person who will give your soul's light air to breathe?"

He kissed her back more deeply, and then whispered against her mouth, "In the grace and form of the most beautiful of women."

Olivia leaned back and frowned playfully. "Then it cannot be me, for I am overly large, am I not? I have ugly hair and big feet, if I am not mistaken."

"Oh, but you are mistaken."

"Truly?"

Ian smiled into her eyes as he stood. "I have learned well, Olivia, I do not make the same mistake twice. I shall now regale you with honeyed words of praise." He helped her to stand and then swept her into his arms as he shoved the door closed with his foot.

"Oh, do," she whispered, sliding her hands about his neck.

"Shall I compare thee to a summer's day?" he asked as he laid her gently upon her bed. "Thou art more lovely and more temperate."

Ian leaned over her and kissed her deeply, and she groaned with pleasure.

"Rough winds do shake the darling buds of May, and summer's lease hath all too short a date." He untied the simple gown from her body, baring her flesh to his ravenous mouth.

"Sometime too hot the eye of heaven shines, and often is his gold complexion dimm'd; and every fair from fair sometime declines, by chance or nature's changing course untrimm'd."

Olivia closed her eyes, reveling in his words and her lover's touch. He kissed her eyelids, her mouth, and then moved down the column of her neck, and she arched toward him.

"But thy eternal summer shall not fade nor lose possession of that fair thou owest; nor shall death brag thou wander'st in his shade, when in eternal lines to time thou growest." He feathered his tongue against the crest of her breast, and Olivia writhed beneath him.

"So long as men can breathe or eyes can see, so long lives this and this gives life to thee." His mouth closed over her nipple, and Olivia laced her fingers in Ian's hair.

"Speak no more."

He lifted his head, and she groaned.

"Did I not speak well enough for you?"

"Yes, yes, 'twas perfect, but I need more than words now, Ian."

"But I praised you well?"

Olivia lifted her mouth to his, and tongued his lips. "You praised well with your words, Ian. Now, praise me with your body."

Ian smiled, and Olivia had to close her eyes because the beauty of him hurt her.

"Your wish is my command, Master Shakespeare." He kissed her again, and Olivia kissed him back with an urgency born in the belief that she had thought never to see Ian again in her lifetime.

He slid his mouth down her neck then, and

she held tightly to his body. "I love your neck," he said.

She laughed. " 'Tis but a neck."

"No," he said, trailing kisses to the hollow between her collarbones. " 'Tis a work of art."

"Ah, yes, your poet's soul has been released."

"Tease me not, fair Olivia, for I plan to spend my life writing odes to each part of your body." His hand trailed up to cup her breast. "I shall begin here." He lightly scraped his thumb over her nipple so that every fiber of Olivia's body trembled with need.

"It shall take years, of course, but in the twilight of our life, I shall, perhaps, reach your toes."

Olivia went very still beneath her lover's hands. He must have sensed the disquiet within her soul, for he tore his gaze from her body and looked into her eyes.

"What is wrong?"

Olivia stared at this new man Ian had become, and her heart wept. His life was new and free, but hers was still the same. And in that moment she knew that she had lost him all over again.

She closed her eyes and tried to move, quickly, for she felt the tears burn the backs of her lids.

"What is it, dearest?" He did not let her run, and so she stopped and squeezed her eyes shut against the anguish.

"Have I spoken wrong yet again?" he said, a desperate edge to his question. "Please, Olivia . . ."

She opened her eyes and laid a finger against Ian's lips. "Shh, you have not spoken wrong. I love you, Ian, and I am so happy that we can have this last time together in our love."

"Last?"

"But you must know that I cannot be with you. You're life is different now, but I still live under the darkness of my birth. That will never change."

"But, Olivia, we . . ."

"No!" She kissed him lightly. "No. I have known always that I cannot ask another to live as I do."

Ian stared at her for a long moment of silence. "You do not trust me, then?"

Olivia frowned. "Of course I trust you."

"No, you do not believe that I can protect you, protect our children."

Olivia caught her bottom lip between her teeth. Their children, how she wanted with all of her heart to bear their children. "Don't, Ian."

"I have laid my infant soul at your feet, Olivia, because I know and trust with everything within me that you will not step on it. I could never have done that as little as twelve months ago.

And I ask you, now, Olivia, to put your life in my hands. Give me your trust."

Olivia searched his face, her heart beating so hard she was sure he could feel it as she did in every pore of her being. "I do trust you, Ian, but . . ."

"Give me your life."

She blinked and knew she was more afraid in that very moment than she had ever been. More afraid than the child that had watched from a hiding place as a man came to kill her.

"I will cherish you. I will cherish our children. I will give you my name, and it will be yours forever, and you shall never again have need to fear, because my name shall protect you as your childhood one did not. I promise you this upon my life."

Olivia swallowed hard, her hand automatically going to curl tightly around Ian's. "If I give you my life, Ian, 'tis a powerful thing that you control."

"Do you trust me?"

She blinked at the intensity of Ian's gaze, and then nodded, slowly.

"Then 'tis not something that I shall control, but something that I safeguard."

A tear, hot and wet and searing slipped from the corner of Olivia's eye and tracked a path down her cheek to drop into her ear. He would, of course he would. She had known it from the first night she had slept within his embrace. Ian Terrance would keep her safe. "You will keep me safe," she said.

He smiled once more, and she pulled him close within her embrace. "I give you my life," she whispered.

"And I give you mine."

Epilogue

Langston Abbey
1623

> To have what we would have, we speak not what
> we mean.
> > —MEASURE FOR MEASURE, II, IV, 118

As Ben Jonson rode up the twisting drive toward Langston Abbey, he realized suddenly that the trees that lined the drive had feet. He squinted out the window of his lumbering carriage.

"How now!" a voice that seemed to be attached to one pair of feet cried. "Who goes there down our dusty path?"

Ben grinned, and stuck his face from the carriage window. A little girl of six stood at the foot of one of the trees.

She clapped her hands as he rode by. " 'Tis Uncle Ben," she said in pure delight, her eyes a bright cerulean blue that reminded Ben of the Mediterranean.

He tossed her a sweet, and smiled as she caught it. Beth was his favorite, and he always brought treats for the girl. Of course, he did also like David, Jonathon, Michael, Stephen, and Martin as well, but he had been ever grateful when Olivia had given birth to his little Beth.

She pounded toward him now, her bare feet brown with dust, her legs encased in breeches. He alighted from his carriage and turned just as she launched herself into his arms. " 'Struth, you have grown five inches since I saw you last."

"Six, I swear, Uncle Ben. I shall be as tall as Jonathon soon, by my troth."

"Jonathon?" Ben set the girl down as his footman gathered his papers for him. "I have just come from seeing Jonathon at university."

Beth circled him as he walked, so that he nearly tripped. "Truly? Is he well? Does he eat his greens? Mother is always upon him for not eating his greens."

Ben grimaced.

"You do eat greens, do you not, Uncle Ben? They are good for you. They make you strong."

"That is hard to believe."

" 'Tis true! Mother swears it."

"Well, then, if your mother says it is true, I shall believe it."

"Mother is very smart. Papa says so."

"Well she took me to husband, that proves her intelligence." A deep voice interrupted his conversation with Beth. Ben looked up to find Olivia's husband bearing down upon them.

"Papa!" Beth was off to jump on another poor and unsuspecting soul. "Ben has been to see Jonathon!"

"He does well?" Ian glanced at Ben.

Ben nodded. "Very well, I'd say, my lord. He excels beyond any other at university. I think he has decided, finally, to study in the sciences."

Ian nodded.

"I am sorry that I missed your speech there a few months ago. Jonathon informed me that his tutors have been testing some of your theories on light. They are very excited."

Ian nodded slightly. "They were just some thoughts I had; perhaps they will come to something. You're here to speak with Olivia?" he asked, changing the subject without pause.

There had never been an easy friendship between him and Olivia's husband. Ben knew, of course, that there couldn't be. How could two men enjoy each other when each adored the same woman?

"Yes," he said now.

"She is in the conservatory." Ian nodded toward the room, though Ben knew well where it was. "I approve this idea of yours, by the by."

"She is excited about it, I know."

Ian's grin was plain. "Her wish is my command. 'Twas told to me many years ago that it must be so, and I have adhered to the dictate ever since."

"She can be quite demanding," Ben agreed.

"Oh no, 'twas from another Beth that dictate came." Ian tweaked the nose of his daughter. "Now, Beth number two, shall we out and find your brothers? I have just let their poor, beleaguered tutor free from the shed, and methinks I shall need to take a stick to their bottoms."

"Oh yes!" cried the bloodthirsty Beth. "I shall show you exactly where they are, Papa."

"Good." He started for the door, and then stopped. "Be careful, Ben, what you print in this book. We are happy, and healthy, and I should like to stay that way. No hints to his true identity?"

Ben nodded quickly. "No hints."

"Hurry, Papa, the boys will get away."

Ian laughed and followed his daughter's directions to his sons' whereabouts.

Ben found his way down the hallway and through the doors to the conservatory. Olivia was kneeling upon a stone path, her arms covered in dirt, a trowel in one hand.

"I think there are servants to do that, Lady Langston."

Olivia looked up quickly, a wide smile gracing her mouth. "Ben."

"Liv."

"I should not allow a servant to do a chore I enjoy so much." She stood, brushing her hands against the skirts of her gown. "I have the most beautiful rose to show you, Ben. It has the most lovely scent! I think I shall name it Ben's Feet."

Ben frowned as Olivia laughed.

"Oh, do not pout so, Ben. I shall always remember the smell of your feet and think of simpler days." She linked her arm through his and guided him toward some comfortable-looking chairs. "Jenny," she said to a maid passing in the hall. "Bring tea for us, please."

Jenny curtsied and hurried away.

"Now, do show me the treasures you bring, Ben." Olivia sat and Ben joined her.

"I have written the introduction as well as the preface and dedication, though I have put other names to the last."

"Can I read them?" Olivia asked excitedly.

Ben handed over the packet in his hands. "I have procured a picture of Shagspeare. I must say, your idea to put up a monument in Stratford was genius. The common view now is that the actor is the author of your plays."

Olivia looked up from her reading. "Wonderful."

"A travesty, really." Ben shook his head. "But, I *am* glad that you have finally agreed to allow me to publish your plays, for truly they are nearly as good as mine."

Olivia rolled her eyes.

"I do hate to see them attributed to some actor who did naught but act as scribe for a few of them, though. And, 'tis passing strange but a group of sonnets have been published under his name as well."

Olivia laughed. "Truly? Someone published them?"

"You have knowledge of these sonnets? Oh yes, the author has a wonderful genius."

"But how did they become linked with Shakespeare?" Ben asked, loving the way the sun brought out the deep auburn highlights in Olivia's hair.

"A rather lofty personage at court put it about that they were mine many years ago. She knew that the author was rather abashed at having his name attached to such unabashed love poems." She giggled.

Ben tapped his finger upon the arm of his chair. "There is more to this story, I think?"

That wide smile graced Olivia's beautiful lips. "Oh, so much more, Ben. But it does not matter now, except that Shakespeare can lend his name to it all so that others may enjoy what we wrote."

"Yes, still, I met Shagspeare once, and he was not at all a nice person. And dull as dishwater as well."

"It doesn't matter what name is upon them, don't you think, Ben?" Olivia put the papers down and took his hands in hers. "A name is just a name."

"A rose by any other name . . ."

"Oh hush!" Olivia swatted him playfully on the shoulder and took her seat once more. "I tell you this, Ben, my name was the bane of my existence until Ian gave me his." She smiled, and the pure joy and beauty of it wrenched at his heart. That she could have felt thus for him had been his keenest wish.

"I have lived my life in truth, not just upon a stage, since I became the lady of Langston Abbey. He gave me children, more dear to me than words could ever be. And that is finally where our name will shine, and there it will matter most. And there it will safeguard many generations to come, I can only hope."

Can the Story that's in your heart touch America's heart?

Everybody has one extraordinary love story to tell. Whether it's their own story, or the story of someone very special to them. We're looking for that story.

To find it, we've created a nationwide contest:

The Greatest Love Story Never Told

All you have to do is visit our website, **www.harpercollins.com**, register, and send us an e-mail describing that story.

So, open your heart and let the love flow. And may the best story win.

Coming in October from Avon Romance

Breathlessly anticipated by her fans . . . it's the latest
in Suzanne Enoch's WITH THIS RING series . . .

Meet Me at Midnight

He's known as the infamous Lord Sin; she's been
called "Vixen" by the *ton* . . . together they enter into
a most unexpected marriage.

··

And don't miss this book by a rising star of romance,
Adrienne deWolfe

Always Her Hero

He's the man she couldn't forget . . . but is he the
man she fell in love with? Or has he changed?

"A jewel of a find!"
Christina Dodd

··